FEAR AND LOATHING

FEAR AND LOATHING

Hilary Norman

Severn House Large Print

London & New York

This first large print edition published 2016
in Great Britain and the USA by
SEVERN HOUSE PUBLISHERS LTD of
19 Cedar Road, Sutton, Surrey, England, SM2 5DA.
First world regular print edition published 2014 by
Severn House Publishers Ltd., London and New York.

British Library Cataloguing in Publication Data

Norman, Hilary author.
    Fear and loathing. – (The Sam Becket mysteries ; 7)
    1. Becket, Sam (Fictitious character)–Fiction.
    2. Murder–Investigation–Fiction. 3. Intermarriage–
    Fiction. 4. Police–Florida–Miami–Fiction. 5. Suspense
    fiction. 6. Large type books.
    I. Title II. Series
    823.9'2-dc23

ISBN-13: 9780727894069

Severn House Publishers support the Forest Stewardship Council™
[FSC™], the leading international forest certification organisation. All
our titles that are printed on FSC certified paper carry the FSC logo.

MIX
Paper from
responsible sources
FSC
www.fsc.org   FSC® C013056

Typeset by Palimpsest Book Production Ltd.,
Falkirk, Stirlingshire, Scotland.
Printed and bound in Great Britain by
T J International, Padstow, Cornwall.

For Linda
With love and so many happy memories

ACKNOWLEDGEMENTS

My gratitude to the following (in alphabetical order):

Howard Barmad; Cécile Campéas; Veronika Dünninger; Gaby Harris; Daniela Jarzynka; Special Agent Paul Marcus (and Julie too) – without your incredible patience and experience, I'm not sure Sam could handle everything I throw at him!; Wolfgang Neuhaus; Sara Porter; Sebastian Ritscher; Helen Rose – always there for those late-night conundrums; Dr Jonathan Tarlow; Euan Thorneycroft.

And Jonathan, with my love always. I could not do it without you.

June 2

The onslaught came without warning.

Relaxation to mortal terror in less than a minute.

One moment, a leisurely, intrinsically Miami Beach Sunday evening scene.

Barbecue in progress on the patio of a small, pretty backyard facing the Intracoastal.

Host Gary Burton flipping burgers on his new American Outdoor Grill with titanium and chrome burners. Molly Burton, his Chinese-American wife, setting down the last dishes of salad and chopped vegetables. Their best friends, Pete and Mary Ann Ventrino, dipping chips, drinking chilled Becks, planning their Fourth of July party.

The boat purring by was blue and white, sleek, well-maintained.

Nothing special about it. Nothing to make the Burtons or Ventrinos do more than glance at it when it docked two houses away.

Gary turned his head, checked out the guys debarking.

Four men. White tees, jeans, boat shoes, navy blue baseball caps. Clean-cut, respectable, wearing sunglasses, one guy toting a navy duffel bag. Looking up and back along the towpath, then noticing the party on the Burton deck and coming their way.

1

Lost, for sure.

'Hey,' one of them said.

Easy, friendly tone of voice.

'Hey,' Gary Burton said back.

The first man opened the steel gate.

'Help you?' Pete Ventrino asked him.

Gary looked back down at his burgers, saw that they were ready, lifted his spatula.

Heard Molly's soft gasp.

Mary Ann's: 'Oh my God.'

Gary turned.

The black muzzle of a gun was right in his face.

'Oh, Jesus,' he said as his heart cartwheeled up into his throat and the spatula fell out of his hand on to the decking.

'Shut up,' the man with the gun told him.

'Goes for all of you,' another man said.

Both voices ice cold.

Gary edged his gaze from the weapon, saw that his wife had a gun held tight against her temple, saw her gorgeous almond eyes huge, staring at him.

He looked toward Pete and Mary Ann. Same deal.

Mary Ann's blue eyes were brimming terror tears, but Pete's had gone jet-black, almost blank with what Gary realized was rage, and Christ, if Pete's impulse was to fight, they had *zero* chance . . .

'Inside,' his gunman said, sharp and clear. A command.

Gary registered that they'd put on black gloves, had to have put them on in a blink of an eye when they took out their guns, and that efficiency made it even more terrifying.

2

'What do you want?' The weapon to his fore-head so damned big he couldn't focus on the gunman's face. 'Tell us, and we'll give it to you. Just please don't do anything crazy.'

'Inside,' the man repeated.

Gary's eyes flicked right toward the towpath, the water, looking for help.

'Don't even think about it,' his gunman said.

'OK,' Gary said. 'Just don't hurt us. We'll give you what you want.'

No one out there anyway. Smooth water. No neighbors, no passersby.

The man leant past him and switched off the American Outdoor Grill.

'Better safe,' he said.

Like lambs to slaughter.

Only quieter.

Small sounds along the way, gasps of fear, Mary Ann's soft weeping. Molly's dark eyes on her husband's face, frightened and bewildered, trusting him, even now, to find a way to stop this. Gary and Pete both silent, their thoughts scrambling wildly.

'Scream or yell for help,' one of the men had told them, 'and you die.'

Their baseball caps were off now, all four tossed on the couch on the way past, the act looking rehearsed, like part of a performance.

Any second now, Gary thought with a flash of hope, they'd toss the guns too, break into song, and this would turn into a joke – a 'killergram' maybe.

No joke.

3

They were all blond – all *golden*, all exactly the same color, which was weird.

Least of their problems.

One gunman per victim. Lousy odds.

Gary and Pete were both smalltime gamblers, friendly poker games mostly, visits to Gulfstream Park, Vegas once in a while, keeping the stakes affordable, both keen to keep their lifestyles intact.

Death-styles now, perhaps, Gary thought.

At least he and Molly had no children, but Pete and Mary Ann had two little ones.

Please, he said inside his head.

The directions were clear and precise, most issued by Gary's gunman, his voice steely.

Guns against their necks now, ordered through the Florida room, the great room, into the square hallway, the only sounds their breathing, Mary Ann's weeping and the tread of the gunmen's rubber soles over the solid wood floors, moving past the jade fu dog statues that Molly had told Gary would guard them against negative energy. Around the corner – the leader plucking keys from the glass dish beside the fish bowl (goldfish meant luck in China, Molly had said) – and along the corridor that led to the garage.

The leader opened the door.

'Inside.'

Gary's mind flew suddenly with scenarios.

It was just his *car* they wanted, his Beemer, until minutes ago his prized possession, but now only a damned *car*. And then his mind cranked up ten notches: they were going to take them on a bank heist, use them as hostages . . . Up another twenty: they were going to turn the car into a *bomb*, make Gary drive it someplace . . . Maybe these men were *terrorists* . . .

They took off their sunglasses.

They all had bright blue eyes.

Shit, but they were freaky, Gary thought.

Blond Number Two, the one holding a gun on Mary Ann, the one with the duffel, reached into it, pulled some things out and gave them to the other three men, the motions almost synchronized again.

Lengths of cord. Precut lengths.

Gary's mind ceased stockpiling plot outlines.

More than enough horror right here, right now.

'You two' – the leader addressed him and Molly – 'against that wall.'

Oh, Jesus.

Firing squad time.

Not yet.

'On your knees,' Blond Number Two told Mary Ann.

She fell on her knees, started crying, big time.

Number Two took a roll of tape from the duffel bag, slapped a length over her mouth. Mary Ann's eyes bulged.

'She can't breathe,' Pete appealed. 'She has bad sinuses. She'll—'

Tape across his mouth before he got another word out.

Molly said something softly, under her breath.

'What did you say?' her gunman demanded, words loaded with menace.

She repeated it.

Gary hadn't learned much Mandarin during their years together, but he knew.

'She's praying,' he said.

'Who to?' Blond Number Three asked. 'Some fat little Buddha?'

'It's the Lord's Prayer,' Molly told him.

He turned, struck her across the face with the back of his gloved right hand.

Rage flamed through Gary, made him bellow, but Blond Number One kneed him in the small of his back, shoved him down on the ground, stuck his gun hard up against his left ear.

'I love you,' Molly told Gary.

'I love you too,' he told her back.

And then their mouths were taped up too, and the next stage began. Working in pairs now, starting with Mary Ann, guns always trained on all the victims as they went about the business of tying them up.

The Burtons watched as Mary Ann was hogtied – hands behind her back, feet tied at the ankles, bonds linked together – and then swung, screaming beneath the tape, into the back seat of the BMW. Then Pete, struggling furiously, hopelessly, dumped in the passenger seat. Then Gary into the back with Mary Ann. And finally, Molly.

Except, in her case, they looped extra cord around her neck, torture style.

If Molly Burton did not keep her neck, arched back and legs still, she'd be strangled.

They deposited her in the driver's seat.

Gary could just see her eyes, tried desperately to send her thoughts: she had to hold on, not *move*, and soon these bastards would go back inside the house and help themselves to whatever they wanted, and then they'd get back in their boat and the four of them would get out of this, *he* would get out of this and free Molly first and then . . .

But they had *seen* them.

Their captors had made no attempt to hide their faces.

The realization cut off every lingering hope.

Gary shifted his gaze, looked at Pete.

Saw that he knew, too.

Mary Ann, beside him, moved a little, just enough so her right leg touched his left knee. He managed a semblance of a smile at her, felt the tape over his mouth tug, glad that she'd stopped crying, that she had clearly, horrifically, understood that if she didn't stop she would suffocate.

He looked back at Molly, met her eyes again, then wriggled a little, trying to see what was happening outside the car, because the men were still in the garage and he could only see two of them, but his hearing was twenty-twenty.

He heard ripping, tearing – knew what they were doing.

Sealing up the place.

He craned his neck, saw duck tape around the up-and-over door and window above.

Knew what would happen next.

Either they'd rig the exhaust with some kind of tubing and run it into the car, or they'd just ensure that the garage was totally sealed, then start the engine.

And leave them to die.

Gary looked at Mary Ann, saw her rising terror. Looked at Pete, whose thoughts had to be running the same route – and, Lord love him, Pete was trying to shuffle himself in Molly's direction, maybe so he could help take some of the strain off her, find some way to keep her from tightening that noose around her neck.

No *way*! They were *not* going to give in, trussed up like four Thanksgiving turkeys. The instant those sons-of-bitches were out of the garage he was going to start rocking like crazy, and if he used every ounce of his strength he thought he'd be able to kick out the window on his side, or else he'd . . .

The men had finished.

The place was sealed.

But they were not leaving.

They were putting on fucking *gas* masks.

Gary felt his guts shrivel.

They were going to *stay* while he and Molly and the Ventrinos were dying. Protected from the carbon monoxide, they'd stand by watching as they lost consciousness – as the noose tightened around Molly's neck.

Watch them all dying.

One of the gang – impossible to tell which one now they were masked – opened the driver's door, leaned in and started the car.

No problem. Gary's Beemer started first time, like always.

Reliable and quiet.

Less than an hour ago, he'd been proud of that.

Now, the shitty truth was that no one beyond the garage was going to hear a thing.

8

The man who'd started the engine rested his hand on the back of Molly's head, pushed, then let go, laughing behind his mask as she gasped.

It was the first time Gary had ever wanted to kill someone.

The man shut the car door.

Gary's eyes met Molly's, suffering yet still beautiful, not giving up. Both of them now asking the same question.

Why?

Andria Carrasco, childminder for Mary Ann and Pete Ventrino's kids, was feeling tired and a little pissed off.

Starting to worry, in fact.

Because Mary Ann had said they'd be home by ten and it was already after eleven, and if the Ventrinos were going to be late, they always called and Mary Ann reminded Andria to let her mom know, so she wouldn't worry. And Andria had called home a while back, and her mom had been cool about it, because Pete would drive her home, and it didn't matter much if she was late tonight because it was Jefferson Davis Day tomorrow, so there was no school.

Still, this was *so* not like them, and both Mary Ann's and Pete's cell phones were going to voice-mail, and Andria was wondering if she should maybe go see what was going on, because she knew they were at their friends, the Burtons, who lived just along the road, and their house had a deck out back same as the Ventrinos, and Mary Ann had said they were barbecuing tonight, which meant all she had to do was scoot along the towpath . . .

She called her mom again to ask if she thought it was OK to leave the children for just five minutes because they were both sleeping.

'You know better than that,' Lisa Carrasco said.

Andria did know, had been minding her own brother and sister for long enough, and her mom had drilled into her that you never left little kids home alone even for a few minutes, because 'anything' could happen.

So she waited another ten minutes, tried both cell phones again, then went to rouse five-year-old Johnny and to lift Mia, his one-year-old sister, out of her crib, hoping she wouldn't start crying.

Mia did protest a little, but settled quickly in Andria's arms, good baby that she was, and Johnny was confused, then excited, wanting to know where they were going.

'To fetch your mommy and daddy,' Andria told him.

'In the dark?' Now he looked doubtful.

'It'll be fine,' she said. 'We'll put Mia in the stroller and you'll hold my hand, and you know where they are, Johnny, it's not far.'

'Why do we have to go fetch them?' he asked in the hall. 'Did something happen?'

'Of course not.' Andria was bright. 'They've probably just been having a great night and forgotten the time.'

'OK,' Johnny said.

'Everything's cool,' Andria said.

* * *

10

Not quite so cool on the towpath in the dark, even for her, walking out here with two little ones, especially since the Burton house was in darkness too, until they reached the gate and the motion sensor lights illuminated it – comforting, but startling nevertheless.

Opening the gate, Andria saw right away that something was up.

Dishes of food untouched. Cooked burgers on the grill gone cold. Two beer bottles on the wooden decking. A spatula on the ground near the barbecue.

Called away unexpectedly, Andria decided. Some emergency, or maybe there'd been an accident, like when her mom had sliced a finger while chopping salad, or maybe Gary had burned himself on the grill, or . . .

She had a weird, lurching feeling in her stomach.

'Where is everybody?' Johnny picked up on her anxiety.

'I guess they had to go out someplace,' she told him. 'I'm sure they're fine.'

'But my mom and dad would have called,' Johnny said.

He was right.

'Probably no signal where they are.' Andria took her Nokia from her back pocket. 'I'm just going to make a quick call, Johnny. Don't move, OK? Watch Mia.'

She moved to the other side of the deck, keeping an eye on the kids, hit her mom's speed dial key and quickly updated her, keeping her voice low.

'That doesn't sound right,' her mother said.

11

'I think I should go inside,' Andria said. 'The door's wide open, Mom.'

'I don't want you going in there. Call out for the Burtons from outside, and if they don't answer, call 911, but do *not* go in there.'

'OK, Mom.' Andria wished she hadn't called.

'You hear me, Andria? There could be burglars inside.'

'I don't think so,' Andria said.

'Stay on the line,' her mother told her.

But Andria had already hit the red button.

Because she knew she was going to – had to – take a look.

Just a quick one.

Sam Becket could not sleep.

In the first place, he just wasn't tired enough. He'd grown so used to fighting through exhaustion, the brain-grinding kind that got you after too much overtime spent either in the pursuit of violent criminals or the endless paperwork battle.

Today, though, had been a real family Sunday. Brunch at his brother's, Saul and Mel Ambonetti, his girlfriend, doing eggs Benedict and smoked salmon omelets. David Becket, his dad – a retired doctor – taking a verbal swipe at cholesterol while tucking in with relish. Mildred, David's wife, spending much of the afternoon playing with Joshua, and Grace helping Mel in the kitchen, then putting her feet up.

All good.

Still, something was keeping him awake, so,

not wanting to wake Grace, he'd given in and gotten up.

On edge, with no real idea why.

Cathy, maybe. Almost five thousand miles away in France and probably – at five-thirty a.m. her time – still sound asleep.

She'd come into her inheritance two Decembers ago. A complex business, presided over lengthily by two Miami law firms appointed, during their lifetimes, by her mother and stepfather and aunt. Everything left to Cathy, who had as a young teen been framed for their murders, then granted the double gifts of freedom and, ultimately, a new chance at life.

Sam, a detective in Miami Beach Police Department's Violent Crimes Unit, had been the cop leading the multiple murder case back then, and Dr Grace Lucca the child and adolescent psychologist originally brought in to care for her. Grace the first believer in Cathy's innocence, even when all the evidence had pointed bloodily at her.

All that had happened before Sam and Grace had got married and adopted Cathy, and years had passed since then, years zigzagged with joys and sorrows and times of fearfulness and a lot of love. And Cathy had deliberately put aside all thoughts of her inheritance because of its unbearable associations, but suddenly it was all upon her.

Arnold and Marie Robbins's and her aunt's combined estates had been buffeted by market crashes and downturns, but Arnie had owned a small chain of restaurants and a house on Pine

13

Tree Drive, and Cathy's aunt's Coral Gables property had made the overall legacy more than considerable.

Infinitely more money than she'd ever wanted to think about, but as the time had approached, two things had become clear. She was going to pay off Sam's and Grace's mortgage and buy Saul – Sam's much younger brother, more like a brother to Cathy than an uncle – the apartment that he'd let her share rent-free for several years.

No matter how much they argued, she'd been determined, and they'd all realized how much it meant to her, and though they were all more than comfortable, Sam was still only drawing a police detective's salary and Grace had been cutting back work hours in order to spend more time with Joshua, their five-year-old. And Saul, though doing well enough with his one-man furniture-making business, would be in a far more secure position to ask Mel to move in with him, so there could be no denying that Cathy's gifts would help them all.

The year in France had been a fantasy Cathy had in common with many at Johnson & Wales University's College of Culinary Arts, where she'd recently graduated with an associate degree. And then she'd heard about the American owner of a restaurant – *Le Rêve de Nic Jones* – in Cannes, who periodically took on a promising graduate for a year, training on the job (apartment included), working under his overall tutelage.

Last November, Nic Jones, a slim, agile man

with dark, brilliant eyes, had come to Miami to interview candidates. After three days of trial, Cathy finally going head-to-head with a fellow student – Luc Meyer, Florida-born son of a French mother and German father, plump-cheeked, bespectacled, sweet-natured, super-talented with pastry *and* trilingual – Jones had offered her the job.

'Close call,' he said. 'I'd have liked you both.'

'Maybe you could.' The idea had suddenly struck her. 'If I worked for almost nothing and rented my own place, Luc could have the apartment that goes with the job.'

Jones had stared at her. 'I'm not often fazed, but—'

'It's just that I've been left some money,' she'd explained. 'Quite a lot, and—'

'Would you work for nothing?'

'No. That would be like saying I feel I'm not worth anything, and I don't feel that.'

Jones had smiled.

'Better brush up your French, if you want to keep up with Luc.'

Cathy was doing great, Sam knew that, yet he couldn't seem to stop worrying, didn't much like the way he'd felt when she'd first told them, didn't approve of the way he *still* felt. Over-protective. Wanting her close so he could be there if she needed anything. So he could keep her safe.

'Like nothing bad ever happened to her here,' Martinez had remarked, wryly.

Alejandro Martinez, his partner in Violent

15

Crimes and his greatly valued friend, who had no wife or children, but had regularly proved over the years that a man did not need to be either husband or father to get on that wavelength.

Sam had experienced a measure of relief when he'd learned that Luc Meyer was going to France with Cathy. But what had helped most had been ascertaining that Thomas Chauvin was *not* presently living in France. Chauvin, the young would-be photojournalist from Strasbourg, who'd come briefly into their lives two years back, displaying an unhealthy interest in both Grace and Cathy because he felt they resembled his idol, the late Grace Kelly.

An Interpol inquiry had informed them that Chauvin had been arrested more than once for stalking – and when Sam and Martinez had entered his rented Surfside apartment, they'd found the walls covered with photographs of Grace and Cathy.

They'd warned him off, seen him on a plane bound for home, but still, within hours of Cathy announcing her job offer, Sam had run a fresh check on him and learned that he'd filed two stories in the UK. Minor publications, published three months apart, one very recently. Sam had asked a pal to run an in-depth check and had learned that the now 'official' photojournalist was living in West London.

With a bit of luck, focusing on some other unfortunate blonde.

Which was not, of course, the right way for a cop to think.

But hell, Sam was a *father*, and his relief at the stalker being in the UK hadn't stopped him from giving Luc a photograph of Chauvin and asking him to keep an eye open for any sign of him.

'What should I do if I see him?' Meyer asked. 'Call the cops?'

'Call me,' Sam said. 'First warn Cathy, then call me, day or night.'

'You think he's dangerous?' Meyer looked alarmed.

Sam shook his head. 'Just a jerk and a bit of a sleaze, but obsessive. And I've learned to take that kind of thing seriously.'

'Especially when it comes to your daughter,' Luc Meyer said.

Sam had felt happier than ever that Meyer was going with Cathy to France.

Not just Cathy he was thinking about tonight, though. Kovac being back in Violent Crimes and giving him grief wasn't helping.

Just when you thought you'd gotten rid of a nagging pain, it came back. Ron Kovac, head bald as a bowling ball, eyebrows and the hairs on his muscular forearms the color of orange marmalade, had never been warmly disposed toward Sam or Martinez. But he'd transferred to Strategic Investigations a few years back, and the transfer had brought them Lieutenant Mike Alvarez – one of the good guys. Sadly Alvarez was now sick, had gone to New York City for lengthy treatment, and though no diagnosis had been disclosed, the detectives feared for him.

17

'Still together, I see,' Kovac had said to Sam and Martinez on his first day back.

'Just waiting for the chance to see you again, Lieutenant,' Martinez said.

'Still with the smart mouth.' Kovac had turned to Sam. 'You'll never get promoted, either of you.'

Ugly man, inside and out.

Grace had asked Sam once if she knew what Kovac's home life was like. If there was some great misery in his private existence that might have turned him mean.

Typical Grace, a major part of her raison d'être trying to find out what might have weakened the apple's skin so the worm could crawl inside. That, and seeing the good in almost everyone.

Only *almost*. She'd seen evil at close quarters more than once, been as glad as Sam when it had been snuffed out.

Grace was one of a kind.

Sam Becket a hell of a lucky man.

Still, tonight he was on edge. And maybe it was just the changes in the unit brought about by Kovac's return, but to be honest, it felt like something more.

Like something was coming.

And not a good thing.

Andria was inside the Burton house.

The layout of the Florida room area looked about the same as in the Ventrinos' house, but with the only lighting coming from the deck behind her, everything felt eerie.

She moved further, into the great room, and paused. To her left against the far wall, a giant flat-screen TV hung blackly; to her right the kitchen area, and she pictured Mrs Burton – who was real pretty, looked almost like Jamie Chung – over there. And maybe she should just look for blood on a chopping board, because then all this would make sense and she could just turn around, take the kids back home . . .

But she did not do that.

Because of the *feeling* she had.

'Andria?' Johnny tugged on her left hand.

'It's OK,' she said.

Except she didn't believe that. But if she called 911 now, for nothing, she'd look like a total loser, and anyway, she felt as if she was being pulled farther into the house by some kind of invisible magnet.

'We'll just take a little look around,' she told Johnny.

Mia, safe in the stroller, was sleeping again, and Andria gripped one handle with her right hand, took the boy's hand with her left, and pushed on into the hallway.

'It's too dark,' Johnny complained.

In the dim light from the deck, Andria saw a switch on the wall to her left, hesitated, then flicked it.

'That's better,' she said softly.

The hall was square, like the Ventrinos', which meant the bedrooms were probably along the corridor over to the right.

'I don't like it here,' Johnny said.

'It's OK,' she said again. 'I'm just going to

call out, and if no one answers we'll go back home.'

She did it, called: 'Mrs Burton?'

No one answered. She tried again.

'Hello? Mary Ann?'

Nothing.

'I want to go home,' Johnny said.

'We will,' Andria said, 'in just a moment.'

She looked to her left, saw a couple of statues of weird-looking animals, and a stone cabinet with a big round fish bowl.

'Hey,' she said softly. 'Fish. Look, Johnny.'

She wheeled the stroller over to the cabinet, hoping to distract the boy.

There was a corridor to the left, a door at the end.

'You stay here, sweetie,' she said. 'Look after Mia.'

'Where are you going?'

'Just taking a look along there.'

'You said we could *go*.' He sounded querulous.

Andria didn't know why she felt drawn along that corridor.

Except, when she reached the door, she stopped, afraid to go any further.

Certainly not through that door.

But she could *hear* something on the other side of it.

Something that sounded like low growling, that made her skin prickle.

And then suddenly she *realized*, grinned at herself for being a prize dork.

An engine.

'Car trouble,' she said out loud, flooded with relief because that was all this was about, and come to think of it, she could smell something . . .

She turned the handle.

The door shifted a little, then stuck fast. She looked down, saw a strip of something at the base, like tape, saw the same thing running up both sides of the door and across the top.

Andria froze.

She didn't know what lay on the other side.

Only that she had to get the kids *out*.

June 3

At a quarter to six on Monday morning, Cathy and Gabe were wrapped around each other in the bedroom of her fourth-floor rented apartment on rue Saint-Antoine, a narrow, historic hill in Le Suquet, the old quarter of Cannes in the south of France.

A day off for them both, pleasures to come.

Most days and nights still feeling like a long, looping dream to Cathy.

Being here on the Côte d'Azur, being here by herself, *being* herself, without her family watching over her. She could not love them more, but it was time to stand alone, at least for now, and doing that in this wonderful place, and then finding Gabe, falling for him . . .

He knew almost everything about her: a lot to know, much of it hard for her to have shared, yet he'd taken it all in his stride, had said that however painful, it had helped create the woman

21

she'd become: the person who loved to cook and run, who could make him hard with a look, who shivered when he touched her and cried when they made each other come.

She'd told him about Kez, the woman she'd once loved, had tried to express her confusions about her sexuality and her feelings for him. Gabe said that loving him now did not mean that she hadn't loved Kez. He said he figured there were many different kinds of love, and that though Kez Flanagan had been a sick young woman who had done terrible things, there couldn't have been anything crazy about her loving Cathy.

Cathy loved hearing what Gabe had to tell her.

Gabe Ryan was, she sometimes felt, part healer – and many other things too.

A mystery package, she guessed, but a good one.

Perhaps the best ever.

The restaurant where they both worked was on Quai Saint-Pierre, facing the port; spectacular yachts and the perfect blues of the Mediterranean beyond, other eating establishments and marine-themed businesses to left and right. Just a gentle stroll from Le Suquet and all things old, yet the broad, modern, smoothly paved sidewalk along the *quai* gave a sense of space and leisure that was distinctly twenty-first century.

Le Rêve de Nic Jones appeared small from the exterior, but its imaginative proprietor had carved out two floors of his four-storey building for dining, with seven tables and a bar on the ground floor, double the table capacity on the first floor and a kitchen that was a marvel, laid out perfectly for efficient flow.

'Our customers expect better than good,' Nic had told Cathy and Luc on the first Monday – the one day each week when the restaurant was closed – after their arrival in March.

They'd arrived at nine, entering at the unglamorous rear entrance in rue de la Rampe, had been welcomed by Jones and introduced to Jeanne Darroze, the general manager – an elegant, formidable, reed-thin woman of around forty.

'You guys will be training in every area of the kitchen,' Jones had told them. 'I'm the *chefpatron*, but there's nothing in this place that I haven't done myself, including dishwashing, and the same goes for Jeanne.'

They'd been given one day's basic training, then begun work next morning, directed by Jeanne Darroze to observe and assist wherever asked to, the boss's only instruction being that they respond swiftly to any request or task and make themselves as unobtrusive as possible when not engaged.

'Less than unobtrusive,' he'd said. 'Invisible, but ready for anything.'

They'd followed Jeanne's daily opening routine, checking temperatures in the coolers and freezer, and by ten Cathy had been at her first post, observing Sadi Guinard, the *poissonière*, a tiny, energetic young woman with cropped red hair and good English, as she sanitized her prep table.

'What can I do?' Cathy asked.

'Just watch me.' Sadi smiled, her small teeth very white. 'Don't worry. There'll soon be plenty for you to do. For now, only look, listen, learn. *Regardez, écoutez, apprenez.*'

'Look, listen, learn,' Cathy sighed later, encountering Luc outside the staff restroom. 'We'll have to have a sampler stitched, put it over our beds.'

Luc was pale.

'Are you OK?' she asked.

'Just a matter of time,' he murmured.

'Till what?'

'Till I screw up.'

'We're both going to do that, surely.'

'It's different for you,' Luc said. 'You're cool under pressure.'

'Sometimes,' Cathy said. 'But you're actually brilliant.'

He shook his head. 'I'm going to mess this up. I always do.'

Much later, she'd gone, tired but still excited, to thank Nic, had been about to knock at the door of his office at the back of the building . . .

'Bad idea.' Sadi Guinard stood behind her, wearing a shiny black leather jacket, a tote bag over her shoulder. 'Did the boss ask for you?'

'No. I just—'

'Doesn't matter what,' Sadi said. 'Just a warning. Never enter Nic's office unless you've been invited. He's a fantastic guy, but he's crazy about his privacy.'

'He seems so easy-going,' Cathy said.

'He is,' Sadi agreed. 'Nic's great. But I've . . .'

She smiled. 'Let's say, I've seen his darker side. We all have one, *n'est-ce pas?*'

And with that, she had gone.

Despite the rotation system used in the appointment of lead investigators, Sergeant Beth Riley was aware that Lieutenant Kovac took every legitimate opportunity to deprive Detectives Becket and Martinez of anything other than routine cases.

As it turned out today, however, neither Riley nor Kovac had any alternative but to get Sam Becket out of bed and to this crime scene *stat* this very early Monday morning.

Because a personal message had been left there for Sam.

Which had begged the question of whether he was the right man to lead the case.

'The lieutenant thought not,' Riley had told Sam.

'There's a surprise,' Sam had said drily.

'But Captain Kennedy agreed with me,' Riley said. 'Your case.'

'I thank you both.'

'Don't thank me too soon,' Riley said.

The message had been stuck to the outside of the windshield of the BMW like one of those nasties that self-appointed parking attendants liked leaving on cars. The kind that took forever to get off the glass.

This one would be removed very differently once Crime Scene was done here, the whole windshield going with it.

For the Personal Attention of Detective
Samuel Becket,
Miami Beach Police Department

It should not be allowed.
Simple as that.
It goes against creation.
I have no quibble with all men being
created equal.
But we were created with differences.
If that was good enough for the Almighty,
it should be good enough for us.
It should not be allowed.
I can't stop you all.
But I can say my piece.

Love Virginia

That '*piece*' – printed in Baskerville font on
white US letter-size paper – had been 'said' with
monstrous clarity, ostensibly by someone naming
themselves 'Virginia'.

Four victims bound, gagged and poisoned to
death by carbon monoxide in a BMW 320d four-
door sedan inside the sealed one-car garage of a
house on Stillwater Drive belonging to Gary and
Molly Burton. Two males and one female hogtied,
but the fourth victim, another female, apparently
having been singled out for maximum torture. A
cord tied around her neck and attached to her
feet, designed to strangle her if she moved the
wrong way.

No right way for her *to* have moved once the
gas had begun working.

26

And one glaringly possible reason why she had been chosen for an even more terrifying death ordeal than the other three.

Molly Burton had been Chinese-American. Her husband, Gary, Caucasian.

The investigators didn't have to be geniuses to believe this was a highly organized, singularly cruel and racially motivated homicide, the author of the windshield message plainly stating her or his case against interracial marriage. The *'I can't stop you all'* line presumably directed at – or at the very least intended to include – Sam Becket.

The crime having been committed in his jurisdiction.

An African-American police detective married to a white woman.

Sam guessed he knew now what had been keeping him from sleep a handful of hours ago. That improbable sense of something coming.

Here it was.

'Bedroom safe's been opened,' Martinez reported after words with officers first on the scene. 'Not forced, but empty.' He paused. 'The babysitter who called this in—'

'Babysitter?' Sam's stomach clenched.

'Not here, man,' Martinez said. 'The Burtons didn't have kids. She was sitting for their friends who live a few houses down.' He checked his notes. 'Pete and Mary Ann Ventrino, here for a barbecue and didn't come home, so she came looking. No ID yet.'

'But probably them,' Sam said.

Fire Rescue had gone in first to ventilate, and on their arrival the detectives had taken their first look at the victims and been sickened. In time, the BMW would be transported to the medical examiner's office with the deceased still inside. Crime Scene would continue processing there, but meanwhile they were working in the garage – dusting, photographing, sketching, peeling off and bagging the lengths of tape that had been used to seal up the death trap – and all over the house, especially the bedroom.

Scene of an apparent robbery.

'Key operated,' Sam said now, looking at the safe.

'So either they made husband or wife open it . . .' Martinez said.

'Or they took care of the victims first, then took the keys and helped themselves,' Sam said. 'No question we're talking "they".'

'The message said "I",' Martinez pointed out. 'Virginia.'

'Boss,' Sam hazarded. 'Of a killing team. Maybe present, maybe absent.' He shook his head. 'Let's do this.'

They started in the bedroom, taking their own photographs, Sam sketching the scene from different perspectives, making notes, then leaving the work to the techs and going back along the corridor to the hall.

They'd seen armed robberies that had spun way out of control for all kinds of reasons, and they'd seen drug-fueled robberies ending in tragedy.

Nothing unpremeditated about this calculated brutality.

'Killers from the off,' Sam said. 'Not armed robbers.'

'Depends what was in that safe,' Martinez said. 'Maybe.'

No jewelry on the victims, so it was likely that the murderers had stolen even wedding rings, maybe waiting until they were unconscious, then leaving through the house door and sealing that up from the other side.

They made a note to check the Burtons' insurance policies, since jewelry, at least, might be traceable. Not so, of course, with cash, though who knew what the couple might have kept in the safe: documents relating to property, marriage, birth or other certificates, raising the slight possibility of identity theft. A minimal consideration, given that this case would soon hit the news, and after sunrise the crime scene tape visible from the Intracoastal as well as the road would bring all kinds of rubberneckers and vultures . . .

'How many you think we're looking for?' Martinez asked quietly.

'No signs they put up a fight, so armed, for sure.' Sam paused. 'One on one, I'm guessing, maybe more.'

'The empty safe's maybe a little extra frosting on their cake, or just water-muddying for our benefit.'

'Much like the signature,' Sam said.

They returned to the front of the house and found Dr Elliot Sanders, Chief Medical Examiner, his Hawaiian-style shirt vivid in the LED lighting, taking his first look inside the car.

'I thought, when I got my promotion,' Sanders said, coming outside, 'that I'd at least get to spend nights with my wife, but we got two on-call MEs down with flu, so here I am looking at another piece of depravity.' He shook his head, took a cigar from his top pocket.

'Doc?' Sam reached out to grab it. 'Flammable situation.'

'I wasn't going to smoke it, Sam.' The ME's eyes were amused as he took back the Romeo y Julieta. 'Enough dead people here already.'

'What do you have?' Sam asked.

'Not much till we get the car to my place – pity we can't move the whole damned garage.' He paused. 'Mrs Burton was probably strangled by that cord before she lost consciousness. The others died from CO poisoning – though, like always, that's subject to confirmation.'

'So her husband had to watch her being tortured to death,' Sam said grimly. 'Part of his "punishment", maybe.' He looked at the ME. 'You saw the letter, Doc?'

Sanders nodded. 'Nice.' He chewed on his unlit cigar for a moment. 'Remember Joseph Franklin? Liked killing mixed race couples.'

'Sure. Joseph Paul Franklin. Member of the KKK and National Socialist White People's Party. Changed his first names as a tribute to Goebbels. Didn't he shoot his victims?'

'Mostly,' Sanders said. 'Though I recall he fire-bombed a temple and robbed banks.'

'He still alive?' Martinez asked.

'On death row,' Sam said. 'In Missouri, I believe.'

'He escaped one time,' Sanders said. 'Was recaptured in Florida.'

'So if it's racist, why the other couple?' Martinez brought them back.

'Maybe they were just here.' Sanders rolled the cigar beneath his nostrils.

'Or maybe they were considered "guilty" too,' Sam said. 'Condoning the Burton marriage.'

The ME looked at him. 'You sure you want to take this case, Sam?'

Sam looked right back at him. 'Never more sure of anything, Doc.'

Andria Carrasco, the fifteen-year-old babysitter, had sounded terrified during her 911 call, unable to remember the Burtons' house number – which was where she thought 'something terrible' had happened – but had told the dispatcher that if the police came to the Ventrinos' house, she would show them.

She'd been as good as her word, according to the patrol officers, had pointed them to the house and then, still badly shaken, had been escorted back along the towpath.

She was in the Ventrino house now, in the Florida room with her mother, Mrs Lisa Carrasco. A female officer sitting with Johnny and Mia Ventrino while attempts were made to locate their parents' adult next of kin.

Andria was still trembling. 'I keep thinking I should have done something, got that door open, turned off the engine, done *something*.'

'There was nothing you or anyone else could have done,' Martinez told her. 'It was too late, Andria.'

'I've been telling her that,' her mother said, 'but she won't believe me.'

'Anyway,' Sam said, 'you did the most important thing of all for them. You took care of their children, Miss Carrasco. They're safe, thanks to you.'

'I could have gone sooner. They were never late coming home – I should have *known* something bad . . .'

Andria stopped talking, buried her face in her hands and sobbed.

Inconsolable, and who could blame her?

It was clear from the off that Andria Carrasco had nothing to offer, that she'd arrived considerably after the crime and had – mercifully for her – not seen the perpetrators. So they'd taken her prints in order that she might be eliminated from the scores of prints at the Burton home, and finally her mother had taken her home.

'We'll need you to make a formal statement,' Sam said, 'when you've had time to rest.'

'Is that really necessary?' Lisa Carrasco asked. 'She's been through so much, and she doesn't know anything.'

'She was the first person on the scene, ma'am,' Sam said.

'I just want her to forget it.'

'I'll never forget it, Mom,' Andria said.

Before she'd left, the babysitter had gone through the phone numbers posted on the refrigerator door, enabling Sam to make one of the calls he hated.

Destroying lives was bad enough in the light of day, but somehow, rousing a sleeping person during the night with the worst news in the world seemed even worse. Sam could have asked Chicago PD to knock on Mary Ann Ventrino's parents' front door, but even in their initial shock, Rose and Joseph Reardon might have questions, and at least Sam, as lead investigator, could vow to do everything in his power to find out who'd done this monstrous thing.

No details, not over the phone. Maybe not every single detail ever – though that was the ME's call, and Sam knew that Elliot Sanders would speak personally to whichever member of these families came to see him.

Mary Ann's father dropped the phone after Sam told him.

Sam heard the clattering, then the first awful, raw sounds of grief, and then the poor man was back on the line, telling him that they would catch the first flight, then adding, distraughtly, that because Mary Ann's brother, her only sibling, lived in Boston, there was no one in their family to call on for immediate help with the children.

Another voice, in the background, female.

'My wife, reminding me that Pete's parents are gone, but he has a sister named Gia.' Joseph Reardon's voice weakened. 'I don't know her surname. I only heard of her as Aunty Gia.'

Sam thanked him, offered renewed condolences and any help needed.

'Gia'. Another name and phone number on the refrigerator door – another life to blow apart.

'Dr Russo.' The man who picked up sounded sleepy, but put his wife on the line in seconds, and Gia Russo sounded almost under control while Sam was breaking the news, but then, after she'd said she would come right away, just before the call was cut off, Sam heard her first great howl.

The sound was still reverberating in his head when he made his next call.

Gary Burton's cell phone had been found; an entry for 'Dad' in his Contacts.

William Burton sounded frail, but remained coherent enough to tell Sam that his daughter-in-law had neither living parents nor siblings, but was close to her uncle in Miami, a man she had worked with.

'James Lin,' Burton said, a note of something – disapproval, maybe – in his tone.

'Do you have his address, sir?' Sam asked.

'I do not.' He paused. 'Are you sure it's them?'

Sam told him that they were certain, though it would still be necessary for someone to make a formal identification.

'That will be me,' William Burton said.

The dignity in his voice almost choked Sam.

Gia Russo arrived less than thirty minutes later, a petite, dark-haired woman aged forty, according to her driver's license, which she'd had the presence of mind to bring with her.

'I thought you might need ID,' she said. 'So you'd let me take the children.' She shook her head. 'It's OK. I know there may be hoops to jump through, but I think—' Tears shone in her eyes. 'I was going to say it would be *best* for Johnny and Mia, but . . .'

'Hey,' Sam said gently. 'You need to give yourself some time. The children are sleeping, and they've been well taken care of.'

'They don't know?' Mrs Russo looked shocked.

'Of course not,' Sam said. 'But Johnny knows something's wrong.'

She looked up at him. 'All the way here, I told myself you were wrong, you'd made a mistake, it couldn't be Pete and Mary Ann. But it's true, isn't it?'

'I'm afraid it looks that way.' Sam saw her flash of hope, knew he had to douse it instantly, that anything else would be cruel. 'We're going to have to ask you to make an identification, Mrs Russo, a little later in the day, but we've seen photographs of your brother and sister-in-law. There's no doubt.'

More dignity.

Another warm June dawn was breaking when Sam and Martinez made their way over the towpath, heading back to the Burton house, keeping to the edge of the crime scene tape so as not to disturb the flags set wherever, say, a shoe print or other evidence had been found, photographed, then lifted. Though even if any of those prints might have been something, Andria and Johnny's shoes and the stroller's wheels had probably spoiled them.

They were avoiding Stillwater Drive, knew that residents had been emerging and were looking on, horrified, because word was spreading and

35

the reality of something so macabre happening in their own street was hideous and, to some perhaps, tantalizing.

The media were already present, news trucks everywhere, reporters there to get the story out, to push lenses and mikes in the faces of anyone who might have seen anything related to what had gone down, anyone who even vaguely knew the Burtons. Soon, boats would gather out on the Intracoastal too, not just those belonging to the big guns but to those who lived to ogle, and, these days, to use their devices to send on-the-spot stories to news websites or simply, ghoulishly, to spread the word and comment on it.

What Sam and Martinez wanted was to get right *on* this, hit it hard.

Their greatest hope for a result from a surveillance camera hooked up to a house two along from the Burton home, trained on an expensive powerboat moored outside.

The house with the camera belonged to a family named Rosenblatt.

Nobody home, the detectives hoping they'd just left Miami Beach for the weekend.

Sam had watched the camera earlier, watched it move, wanting it to be a top-of-the-range model complete with pan, tilt and wide range and – a cop could dream – maybe face recognition thrown in.

It seemed to be moving sluggishly and Martinez had said: 'At least it's not dead.'

'Surprising, with a crime this organized,' Sam said. 'I'd have expected those sons of bitches to take it out.'

36

'Maybe they didn't have time,' Martinez had said.

'Maybe they were confident of evading it,' Sam said.

Now, hours later, search warrant for the camera applied for, they paused again at the same spot.

'Cutter and Sheldon are going to watch for the Rosenblatts while they canvas the street,' Martinez said.

'Meantime, all we need is a credible insomniac,' Sam said, 'with twenty-twenty vision and a pair of camera binoculars.'

'With zoom,' Martinez added.

The victims' faces came back to both men. The torture-style cord around Molly Burton's neck. No further information yet about her uncle, or any other next of kin.

Sam stirred himself out of negativity.

They *did* have something.

The message to him – a cop whose private life had gotten into the public domain more than once over the years. Which might therefore have been written in malice or as a threat – or merely to mislead.

Whatever its intent, it was evidence that might yield as much or more than those four poor people and the scene.

'Let's go,' Sam said.

'Where?' Martinez asked.

'To get this investigation moving,' Sam said.

Cathy's first sighting of Gabe had been during her first dinner shift.

Good waiters were supposed to blend in, but she had noticed him immediately – in the three-second hiatus she'd had before Jacques Carnot, the *rôtisseur*, had dispatched her to the linen store for a clean apron.

'*Vite!*' he'd yelled, and after that she'd forgotten about the young man, with scarcely enough time to draw breath, and by the time her shift was over, he and the others had gone for the night, and anyway, Cathy didn't think she'd ever felt so tired in her life.

'Are you OK to get home alone?' Luc had asked her.

Living in the small top floor apartment above the restaurant – another, much larger residence on the third, one of the boss's homes, rumor had it, generally unoccupied – it was to be part of Luc's duty to take over the closing rituals, logging any problems, checking equipment and hygiene and, most crucially, lowering the shutters, locking up and setting the alarm.

'Sure,' Cathy had answered his question.

'I never thought I'd say this,' Luc had said, 'but I'm too exhausted to eat.'

'But we survived,' Cathy had said.

'For now,' Luc had replied.

She'd been jogging early next day, a gray, misty March morning, when she saw him again.

She'd meandered around the port, going gently, had passed the Palais des Festivals and was moving along the Promenade de Pantiero, the broad walkway between the Croisette and the beach – and there he was, the guy from last evening's shift, strolling toward her.

38

He wore a white T-shirt, jeans, sneakers and a thin parka, his brown hair longer than she'd thought, had probably been tied back for work, his face lean, and there was a particular *grace* about him that made her catch her breath.

He smiled as he recognized her, straight into her eyes.

They both halted, a few feet apart.

'You're an athlete,' he said.

'You're American,' she said, surprised.

'And so are you,' he said, teasingly, and put out his right hand. 'Gabe Ryan.'

'Cathy Becket.' She liked his grip.

'This year's winner,' he said. 'From Miami Beach.'

'And you?'

'From here now.' He smiled. 'Originally from Boston.' He paused. 'You do this every morning?'

'If I can.'

'Going west's even better.' Gabe Ryan nodded toward the area called La Bocca. 'Great views of the Estérel mountains.' He paused. 'Breakfast tomorrow?'

'Sure.' Cathy felt a small kick in her stomach, recognized instantly how long it had been since that had happened. 'Where?'

'The beach? Anyplace along here.' He gestured toward the sand.

'Do they allow eating?' She thought of Miami Beach and the long list of regulations posted at intervals all along the expanse of public beach.

'I'll bring the coffee and croissants, and I guess we'll find out.'

'Are you working tonight?' she asked.

'Not tonight,' Gabe Ryan said, and walked on.

She'd come next morning armed with two Tupperware eco-bottles of OJ, not sure that he'd show, but he'd been waiting for her, sitting crosslegged on the sand with croissants in a napkin-lined straw panier – feather-light and buttery, she discovered – and a pot of delicious dark jelly.

'Wild blackberries,' he told her.

'Where can I buy some?'

'You can't,' he said. 'I made it.'

'Now I'm impressed,' Cathy said.

'Hey, you squeezed oranges.'

Cathy grinned. 'And later, I may be scrubbing prep tables or shaving truffles.'

'Who knew?' Gabe's brown eyes were dancing.

'Knew what?'

'That truffles grow beards.'

'Only the females,' Cathy said.

'Matter of fact' – Gabe stretched out – 'I went truffle hunting with a friend's dog last year.'

And so their first real conversation had continued gently and easily on that cool, early March morning, the coffee pleasantly warming, and by the time they'd gone their separate ways, Gabe knew that Cathy lived in Sunny Isles Beach and that she'd found an apartment here in rue Saint-Antoine; and Cathy knew that Gabe worked four evenings a week at the restaurant and that he and a friend ran a stall at Forville Market every Tuesday to Sunday, that generally his friend set up at around six a.m. and Gabe took over from ten till one.

Beyond that, she knew nothing.

Not even the name – or gender – of the friend.

But she liked what she did know.

Which had thrown her because there was no doubting that she had found Gabe physically attractive, which was kind of extraordinary in itself, given that since Kez Flanagan had blown into and out of her life, Cathy had semi-accepted that she was gay. Never an absolute conviction, because though her love for sad, psychotic Kez had been very real, she also knew that the other woman had psychologically overwhelmed her.

No one significant before or since. Till Gabe Ryan.

He was so easy to be with. Even the sense of mystery that remained seemed delicious, in no way disturbing, certainly not threatening.

They'd made love for the first time in her small apartment after Cathy had made *moules marinière*, and seeing him naked beside her, Gabe was even more beautiful than she'd first realized. Except that in the midst of sex, right at the *nub* of early arousal, a memory of Kez flew back into her mind, because the fact was, a woman had given her the first powerful orgasm of her life, and Cathy still remembered the sense that she had come home . . .

'Hey,' Gabe had nudged her. 'Come back.'

She'd told him she was sorry and he'd kissed her, said it was fine.

'But if you want to talk about where you went . . .'

'No,' Cathy had said. 'I don't. It's gone. I'm here.'

And it was true, because this was immeasurably different – and oh, Lord, she wanted this to be different in so many ways.

She had looked at Gabe in the light from the small open window.

Looked at his body, then back up at his face, studying angles, shadows, lines.

'Hey,' he'd said, and kissed her again. And then there were no more words or even thoughts. Only feelings, sensations, emotions; the rest of the world vaporizing into space.

Only Gabe now, inside her, all around her.

They had begun setting up for a major case in the squad room. Just Sam and Martinez for now, focusing on the windshield message. Everything to play for during the first twenty-four hours, and if the neighborhood canvassing got so much as a sniff of *something*, they'd be back on Stillwater Drive post haste.

A lot of grim things would happen this Monday – a holiday for some, but not the investigators – as postmortems got underway and shattered relatives suffered through the nightmare of identification and full realization. Those life-wrecking moments taking place in the Family Grieving Room at the Joseph H. Davis Center for Forensic Pathology; a good building, the visitors' areas sympathetically thought out and designed, but still the morgue.

Sam didn't envy the ME investigators who dealt with the mourners at that time, though their own job was often little better. They treated those poor

grieving people with gentleness and respect –
then began perpetrating their own brand of
professional cruelty by persuading them to share
secrets, sometimes intimate details, stripping off
outer layers, another kind of violation of the
victims in their quest to find answers.

To discover *enemies*, ideally: to discover who
had wanted the Burtons dead – and perhaps Mary
Ann and Pete Ventrino too, unless they'd been
just so much collateral damage.

For now, they'd put the basics up on
whiteboards.

Crime scene photos of the victims, names, ages,
occupations.

Gary Burton, thirty-three, proprietor of a fitness
club. Molly Burton, thirty, bookkeeper, working
for her uncle. Pete Ventrino, thirty-four, mechanic
with his own workshop. Mary Ann Ventrino,
thirty-two, homemaker and mother.

On another board, a blown-up copy of the
message left for Sam.

'So who's Virginia?' Martinez said, his feet up
on a desk, staring up at the signature: *'Love
Virginia'*.

'I don't think it's a person.' Sam sat astride a
chair close to the boards. 'I think it's part of the
statement. Maybe of the game.'

'Game'. A word he'd come to hate, because so
many of the psychos they'd come up against over
the years seemed to exult in game-playing. But
this particular piece of significance had struck
Sam as soon as he'd read the message.

'You ever hear of *Loving v. Virginia*?'

43

Martinez's forehead furrowed. 'You told me about it – they made a movie?'

'They did, but I learned about it from my dad a long time ago.'

Born Samuel Lincoln, he'd been seven years old and injured in the accident that had killed his father – a Miami policeman – his mother and little sister, when David Becket, a Jewish pediatrician, had first encountered him. A year later, the doctor and his wife, Judy, had adopted him and lengthened his name to Samuel Lincoln Becket. David had taken pains to research their new son's heritage, had learned that Sam was a descendant of a runaway slave from Georgia, and after that David had made a point of studying African-American history alongside Sam.

Hence, his fascination with *Loving v. Virginia*, a huge landmark case concerning a couple named Mildred and Richard Loving: Mildred of African and Native American descent, Richard a white man. The couple had left Virginia – where state law banned mixed marriages – in the late fifties to be married in DC, but when they'd arrived back home, they'd been arrested.

'Bottom line,' Sam told Martinez now, 'after a whole string of law suits, the Virginia Supreme Court upheld the convictions, but finally, almost ten years after the marriage, the US Supreme Court ruled against Virginia.'

Martinez shook his head, looked back up at the whiteboard. 'So you really think this is some sick racist fuck playing name games?'

'Seems to fit right in with the rest of the message.' Sam stood up and wrote, in marker

pen, *Loving v. Virginia* to the right of the windshield letter. 'And it suggests that maybe if the
Burtons' friends hadn't been there, they'd still be
alive.'

Martinez's sharp dark eyes were grim. 'I don't
like that it's addressed to you. Or the *"I can't
stop you all"*.'

Sam sat down at the table, opened his laptop,
typed something into Google.

'I hate to say it, man,' Martinez said, 'but I
think maybe, just this one time, Kovac might be
right. Maybe you do need to be home with Grace
until we catch these scumbags.'

'Now either hell really did freeze over' – the
unmistakable nasal twang of Ron Kovac's voice
said from behind them – 'or I just heard one of
my two most esteemed detectives saying I was
right?' He raised both hands. 'Sorry, *might* be
right.'

Sam went on typing for another moment, then
sat back. 'Are you planning on taking the case
away from me, Lieutenant?'

'No.' Kovac sat down. 'Just expressing my
concerns. Not just for you, but for your wife and
son.' He regarded the boards. 'In the
circumstances.'

Sam looked at the lieutenant, trying to believe
him, finding it hard.

'I think it's a threat,' Kovac went on. 'The
captain and I have talked it over, and he's
concerned too.'

Sam took a moment, bit down on the anger
that he knew he ought to be directing at the
killers, not the men on his side, even Kovac.

45

'I'll talk to Grace tonight,' he said.

'Good,' Kovac said. 'Maybe talk about taking some measures.'

'Best measure I can think of,' Sam said, 'is catching these bastards.'

'True enough.' Kovac looked at what Sam had written beside the note. 'What's that about?'

'Famous civil rights case,' Martinez told him. 'Sam thinks the message writer was just playing a game with the signature.'

'So you have nothing,' Kovac said. 'Not even a real name.'

'Motivation,' Sam said. 'Not much else yet.'

'Best carry on then,' Kovac said. 'And talk to your lovely wife, Detective.'

Sam waited till he'd left the room, then tapped his keyboard to restore his screen. 'So we know the message was printed in a font called Baskerville.'

'Like the hound,' Martinez said.

Sam nodded, then read aloud: 'The refined feeling of the typeface makes it an excellent choice to convey dignity and tradition. Created by a John Baskerville, who used it to print a Bible.'

'So a religious nut, maybe?'

'The font's used by a university in the UK and Castleton State College up in Vermont . . .' He read on. 'Modified version also used by the Canadian government in some corporate identity program.'

'Religious nut or Canadian professor,' Martinez joked grimly.

'There's certainly a preachy, fundamentalist feel.'

'So *possibly* a religious, pontificating, slaughtering sonofabitch.'

'With followers.' Sam was deadly serious.

'Bought or persuaded. Fanatical, maybe.'

'Let's hope bought,' Martinez said. 'Maybe with the proceeds of the robbery. Might make them easier to trace, and I'd take a hit squad over fanatics any day.'

'I'd take either,' Sam said, 'so long as we put them away.'

His cell phone rang. Detective Cutter calling.

'Putting you on speaker, Mary.'

'Possible eye witness,' she told them. 'One of the Rosenblatts' neighbors – who don't know where they've gone, by the way. But the husband, Mr Philip Blauner, answered our first knock, said he hadn't seen or heard anything, was watching TV, and his wife had been out all evening at her sister's, took a sleeping pill when she got home and was still out for the count.'

'Any chance you could cut to it, Cutter?' Martinez said.

'Mrs Elaine Blauner found us ten minutes ago, says she came home earlier than her husband thought, says she did take a look out of their bedroom window before she took her pill, and she thinks she might have seen them leaving.'

'Them?' Sam said.

'Four males. That is, she can't be sure they were males, because it was dark and they were wearing baseball caps, but they were walking along the towpath from the direction of the Burton house.'

47

'She didn't see them leaving the house,' Sam checked.

'Negative. They boarded a boat – maybe black-and-white – tied up in front of the Rosenblatt boat, started the motor and left. Nice and smooth, though one of them stumbled boarding and one of the others caught him.' Cutter paused. 'You want her to come in, Sam?'

'Tell her we'll come to her later, see if she remembers anything else.'

'Pity it isn't conclusive.'

'At least we know there were four of them,' Martinez said.

'If it was them,' Cutter said.

'It was,' Sam said. 'I'd bet the farm.'

At eleven – with initial computer trawls bringing up no unsolved cases anyplace with matching or similar modus operandi; violent hate crimes, too damned many; hogtied victims, mostly sex crimes; some homicides by carbon monoxide poisoning; any combination of the three, *zero* – and with details entered into ViCAP (the FBI's Violent Criminal Apprehension Program), Sam had a call from Gia Russo.

'I figured you'd want to talk to me, Detective.'

'We'll fit in with your needs,' Sam told her. 'How are the children doing?'

'Mia's unsettled, and Johnny still doesn't know.' Her strain was audible. 'But just to say I'll be available as soon as my husband's locum shows up – he's a doctor – so he can come home and help take care of them.'

'That would be good,' Sam said.

48

'Though I can tell you right now that if you're hoping I'm going to come up with someone who hated Pete or Mary Ann enough to do *that*' – her voice choked – 'you're going to be disappointed.'

'I'm sure, Mrs Russo, but the fact is you never know what you might be able to help with. It doesn't have to be a question of personal hate. It can be a grudge going back a long way, or it can be work-related or even something going back a generation.' He paused. 'Or it could be nothing to do with Mr or Mrs Ventrino at all.'

'You mean just because they were with their friends,' Gia Russo said. 'Oh, dear God.'

They went to the morgue, and learned that after identifying the bodies of his son and daughter-in-law, William Burton had collapsed and been taken to Jackson Memorial. Word was he wanted to talk to them, but Sam and Martinez knew that no doctor worth his salt would let them near him for a while.

The Reardon family, arrived from Chicago and Boston for the same awful purpose, were waiting in one of the family rooms, sharing the same pinched, hollow, shattered expressions, the father sitting shaking his head, the mother sitting straight, hands twisting in her lap, the brother pacing as they entered and introduced themselves.

'Do you have news?' Sean Reardon was as fair and blue-eyed as his sister.

'Not yet, sir,' Sam told him. 'But I promise you we're doing all we can.'

'Not enough,' the young man said violently, raking his hair.

'Not yet, no,' Sam said. 'But we won't rest until we get them.'

'Them?' Joseph Reardon's dark hair was threaded with gray, his bottom lip bleeding as if he'd gnawed on it. 'Do you know that for sure?'

'We know it had to have been more than one perpetrator, sir,' Martinez said.

'Why?' Rose Reardon pleaded softly. 'Why did they do it? Mary Ann was the sweetest person. All she wanted was for the children and Pete to be happy and safe.'

'Why any of them?' Joseph Reardon said. 'They were all good people.'

'We don't know that for sure,' his son said. 'We don't know what Pete might have gotten into, let alone the other two.'

'I've met them.' Rose Reardon was reproachful. 'They seemed like nice, normal people.'

'Not exactly.' Sean Reardon shrugged. 'Normal, I mean.'

'In what way?' Martinez's eyes sharpened.

'You know what I mean,' Reardon said.

'Not really,' Sam said. 'It would be very helpful if you explain it, sir.'

'White guy, Chinese wife,' the younger man said flatly.

'You think that might have a bearing, Mr Reardon?' Sam said.

His tone remained even, and all Sean Reardon had actually done was speed them to the subject they'd have arrived at in due course. And though

50

no one outside the investigation had been told either that Molly Burton had been tortured, or about the windshield message, the fact was that this bereaved brother was probably right about the mixed race issue.

'I don't know if it might have a *bearing* or not,' Reardon answered, 'but you hear about hate crimes all the time.' He sank down onto one of the chairs. 'Jesus.' He held out his trembling hands, stared at them, balled them into fists. 'I can't believe I'm saying that about my sister's friends. I can't believe any of this.'

His shoulders heaved, and Joseph rose to put his arms around his son, both men now weeping openly.

'Please,' Rose Reardon remained in her chair, beseeching the detectives. 'Help us. Catch those evil people.'

'We'll catch them, ma'am,' Sam told her.

'A lot of people out there right now,' Martinez added, 'all wanting to do just that.'

'Thank you,' she said, and covered her face with her hands.

Sean Reardon had made reservations at a First Choice Inn, though he said that Gia Russo had left word that they were welcome to stay with them.

'Which would be good,' Rose said. 'Because we could be with the children, but my husband . . .'

'I'd rather not be with strangers,' Joseph said flatly.

No warm joining of the Ventrino and Reardon clans then, Sam surmised.

51

'They're your grandchildren, Dad.' Sean let his irritation show.

'We'll stay at the hotel.' Rose Reardon flushed. 'But we'll go visit with them.'

Bad blood, Sam thought, or maybe Joseph was just a private man, and these poor people had no inkling yet that a family murder brought with it an end to privacy for a long time. The bereaved could carve out portions of days and nights for themselves, but with no clear prime suspect drawing fire, every skeleton would be dragged from its closet, every secret, quarrel or debt inspected before they would be left in any semblance of peace – and that was discounting the media searchlights.

Sean Reardon's remark might not have been malicious, but he had nevertheless lit a small flare over his own head. He might have betrayed personal prejudice, or he might merely have been remarking on the sorry truth of still all-too prevalent bigotry, but ahead of any further conversations they'd be taking a long, close look at Mary Ann's brother.

One more newly bereaved, significant relative had presented himself that morning. Molly Burton's uncle, James Lin, had been watching the early news when he'd caught the images of his niece's home behind the BREAKING NEWS caption.

No words to describe how that must have felt, but Mr Lin had made a number of phone calls, then made his own way to the morgue and, according to Ida Lowenstein in Elliot Sanders's office, if the small, trim, silver-haired Chinese-American gentleman had chained himself to the doc's office door, he could not have been more forcible in his insistence on being seen by the chief medical examiner himself.

The Miami Beach detectives came upon Doc Sanders and Mr Lin having tea together in the chief's office – tea, that was, amply fortified with Chivas Regal from the ME's personal supply.

'This,' Sanders said to Sam and Martinez, 'is a very special man.'

James Lin wept openly when Sam told him how sorry they were for his great loss.

'You couldn't know how great,' he said.

And then he went on to tell them about his late brother and sister-in-law's daughter. Born Mo Li Lin in San Francisco, a beautiful, intelligent, independent young woman, a qualified CPA who had liked numbers but not accountancy and who had, in the fall of 2006, been sharing an apartment with a girlfriend and working as a bookkeeper for a restaurant on Stockton Street, when she'd gone with friends to a bachelorette party in Las Vegas and met Gary Burton.

'Her fate, perhaps,' Lin said.

Burton had been there with his best buddy, Pete Ventrino, and they'd all hit it off right away. Gary had flown back west with her and had proposed just three days later. Molly, not by nature – according to her uncle – an impulsive person, had said she needed time to consider.

'He did not respect her wish,' James Lin told them now.

There'd been daily flowers and phone calls,

Burton begging her to come to Miami so he could show her the house he wanted to buy for her; he told Molly it was a foreclosure, which was why he could afford it, but he needed her to love it, that he knew she was the only woman for him and saw no sense in wasting precious time.

Mr Lin was weeping again. 'In that, of course, he was right.'

'More tea, sir?' The ME poured another hefty shot of Chivas into Lin's cup.

'Her parents chose the name Mo Li – meaning jasmine – because they guessed the two parts would be joined, and they liked the name Molly too.' Lin paused. 'My given name is Jie, meaning successful.' He shrugged. 'James seemed more suitable for business. My business is called James Lin International Air Freight, and it has done well, so I guess the name change didn't hurt. My niece came to work for me when she moved to Miami.' His smile was very sad. 'She enjoyed her days at the office with me, though not, I think, as much as I did.' He rose, calmly and steadily, from his chair. 'For purposes of the death certificate, her first name should be Mo Li.'

Elliot Sanders and the two detectives were on their feet too.

'I'm grateful, Doctor,' Lin said to the ME, 'for your hospitality and kindness.'

'I'm grateful, too, Mr Lin,' Sanders said, 'to have had this opportunity to hear about your niece.'

James Lin turned to look up at Sam, who, at six-three, was taller by at least eight inches. 'I expect you have questions for me, Detective

Becket. The primary one being do I know of anyone who might have had reason to do this to Mo Li.' His face was grim now. 'I do not. I don't know anyone who didn't like, if not love her. She was very easy to love.'

Sam offered Lin a ride home, but he refused, said he wanted to remain in the building a while longer, would sit quietly in the lobby, not yet ready to leave the place in which his niece's body lay.

'If I need help, I'll ask. And I'll be available to you any time.'

'One immediate question, sir,' Sam said.

'Sure,' Lin said.

'Do you know of anyone who might have had a reason to want Mr Burton dead?'

Lin looked up, his gaze steady. 'If I had known seven years ago how my niece's life would end, I might have killed him myself.'

'Has anyone else felt that way, Mr Lin?' Martinez asked. 'More recently.'

'Not that I know of,' Lin said.

'May I ask how your brother and Mo Li's mother died?' Sam said.

'My brother's given name was Zhu, but he was always known as Joe. His wife was named Meihui, but most people called her May. Joe's car went off a bridge into a creek near Santa Barbara. His steering failed. So they told me.'

'Did you have any reason to doubt it?' Sam asked.

'No reason. Yet I did.' He sighed. 'It happened a long time ago. If you're thinking there might

55

be some connection with what's happened to my niece, don't waste your time or energy.'

'It didn't just happen to your niece, Mr Lin,' Martinez said. 'So forgive us, but if you had cause to believe your brother's accident was suspicious, we need to know.'

'There was no logic to my doubts,' Lin said, 'only grief. And please don't imagine I don't feel for the others, but my heart isn't breaking because of them. Not even for Mo Li's husband.' He looked up. 'I'm sure you understand.'

'Of course,' Sam said.

And saw Martinez's dark brows rise just a little.

Two calls to make before their working day ended.

The first to Jackson Memorial to check on William Burton.

Resting, they were told, and not to be disturbed till tomorrow, at the earliest.

They headed back to Stillwater Drive to see Elaine Blauner.

Her account differed in no way from the one she'd shared with Mary Cutter, with one addition: the boat in question had been 'parked nose out toward the Intracoastal'.

'I do know that isn't a boating term,' Mrs Blauner said, 'but as my husband will confirm, I'm seriously anti-boats.'

She had not seen the four men's arrival, had presumably still been at her sister's, though if only she'd known . . .

'Nothing you could have done.' Sam saw her distress.

'I could have called 911,' she said. 'Found our binoculars, given you more.'

'You're giving us plenty, ma'am,' Martinez said.

Their only witness so far.

Lot of hope pinned on the camera next door.

Coming home to Grace and their son felt even more precious than usual.

The small house itself, on Bay Harbor Islands, with its lovely white frontage, twin palms and bottle brush tree had seemed welcoming to Sam the first time he'd visited, back when Dr Grace Lucca had still been a stranger. Many happy years since then, even if there had been too many bad times interwoven with the good. But they'd all come through, stronger for what they'd survived, grateful for what they still had.

Sam was damned if he'd let another psychotic game player threaten that.

Grace had cooked one of his favorites, *pollo all'arrabiata*, and in return, he told her about the killings and the implicit threat to them.

'This might be a good time for you and Joshua to go stay with Cathy.'

'I don't think so,' she said.

'This was brutal stuff,' Sam said. 'And that message was personal.'

'Clearly,' Grace said. 'And you're afraid for me, because they were especially brutal to the Chinese-American wife. But following that train of thought, you're as much at risk as me – perhaps more.' She paused. 'Maybe you should hand over

57

the case, and then we could all leave town until the killers are caught?'

'I don't want to do that. Though I will, if you ask me to. For one thing, my leaving would be giving them exactly what they want. For another, this feels like some kind of challenge.'

'It doesn't make you responsible, Sam.'

'I know,' he said.

'Yet I know that's how you feel.' Grace paused. 'You must know that I won't go anywhere without you, especially in these circumstances. If our marriage is behind this, we've always known that such dregs still exist.'

'Doesn't make me prepared to put you and Joshua at risk.'

'Of course not. But I don't think we should overreact. We're not as low profile a family as we'd like. We've both made the news too often, which means that addressing that message to you was probably just game-playing, as you said.'

'Possibly.'

'I'm hoping probably,' Grace said.

'So we sit tight,' Sam said.

Grace nodded. 'I think so. We sit tight while you and Al find these new monsters and put them away.' She picked up her plate and glass, and Woody, their ageing mini dachshund-schnauzer cross, eased out of his bed, hopeful of tidbits. 'And if we have to change our minds, by the way, we won't be ruining Cathy's precious time, we'll find somewhere else to hide.'

They were both quiet for a few moments, clearing the table, and then Grace asked suddenly: 'Have you checked on Chauvin lately?'

'Sure,' Sam said.

'Why didn't you tell me?'

'Because I hoped you'd put him out of your mind.'

'Like you have,' Grace said.

Sam smiled. 'It's all good. Another piece published in a local paper. In Bath, England. He seems settled for now. Maybe he's found another blonde.'

Grace moved closer, leaned against him. 'If I say I hope so, does that make me a very selfish person?'

'No more than me,' Sam said.

'Maybe he's found someone to love him back,' Grace said.

'You're still a romantic then,' Sam said.

'I am, if it gives us one less thing to worry about,' Grace said.

Monday evening in Miami, the four members of the Virginia Chapter were celebrating.

Reaping their respective rewards for a job well done.

Targets terminated in the manner laid down in their instructions.

The message for Becket left as directed.

The golden-blond washed out of their hair, blue contacts out of their eyes.

Their boat, its forged decal removed, scrubbed and power-steam-cleaned of every residual trace of their presence, gently bobbing in its mooring. One of many in No Name Harbor in Bill Baggs State Park. A good distance away.

The weapons returned. Proceeds of the robbery locked in the Safe Lock Company vault. Their killing clothes and masks disposed of, even contacts and sunglasses. Those parts of the mission taken care of by Leon, the front man. Team leader. Hardest and coldest of the bunch. The right man for the job. The one trusted most by the boss.

Not that she actually trusted any of them. They all knew that. Same as they knew that none of them trusted each other.

She called them her Virginians and her Crusaders and, sometimes, her Knights, and Leon had seen *Kingdom of Heaven* and Andy had seen *Robin Hood: Prince of Thieves*, and it had been Leon who'd first called her 'Mrs Hood', which she had liked and which had stuck with them all after that.

All their names were aliases, chosen by the boss, and having another identity had made the mission a little less hard for CB, who had felt he was living through a nightmare, had been aware that Andy, too, had been burdened by the sins they were committing.

Not so Jerry, who seemed to have sailed through it, while Leon had patently enjoyed the events of Sunday evening.

Hell, Leon had fucking *loved* it all. Especially putting the noose around that poor woman's neck.

It made CB sick deep in his soul – if he had one – and that scared him.

Though not as much as *she* scared him. Mrs Hood or Virginia or her *real* damned name, which they all knew, but were too terrified to ever tell anyone.

60

She knew how to tailor her threats, custom-made for each individual.

Better this, then, than the alternative.

And for now, this evening, they had their rewards.

She had chosen carefully, had enjoyed choosing. For Andy, divorced and living alone, a thousand dollars and a sixty-inch all-singing, all-dancing TV that she guessed he'd slump in front of most nights, eating pizza, drinking beer and watching cop shows and salacious channels.

For Jerry, his cash and a room at Zoop's Motel with a multi-pierced woman promised to him for two hours, an exotic creature who would bind and gag him and help him fulfill some of his strongest urges, which *she* knew were to be on the receiving end of all kinds of sexual viciousness.

For CB, who had been suffering disabling toothache for weeks, the same payment and torture of another kind in a downtown Miami dentist's chair. The weakest of the team, she knew, the one most burdened by conscience, to whom she suspected that the pain of drilling might almost be a blessing if it blocked out the memory of what he had helped to do to those people.

And for Leon, his money and dinner at Nobu, and she'd been amused by his surprise when she'd suggested that, amazed that she knew he'd yearned to go there; especially intrigued too, she guessed, because of the connection with his hero, De Niro, and his fabulous black wife. She didn't know if Leon actually understood irony, but she had made it clear to all her Crusaders at the outset that she did not expect them to feel as she did, did not give a damn how they felt about anything, so long as they did her bidding and kept their mouths shut.

She had gone so far as to run through the menu with him, observed him selecting. Sashimi first, including bluefin *toro*, then hot black cod, then Wagyu flank steak, washed down with a ten-year-old sake, aged (according to the menu) to classical music. Followed by Satandagi and Pacific Rim dessert wine.

A glutton, but a competent man who had enjoyed his work. A killer, who had earned his reward.

As they all had. For services rendered to the cause.

And more to come.

June 4

At four a.m. Tuesday, Central European Summer Time, the man who Sam and Grace believed to be in the English spa town of Bath turned over in bed and gazed up at his ceiling.

At her.

The woman of his dreams.

His fantasy-reality *mélange*. Cathy Becket transformed from an American student-cum-athlete into one of the sexiest women ever photographed. So much like the real Grace Kelly as she'd looked leaning in over Jimmy

Stewart in *Rear Window*, lips tantalizing, the black dress with its perfect décolletage, the single strand of pearls, all just restrained but exquisitely tempting . . .

Almost impossible to believe that the blown-up photograph he was looking at was not of Kelly, but of Catherine, as he'd renamed Cathy.

He said it now, enjoying the sound of it spoken the French way, the last syllable elongated. '*Cat-er-een.*' His make-believe fantasy child of her late, great Serene Highness.

He'd thought no one could ever replace the princess in his imaginary world, the place in his mind that he inhabited whenever possible, when the frustrations and tedium of everyday life permitted. GK had lived in his mind-cocoon for years, until he'd traveled to Switzerland and happened upon Grace Lucca Becket for the first time – and she'd blown him sky-high, had galvanized him sufficiently to travel to the United States in search of her, or at least another fix of her.

But then the Beckets had invited him to their home.

And he had seen *her*.

Their Cathy.

His Catherine.

He gazed up at her now and murmured her name again, like a long, breathy kiss.

He had already taken her places she'd probably never dreamed of going. He'd been practicing Qigong for almost a year now and felt extraordinarily better for it, mentally and physically; and he knew that some people – his parents, among others, needless to say – viewed the practice with skepticism, but through his adaptation of Qigong he had not only strengthened his body and improved his physique, but had also learned to mind-travel. He and Catherine had gone to Caribbean islands and lain on white sand, had walked together – both naked – around the Sully Wing on the ground floor of the Louvre, had stood, arms linked, gazing at the mutilated, exquisite Venus de Milo, so enigmatic, so aloof. It was just a matter of time, he was certain, until his Catherine would pose for him as the goddess, semi-draped; only his Venus would be whole, sublime, perfect.

Just a matter of time.

It was Cathy who found them.

Three months since she and Luc had arrived in Cannes. Gray, mild winter transmuted into gorgeous early summer, a time of unsurpassed beauty for Cathy, much of it seen from the back of Gabe's Ducati Monster.

No beauty this morning, early on the Tuesday that Gabe was due to return after a week on his uncle's farm in the Var interior.

Cathy had been assisting Jeanne with opening, was running checks in the dry store when she spotted them between the olive oil and spices. Thought for a moment that a large ketchup bottle must have broken.

Until the vivid red stain shifted. Came to life.

'Jeanne!' Cathy jolted back into the doorway, horrified, as a moving blanket of huge red cockroaches spilled over the shelf and spread like a moving blanket over the canned goods. '*Jeanne!*' '*Qu'est-ce qu'il y a?*' The older woman came in, saw them. '*Dieu.*'

She backed out, Cathy right after her, and Jeanne slammed the door shut.

'What do we do?' Cathy's heart was pounding. 'They're *everywhere.*'

Jeanne was pale, but composed. 'First, I phone the exterminators and Nic, then you and I must check over the whole restaurant.' She pulled her cell phone from her blazer pocket and checked her watch. 'It will be voicemail, but they'll call back immediately.' She found the number, pressed the key, waited, then left a brief, clear message.

'Have you had them before?' Cathy asked.

Jeanne shook her head. 'I'm going to call Nic from his office. Wait for me, please.'

'Do you want me to start checking around?' Cathy felt sick at the thought.

'No,' Jeanne said. 'We'll do it together.'

Half a day lost. Nic and Jeanne, Cathy, Luc – surprisingly calm, having lived for a time in an infested Manhattan brownstone – and the other early arrivals assisting in the search for some entry point previously unknown, finding no holes or gaps, then waiting for the exterminators to declare that cleaning could commence.

'What I don't get,' Cathy said to Luc as they scrubbed the floor around the work stations, 'is how come there were no signs yesterday.' Monday being the weekly deep-clean day.

'They were probably lurking in the walls,' Luc said darkly.

'I'm not sure they would dare.' Sadi violently scraped her own prep table. 'Every cockroach in the neighborhood must know how obsessive Nic is about hygiene.' She paused. 'Though I've never heard of red *cafards* on the Côte d'Azur.'

It was certainly true that preventive measures were taken daily, and Cathy had often seen Jeanne on her knees in corners checking for cracks between monthly visits from their pest control firm.

'If they're anything like American roaches,' Luc said, 'that might make them even more determined.' He leaned back, shifted to ease his knees. 'Horrible little bastards.'

'These weren't little, though.' Cathy shuddered. 'They were huge.'

'Maybe they didn't just crawl in,' Marcel Simon, the barman, said, coming in from the bar with one of the waiters, a Parisian named Michel Mont.

'What do you mean?' Luc asked him.

Marcel shrugged. 'It could be like the other things.'

'What other things?' Cathy asked, still scrubbing.

'Nothing.' Aniela Walczak, the beautiful Polish *gardes-manger*, waiting for the order to restack the coolers and storage room, gave the barman a look. 'Marcel has a vivid imagination.'

'Maybe,' Marcel said, and headed off to the wine cellar.

'What did he mean?' Cathy asked Sadi a moment later.

Sadi looked around before she answered. 'A few things have happened here. Nasty tricks, and—'

'And what?' Luc asked curiously.

Sadi shook her head.

Cathy, about to speak, saw that Jeanne had come in from the dining room. She looked up at Sadi, saw that her mouth had set in a straight line. No more gossip out of her for the moment. Cathy remembered the seething red blanket of bugs, shivered again, and carried on scrubbing.

The squad held an early meeting Tuesday morning, prior to a hastily arranged press conference.

Too damned little added to the boards, though Sam had posted four empty *Wanted* frames, just waiting for the photos to fill them, and James Lin's name and image (lifted from an old copy of the *South Florida Business News*) had made it onto a board, with checks underway into Molly Burton's parents' deaths and into Mr Lin and his company.

Mary Cutter came in ten minutes late, looking upbeat.

'Mr Rosenblatt just called. They came back late last night, and he knows we wanted them to wait for us, but he already checked the camera. Remotely,' she added swiftly, seeing Sam's expression. 'He understands the importance of the warrant, swears no one's touched the camera itself.'

'And?' Martinez said impatiently.

'And he's pretty sure they've got them.'

'Way to go, Mary,' Sergeant Beth Riley said.

'Not my camera,' Cutter said. 'Four men, baseball caps.'

'On our way.' Sam was already halfway out the door, Martinez putting the lid on his coffee and grabbing his phone.

'Press conference,' Riley called.

Sam wheeled around. 'You want us to delay this, Sarge?'

Riley hardly hesitated. 'I'll tell the captain. Go, guys.'

Sam glanced at Martinez. 'Warrant?'

Martinez patted his jacket pocket. 'Right behind you.'

They had the four men on tape, on departure presumably, not arrival, because due to the camera's slow swivel, one minute – six fifty-four Sunday evening, according to the clock – there was an empty space just ahead of the Rosenblatts' mooring, and then, at six fifty-eight, that space had been occupied, as if by magic, by a dark blue-and-white Fountain power boat, its portside decal visible, moored and already empty – and Elaine Blauner had been right about the boat facing toward the Intracoastal.

By thc time the camera had traveled back toward the Burton house, the towpath was deserted and the Burtons' backyard was not in range of the device.

Still, they did have footage of the suspects – or at least, persons of interest – walking back toward the boat at eight thirty-four, almost half an hour after sunset. No record of the stumble that Mrs

Blauner had told Cutter about, but four men – male, for sure – wearing white T-shirts, jeans, dark boat shoes, dark baseball caps and sunglasses, one man carrying a bag – proceeds of the safe robbery, perhaps, maybe weapons, who knew what else?

Nothing more for now, but the images would be blown up and worked on, the men's individual walks, bearing and any observable idiosynchrasies jumped on, though darkness, the caps and sunglasses made facial recognition software unusable.

They did have the boat's registration number and validation decal.

'Like that's not going to be phony,' Martinez said on their way back to the station.

'Maybe just stolen,' Sam said.

Which would, at least, give them the possibility of a trail if, say, some other camera or witness had seen the Fountain being taken.

Not holding their breath.

'Still wondering why they didn't disable the Rosenblatt camera,' Martinez said.

'Probably too risky to tamper with it,' Sam said.

'Maybe cocky about not being recognized.'

'Maybe whoever paid them was just very confident.'

'You really don't think the boss was one of them.'

'Uh-uh,' Sam said. 'My gut tells me we have another game player who doesn't like getting his hands dirty.'

* * *

69

They checked in, heard that the press conference had gone to plan, then went to Markie's for coffee and Danish and more mulling over what they had.

James Lin still on both their minds.

'He said he wouldn't have minded killing Gary Burton,' Martinez said.

'If he'd known what was going to happen down the line,' Sam reminded him. 'Could be something else behind that, though.'

'Probably wanted Molly to have married someone from the same background.'

'No crime just wanting that.' Sam shrugged. 'Let's wait on what we learn about her parents' accident, see if Mr Lin had cause to be suspicious.' He drained his Americano. 'And let's see what he imports or exports.'

'What are you hoping for, man?' Martinez's grin was wry. 'A cover operation for ivory poachers?'

Sam took out his iPhone, tapped in, waited. 'Top five US exports to China: waste, seeds and grains, aircraft and aircraft parts, electronic components and cars. Just bringing you back to the real world.'

'Where all people are what they claim to be,' Martinez said.

Gary Burton's business partner was waiting for them at the station.

Nick Gibson, about six-one, thirty-something, looked a little like Richard Gere at that age, lean and tanned. A poster boy for the fitness club he'd run with Burton, and from the laugh lines around his eyes, Sam guessed he usually smiled a lot, though this afternoon he looked wretched.

'I was in Cancun,' he explained. 'I didn't know until I landed and saw a text from the office. The guys knew I was flying back, and no one wanted to tell me before.'

Sam told him they were sorry for his loss, and Gibson lost it for a moment, cried like a baby, then blew his nose, pulled himself together and apologized.

'No need, Mr Gibson,' Martinez told him.

He didn't want coffee, tea or water. All he knew so far about the killings was that his friends had been tied up in a car and left to die of carbon monoxide poisoning. He wanted to know if that was true, what the cops were doing about it, and what he could do to help.

'So you and Mr Burton were friends,' Sam said, 'not just business partners.'

'We were friends over and above the business.' Gibson's eyes filled again. 'We opened the first GG Fitness – on Collins and Seventy-second – the only one left now – eight years ago. Pete and Gary were best buddies, but I think I was second in line for Gary. He was my best friend in the world. He made every day seem like fun.' He shook his head. 'Even when we agreed we had to shut down the other two clubs, we had our priorities straight, you know? Families, good health, nice homes, enough to eat. The rest would have been a bonus if it had gone right, but it wasn't that important.'

'Easy come, easy go?' Martinez said lightly.

Gibson's laugh was harsh. 'You're kidding,

71

right? It was damned hard working our butts off to open two more clubs, then having to shut them down again. But at the end of the day, it was only business, and we both knew that.' He turned his face away. 'And here it is. The end of the day.'

Sam gave him a moment, then asked about enemies. Gibson said he'd stake anything that Gary had none. Martinez asked about the Burtons' marriage. Gibson said they were nuts about each other. Sam asked if there had been any family issues, any long-term arguments or maybe disapproval when they'd married, and Gibson said none that he knew of.

'Definitely not from Gary's side. His old man loved her.' He stopped. 'William. I haven't talked to him. You've seen him, right? Is he alone?'

Sam told him that Burton had been hospitalized, but was stable and would be discharged later that day.

'I hate to think of him alone,' Gibson said. 'Do you think he'd come stay with me?' He rubbed his face hard, trying to pull his thoughts together. 'Ask him,' Sam said.

'What about Molly's family?' Martinez brought them back on track. 'Any issues about the marriage from that side?'

Gibson stared at them. 'What are we talking about here? Is this about her being Chinese and . . . Are you saying that could be relevant to *this*?'

'We're just building a picture,' Sam said. 'Anything that helps us get to know Gary and Molly better, to know anything they might have been up against.'

Gibson was silent for a moment. 'OK. I guess I was never sure that her uncle – you know he was her only close relative . . .' He broke off.

'I'm sorry, I've lost the thread.'

'Molly's uncle,' Sam supplied. 'Do you think he didn't approve?'

'Maybe. Gary mentioned that he was cool early on, but it didn't seem a real concern.'

'How close were you to Molly?' Sam asked.

'I loved her,' Gibson said. 'Most people did. She was a delight.'

'You said "most" people loved her,' Martinez said.

'No one could have hated Molly, if that's what you're reaching for.'

'The only thing we're reaching for is the truth, Mr Gibson,' Martinez said.

Gibson looked suddenly tired. 'I know. I'm sorry. Molly was kind, she was smart, she had a sense of humor, she was pretty. And she loved Gary, which was what counted most for me.'

'GG Fitness.' Sam changed tack. 'Any unhappy members, recent or going way back? Any ugly scenes or long-running issues? Anyone barred or thrown out? Employees fired for reasons they might have thought unjustified? Someone who might have harbored some kind of grudge, maybe the kind that festers?'

'Enough to lead someone to kill four people?' Incredulous, Gibson ran a hand through his hair. 'Jesus. No one that springs to mind. I could ask a few of the guys, see if they ever witnessed anything like that.' He paused. 'I know we've had to close a few people down because of unpaid dues or health issues.'

'What kind of issues?' Martinez asked.

'People sometimes become obsessed with bodybuilding or weight loss. You see members repeatedly overdoing workouts, maybe insisting on using unsuitable equipment or just not understanding that they need to respect their bodies.'

'Names would be helpful.' Sam saw Gibson nod. 'What about steroids? Anyone ever ask for them?'

'You mean ask us to supply them?'

'Maybe,' Sam said.

'If they did ask, they'd get turned down flat,' Gibson said. 'If they persisted, they'd be told to leave and not come back.'

'And that's never happened?' Martinez said.

'Not that I'm aware.' He hesitated. 'We've had members who've asked about performance-enhancing drugs. We educate them, tell them about vitamin supplements, glucosamine, the right sports drinks, if and when to use them. Our policy on steroids and other illegal substances is very clear, very firm.'

'Did you and Gary work the same or split shifts?' Sam asked.

'When we were running three clubs, we both worked crazy hours, and it was tough, but we were young. Once we scaled back down to just Collins, we divided the hours. Gary took care of the paperwork, while I've always been more front-of-house.'

'Didn't Molly do the book work?' Martinez said.

'She didn't have time,' Gibson said. 'Her uncle kept her pretty busy.'

Sam nodded. 'Just one last thing. Strictly for

the record, can you tell us where you were Sunday evening?'

Gibson shook his head. 'In Cancun, like I told you. I can give you the paperwork. The hotel and the restaurant where I ate Sunday evening.' His jaw worked for a moment. 'If that's not enough, the hotel spa's manager could confirm that I had dinner with him.'

'We appreciate your help,' Sam said.

Gibson took a breath, steadying himself. 'Could this have been a robbery turned bad, something like that? Because I'm telling you, these were all decent, sweet people.'

'You know much about Mr Ventrino?' Martinez asked.

'He was a mechanic with his own place, selling used cars and vans, doing well enough to afford a nice house. A good guy.' His forehead was deeply furrowed. 'I still can't believe it's even true, you know?'

'We know,' Sam said.

A little after noon, Kovac summoned Sam to his office to ask if he'd reached a final decision about the case.

'Not too late to change your mind. You weren't named as lead at the conference.'

'I won't be changing my mind, Lieutenant,' Sam said.

Kovac shrugged. 'Your call. Is Grace OK with this?'

'Of course,' Sam said.

And after that the afternoon continued according to plan.

Bereavement. Grief. Shock. Mourning.

William Burton had accepted their offer to drive him home from Jackson Memorial, on the understanding that they would speak to him honestly.

'I'm not sick,' he said in Martinez's Chevy. 'My family were just murdered.' He looked haggard, like a man who'd been hit by a wrecking ball. 'So you can interview the crap out of me, whatever you need, so long as I can do something for my boy and his sweet wife and their poor friends. Just let me do *something*.'

His Surfside apartment was semi-dark when they arrived, the blinds still drawn, the kitchen garbage smelling bad, sections of last Sunday's *New York Times* strewn over the couch and floor in the sitting room.

'Nick must be in a bad way,' he said, after hearing about Gibson's concern.

'He seemed very shocked,' Martinez said. 'He'd been traveling and only found out this morning.'

'Not "seemed",' Burton said firmly, and sat heavily on the *Sunday Review* on the couch. 'I guess your line of work must make you suspicious of everyone, but I can tell you those boys were real close. If Nick Gibson tells you he's shocked, believe him.'

'Good to know,' Sam told him.

'So,' Burton said. 'Why don't you both take a load off so we can start?' He paused. 'I'm assuming you haven't arrested anyone yet?'

'No, sir,' Sam said.

'Could I make you a cup of something, Mr

Burton?' Martinez asked. 'Maybe get a little light into the place?'

'Later,' Burton said. 'Sit down, please.'

They sat.

'No suspects?' Burton asked.

'Not yet,' Martinez said.

'Lines of enquiry?'

'Several,' Sam said.

'Which you can't discuss with me, right?'

'Not at this stage, no, sir.'

Burton's pain was palpable, and both detectives felt that if he were alone he'd break down, had probably had no privacy since the identification and his own collapse.

'So, what can I tell you?' He rallied. 'I can tell you about my son. That he was a good, decent boy growing up. That he loved his mother and me, too. That he was never big on learning, more the athletic, lighthearted type. Gary laughed a lot, was never moody. When he met Nick and they opened the club, it made him happy.' Burton's eyes glistened with tears. 'Which made us happy too, because Gary liked sharing things with people he loved. He was an optimist.'

Neither Sam nor Martinez spoke.

'They made mistakes,' Burton continued. 'Opened more clubs when they should probably have stuck with the one and paid a price for that, which scared Gary, I can tell you, because Molly was in his life by then. But she helped him keep their heads above water. They were a team. They would have made fine parents.'

The sorrow, the waste, pierced Sam to the core.

'Molly miscarried twice,' Burton said softly. 'I'm not sure how to feel about that now. Maybe it's better there aren't any little ones.'

Sam gave him a moment. 'Did your son talk to you about those rough times? About anyone who might have lost money, perhaps held that against Gary?'

Burton shook his head. 'He always hated us knowing if he'd flunked an exam at school or got in any trouble, so no, if there were people like that he probably wouldn't have told me.' He paused. 'I don't know if anyone else mentioned it, but Gary and Pete were pretty keen on gambling.'

'No, sir,' Martinez said.

'Strictly small stuff, so far as I know. Molly used to tease him about it, complain a little about their poker nights and Vegas weekends – did you know that's where Gary and Molly first met?'

Sam nodded. 'Molly's uncle told us about that.'

Burton made a disparaging sound.

'Mr Lin not your favorite person, sir?' Martinez asked.

'I only met him twice,' Burton said, 'so I may have been mistaken, but let's just say I got the impression Mr Lin didn't feel that Gary was good enough for his niece. I didn't take kindly to that.'

'Did he object to the marriage?' Sam asked.

'Not that I was told. But Molly was strong, and it was plain from the first time Gary introduced her to us that she was in love with him. If James Lin had tried to split them up, he wouldn't have stood a chance.' The pain came back into his face. 'I can't stand to think about what they did

78

to her and my boy.' He shook his head. 'I just can't.'

'How about that cup of tea now?' Martinez said gently.

'No tea.' Burton stood up. 'Thank you for your kindness.'

Sam and Martinez rose too.

'Perhaps we could let Mr Gibson know you're home?' Sam said.

'I imagine he'll be in touch soon enough,' Burton said. 'You don't need to worry about me. Just do whatever you can to put them away.'

'You can depend on it,' Sam said.

'I am,' Burton said. 'I'd say it's about the only thing holding me together – that you seem to care.'

They walked toward the front door, Sam and Martinez uncomfortably aware of the blinds still drawn, the garbage still not taken out.

'I know the place stinks,' Burton said. 'I'll be dealing with that.'

'It's no problem for us to lend you a hand, sir,' Martinez said.

'It would be a problem for me,' Burton said. 'I'm grieving, not losing my marbles.'

'No, sir.' Sam hesitated, then had to ask: 'Do you think that your son might ever have got in over his head, maybe playing poker? Any big debts?'

Burton stood up straighter. 'Big enough for someone to arrange a hit, you mean?' Even in the dim light, his outrage showed. 'No way on earth. My son had his head screwed on, and he wouldn't have done that to Molly, believe me.'

'We do,' Sam said.

'Are you sure there's nothing we can do for you?' Martinez tried again.

'I'm all right. Or as right as I'm ever going to be.' Burton paused. 'There'll be a funeral to arrange soon enough, and then I'll just wait my time.'

Neither detective asked for what, both all too sure they knew.

William Burton felt he had nothing left to live for.

Next stop the First Choice Inn and the Reardons.

Joseph Reardon came down to the lobby, told them that Rose was finally sleeping, that he'd be grateful if they could put off their interview for another day.

'It's not as if we feel we have anything to tell you that would help,' he said.

Sam asked if their son might be ready to talk.

'Sean isn't here,' his father said. 'He's out walking. He's always done that when something's upset him.' His eyes, behind their spectacles, became rheumy. 'This has hit him very hard.'

They left a note for the son, asking him to call so that they could continue their conversation with him.

'Want to go look for him?' Martinez asked on their way back to the car.

'Big haystack,' Sam said. 'Let's go see what we can dig up about him.'

'And Molly's Uncle James too.'

'Then I guess we go talk to a few people at GG Fitness,' Sam said.

'The usual,' Martinez said, getting into the Chevy.

Nothing yet but a few niggles, none of them pointing to multiple homicide.

And then, of course, there was 'Virginia'.

Gabe arrived early Tuesday evening, back from the Var with a large jar of olives and an armful of fresh lavender, and they went straight to bed. Cathy told him that she'd missed him, and he said the same back.

They agreed on many things. They disliked the mega-rich end of Cannes, hated Monaco, loved the stunning coast, spent many hours of their spare time swooping in and out of traffic, taking in breathtaking views, riding up to St-Paul-de-Vence, enjoying the Chagalls and Picassos and Giacomettis; and once, after they'd drunk too much wine in a small restaurant up in Eze, as the Ducati roared around bends on the way back, Cathy had thought that they might be killed, but each time Gabe had steadied the bike and laughed, she'd felt more certain that she loved him.

She hadn't told him that, nor had he told her how he felt. Nor had he shared much more about his past or family or any innermost secrets. She knew more than she had: that his home was a small apartment on the top floor of a little pale green house in Golfe-Juan, that his market partner was a forty-something man named Rafael Fillon who rode a Harley Davidson and lived alone in a small apartment in the rue de la Miséricorde, where Gabe sometimes stayed. That he'd been

81

given a *lopin de terre,* a small parcel of land, by his Uncle Yves – Yves Rémy, his mother's brother, a farmer – and she *thought* that was probably where he went when he left town for a few days at a time, and she'd asked what grew there, olives or fruit trees or lavender, perhaps. But Gabe had just smiled and told her that he'd take her there some day when the time was right.

That time, apparently, had not come, though it scarcely seemed to matter, because he shared *himself* with her almost daily, and she thought she could ask for no more.

That, perhaps, she wanted no more.

'I keep remembering the roaches,' she told him tonight, in bed.

'Try thinking about other things,' Gabe said. 'Like what we just did.'

She smiled. 'So what were the nasty tricks Sadi and Marcel mentioned before Aniela shut them down?'

'Couple of things,' Gabe said. 'A plague of carpenter ants last year.'

'Yuck.'

'Legions of them. The restaurant was closed for two days before CHSCT – health and safety – pronounced it clean.'

'But those things happen, surely?'

'Not usually in a place run as rigorously as *Le Rêve.*'

'OK,' Cathy said. 'What else?'

'Something more subtle, but a lot worse. A big copper pan switched with an unlined pan. If Jeanne hadn't spotted it—'

'Verdigris poisoning,' Cathy said.

'Potentially,' Gabe agreed, and stretched.

'Is that all?'

'In my time, yes,' he said.

'So what's Nic done about it?'

'Beats me.'

'Didn't he bring in the police?'

'I doubt it.' Gabe paused. 'Did he call them today?'

'Not that I know of. He joined in with the cleanup for a while, but then he disappeared into his office. Jeanne told us later that although we were closed till evening we'd all be paid for our shifts, and Nic paid for us to go to *La Pizza* for lunch, which was nice of him.'

'He's a great guy,' Gabe said. 'But I'm not surprised he didn't call the cops. More risk of damage to the restaurant's reputation, besides which, I imagine Nic has his own ways of dealing with things.'

'You think he knows who's done these things?'

'If he does, he won't be sharing it with us.' Gabe yawned, closed his eyes.

'But—'

'Goodnight, Marple.'

June 5

By noon on Wednesday they'd all seen their images on TV, in newspapers and on the Internet, including a video on Channel 6 of their walk back from the Burton house – the *kill house*, the boss called it – to the boat.

The Boss.

Who hadn't laid a hand on the victims, but was the scariest of them all.

None of them ever spoke about her among themselves. Fact was, despite the rewards and cash and promises of more to come, they were all scared to death of her.

Death linked them all now.

This was the first time they'd all gotten together since early Monday morning, when they'd gone about their respective post-job tasks as laid down for them by the boss.

Mrs Hood.

This was to be a short meeting, she'd told them, summoning them individually with brief phone calls, her orders clear and concise, her manner affable.

She came for them, one by one, in a black stretch limo with driver and tinted windows, had pre-arranged pickup points, told them to dress respectably but not in a way that would draw attention.

'What do you want me to wear?' Leon had asked.

The only one who'd dared ask for clarification, she'd noted.

Still team leader quality.

'Not the same look as Sunday,' she said.

She picked him up first, outside Dunkin Donuts at the corner of Sheridan and Arthur Godfrey, saw that he was wearing beige chinos, a navy short-sleeved shirt and sunglasses. He looked like a thousand other men in Miami.

'I figured no baseball cap,' he said, right after climbing in.

'No one's going to recognize you,' she told him.

Leon looked around the back of the limo, saw the bar, the chilled champagne, felt a buzz and saw Mrs Hood smile a little, though she didn't offer him anything, said nothing more as they drove on.

Next pickup still on Sheridan and West Forty-second, where Andy was waiting outside the HSBC, then right onto Pine Tree Drive, left back onto West Forty-first, over the Intracoastal to Collins and Forty-third for Jerry, standing out front at the Days Inn in denims and a skin-tight red T-shirt.

'Afternoon, Boss.' He nodded at the others. 'Guys.'

'Showing off your oily biceps and six-pack is not my idea of trying not to stand out in the crowd,' Mrs Hood said.

'Just my regular look, Mrs H,' Jerry said.

'Tone it down next time.'

They continued up Collins, getting snarled up in traffic, finally making the Fontainebleau bend before ducking into the Hertz Rent-A-Car fore-court to pick up CB.

'Now here's my idea of a man no one would look at twice,' Mrs Hood said.

'You really know how to pay a guy a compli-ment, Mrs H,' Jerry said.

She looked at him, her eyes cold as frostbite.

CB kept silent, sat back in his seat, dread tight-ening his gut, and wondered for the umpteenth time how he'd ever gotten himself caught up in this ungodly horror.

No one spoke again until the driver – in chauffeur's hat, all but invisible beyond dark glass – had pulled into a strip mall just past Sixty-fifth and parked the limo near Domino's Pizza.

'Hey,' Andy said. 'Good choice. I'm starved.'

'We're not here to eat,' Mrs Hood said.

CB saw Andy's face grow hot, felt a glimmer of relief at not being the only man in the car ill at ease. Ease, hell – they were among killers. They *were* killers. Wanted men.

'I thought you might need a little reassurance,' the boss said, 'after seeing how famous you've all become.'

Clearly she was unfazed by the coverage, Leon saw, his admiration growing.

CB saw Leon's approving gaze, looked at Jerry, strong enough to snap a man's neck, then at Andy, whose eyes were currently fixed on the limo's carpet.

No one as afraid as he was, he felt sure, scared to death every minute, day and night, and his toothache had been worse than ever since his treatment, and he wasn't sure he believed the dentist's assurance that it would ease with antibiotics and time. Not that he was complaining. First because he wouldn't dare, but mostly because he deserved pain.

'You must realize there's no way any of you could be recognized from that recording.' Mrs Hood's blue eyes were calm.

'Only because we dodged the damn camera on the first walk,' Jerry said.

'We should have timed it better on the way back.' Leon regarded the boss squarely. 'I screwed up.'

'No harm done,' Mrs Hood said. 'It was dark and you were well disguised.'

'How do we know it didn't catch us when we got off the boat?' Andy said nervously.

'They got computers that recognize faces,' Jerry added to the angst.

'Facial recognition doesn't work well on subjects in big sunglasses,' Mrs Hood said. 'And unless the sun was full on you, the caps would have shaded you too. Darkness makes it a total no-no.' She paused. 'I imagine you were all paying better attention when you arrived. You need to watch those nerves, gentlemen.'

'I wasn't nervous,' Jerry said.

'Then you're a damned fool,' she said. 'And if you weren't at least edgy after that job, then you were probably high on adrenalin, which can be just as dangerous. We'll all be more observant next time.'

'Next time,' CB echoed.

'You know there's going to be a next time, CB,' she said.

'When?' Leon asked.

'Soon, very soon.' She smiled at him. 'Patience, eager beaver.'

Leon nodded.

'Now,' Mrs Hood said, 'what I really want to know is if you all enjoyed your treats.'

CB listened as, one by one, the others told her they had; Leon almost fawning, Andy teetering between too much or too little enthusiasm, Jerry smirking his thanks.

'Still painful, CB?' she asked.

He hadn't even been conscious of touching his jaw.

'A little.' He flushed. 'Less than before.'

Pain aside, he felt at a great disadvantage. He had no idea, didn't want to know, what the other three had been rewarded with, yet *they* all knew about his dental problems, which he found humiliating.

'The doctor says two more sessions should improve things,' Mrs Hood said.

Just the thought of that made him want to weep.

'I'm very grateful.'

'Me too,' Andy said.

'That's what I like,' she said. 'A little gratitude. And more to come, for you all.'

'That's what I'm counting on,' Jerry said.

She turned her eyes first on him, then the others, one by one.

Cold, empty eyes now, CB thought, suppressing a shudder.

'We're all counting on each other, aren't we?' she said.

'Yes, ma'am,' Leon said.

'*Aren't* we?' she repeated.

'Yes, ma'am,' they all said, in unison, like a school sports team.

'So,' Mrs Hood went on, 'are we ready to hear about Number Two?'

Already. CB's dread expanded again. He glanced at Andy, whose eyes met his, then veered away again.

'I'm ready,' Leon said.

CB chanced a swift look at him, saw something close to dark delight.

'Me, too,' Jerry said.

CB didn't look at him.

'Andy?' the boss said.

'Yes, ma'am. I'm ready,' Andy said.

'And what about you, CB?'

He felt her gaze, those eyes that changed from gentle to brutal in an instant.

'Yes, ma'am,' he said.

'I could use a little more gusto, CB,' she said. He nodded. Forced his lips into a smile.

'Yes, ma'am,' he said again.

Sean Reardon had a record, had been convicted in 2006 of a Second Offense Battery charge on a family member, now his ex-wife; had pled guilty and served time.

'There's more,' Martinez told Sam early Wednesday afternoon. 'The ex was – is – Vietnamese.'

Sam leaned back in his chair, remembering Reardon's reference to the Burtons' marriage, his swift attempt to buy back credibility.

'He got real upset about hate crimes, didn't he?'

'Maybe his own?' Martinez said.

'Let's see what else we can get from Massachusetts,' Sam said.

'Reardon still hasn't called us back.' Martinez's eyes were sharpening.

'His sister was murdered,' Sam said. 'His grief seemed real to me.'

They both absorbed the implications of a supposedly loving brother *possibly* being involved in the brutal killing of his sister and three others. By no means out of the question; Sam had witnessed firsthand a hideous fratricide a couple of years back.

'Back to the hotel?' Martinez said.

Sam thought about the parents, and sighed. Got to his feet. 'Let's go.'

He was easy to find this time. The only customer in the First Choice Bar, drinking Beck's.

Sam hoped he hadn't been doing that for too long.

'Do you have them?' Reardon's first words, soon as he saw them, precise and clear.

Sober enough to interview.

'Not yet,' Sam answered. 'But we would like to talk to you, Mr Reardon.'

'We left a message for you yesterday,' Martinez said.

'Maybe you didn't get it,' Sam said.

'I got it,' Reardon said.

His hostility was plain, and Sam checked again to ensure that they weren't about to embark on a pointless conversation, because a beer or two might loosen the tongue, but anything more . . .

'I'm sorry I didn't call,' Reardon said. 'I guess I just wasn't up to talking.'

'No problem,' Sam said.

'I'm all yours now.'

'We should probably take this somewhere more private,' Martinez said.

'What's wrong with here?'

'Not really a bar stool conversation,' Sam said.

'OK.' Reardon slid off his stool, picked up his Beck's and pointed to a corner table. 'Private enough?'

'Sure,' Sam said. 'So long as the place stays empty.'

He studied Reardon as he moved, almost certain already that he was not one of the *four*, but aware that if this man was party to the killings, it didn't mean he'd had to have been at the scene or even in Florida.

'Is this to do with my ex?' Reardon paused. 'My history?'

'Your conviction, you mean,' Martinez said.

Reardon sighed, then shrugged. 'I guess I can't offer you guys a drink, but maybe a cup of coffee?'

'We're good, thank you,' Sam said.

He motioned to one of the chairs and Reardon sat, facing them and the faux wood-paneled walls, while Sam sat on the banquette, Martinez between him and the other man, the detectives keeping the entrance in view, wanting early warning of the older Reardons perhaps coming to look for their son.

Sean Reardon shifted in his seat, fingered the bottle on the table.

'Times like this, I really miss smoking.' He paused. 'Not that I've ever known a time like this.' He shook his head again. 'God.'

'When did you give up?' Sam asked.

'I didn't. And I get it in restaurants, sure, but in bars?'

'Where were you on Sunday evening, Mr Reardon?' Sam asked.

'Boston.' He paused. 'Why?'

'Routine questions,' Martinez said. 'Where in Boston?'

91

'I was at a birthday party at the Union.' Reardon paused. 'That's the Union Oyster House. Oldest restaurant in America, so they say.'

'Big party?' Martinez asked.

'About twenty people. Why?'

'I already told you,' Martinez said. 'Routine.'

'I wouldn't know,' Reardon said. 'My sister was never murdered before.'

Sam saw his jaw clench, the still-fresh wounds behind the anger, believed his pain was real, knew it ruled nothing out.

'When were you last in Miami?'

'January two years ago,' Reardon said. 'Pete threw a surprise party for Mary Ann's thirtieth. Our parents came too. It was a happy time.'

'Was that the last time you saw your sister?' Martinez asked.

'No. Mary Ann came to Boston at Christmas. She loved it, preferred it to Miami, but Pete was a real Florida guy. Though he liked visiting well enough too.' He took a drink, put down the bottle again. 'Next question.'

'On Monday, at the medical examiner's office,' Sam said, 'you talked about hate crimes.'

'What is this crap?' His face turned red. 'You think I'm a racist? How the *fuck*—?'

Sam noticed the bartender's eyebrows lift.

Reardon leaned forward in his chair, his voice lower. 'I married a Vietnamese girl, you *jerks*.'

'You assaulted your wife,' Sam said quietly. 'More than once.'

'And I served my time,' Reardon said. 'I'm not proud of what I did, but it had nothing to do with race. Kim used to push my buttons, and I lost it a few times. I've had anger management counseling since then.'

'Has it worked?' Martinez asked.

'I'd say so, yes.'

It seemed to dawn on him suddenly, sheer horror widening his eyes. 'You're not serious. You can't be going there. Because Molly was Chinese?'

Sam and Martinez said nothing.

'My own *sister* is dead.' Reardon picked up the Beck's, his hand shaking, then put it down again. 'You're out of your minds, or maybe you're just sick.'

'Were Mo Li Burton and your sister friends?' Sam asked.

Reardon shook his head in disgust. 'Sure they were. And by the way, Molly never pronounced her name that way; she was Molly, plain and simple. Except she wasn't plain and she certainly wasn't simple.'

'Living so close to Mary Ann,' Sam went on, 'I guess they were probably in and out of each other's homes all the time?'

'I guess. Maybe. I wouldn't know.'

'Did you ever see them together, Mr Reardon?'

'Sure. A few times. Not often.'

'At Mary Ann's thirtieth?' Martinez asked.

'Sure.'

'Any other times?' Martinez asked.

'A couple of times, when I was down here, yes. So what?'

'Did you mind seeing them together?' Sam asked. 'Them being such close friends?'

'Why in hell would I mind?' His anger was rising again.

93

'Maybe Mo Li might have reminded you of Kim,' Sam said.

'What, are you stereotyping now?' A sneer in with the anger. 'Saying all Asians look the same?'

'Is that what you think, Mr Reardon?' Martinez said.

'I'll tell you what I think.' Reardon rose. 'I think I'd like to tell you both to fuck off and leave me alone so I can take care of my parents.'

'I'm sorry,' Sam said.

'Jesus,' Reardon said, and sat down again. 'Jesus Christ.'

'We had to ask,' Sam said.

'Given your record,' Martinez said.

'I have something I'd like to ask,' Reardon said, his voice lower.

'Sure,' Sam said.

'Are you going to catch the stinking bastards who did that to my sister and her husband and their friends? Or are you going to carry on wasting time rubbing my nose in something I'm so ashamed of it hurts.'

A group of men entered the bar, and Sam stood up.

'Where are you going?' Reardon said. 'We're not finished.'

'I'm going to buy you another beer,' Sam said. 'I'd say it's the least I can do.'

'You saying you believe me?' Reardon looked up at him.

'I'm a cop,' Sam said. 'I'm not allowed to just *believe* anyone.'

Martinez got up. 'I'll get it. Another Beck's, or something stronger?'

94

'Scotch,' Reardon said. 'Rocks. Thank you.'
Sam sat down again. 'So. Let's start over.'

It had gotten them nowhere, they reflected on their way back to the station.

Reardon supposed, theoretically, that Gary or Pete, or both, might have gotten themselves in deep with their gambling, but he doubted it, and he knew nothing about Molly's family business. He could not imagine anyone hating any of the victims, found it hard to imagine the kind of people capable of such a crime.

Sam and Martinez had both, going on instinct, pretty much ruled him out, even if he had beaten up on his Vietnamese wife. Reardon was still in shock and grieving for his sister, of that they were as sure as they could be.

Martinez gave a sigh. 'I guess it would have been too easy.'

'Is it ever?' Sam said.

June 6

Dr Sergio Antonio Gomez Vega, his wife Luisa and their children, sixteen-year-old Roberto and twelve-year-old Laura, had arrived back at Miami International early Thursday afternoon, their flight from Madrid on schedule; but by the time they'd retrieved their bags and car and taken Laura to Coral Gables (where she was staying over before her best friend Danielle Loeb's eleventh birthday party next day), and Wendy Loeb had insisted they stay for a cup of coffee, it was after six when they finally pulled up in the driveway of their own house on Emerson Avenue in Surfside.

'Hey, Rob, want to help your old man unload the trunk?'

'Can't we stick the car in the garage and do it later?'

'So you can slump on the couch and leave your dad to do it?' Luisa said from the front. 'I don't think so.'

Dr Gomez popped the trunk. 'Come on, son.'

Rob opened his door. 'I can do it without you, Dad. You'll only put your back out.'

'Good boy.' His mother got the keys out of her purse. 'I'll go ahead, see what we have in the freezer.'

'Couldn't we have pizza?' Rob asked. 'I'm starved.'

'Sounds good to me,' his father said.

'I'm not arguing,' his mother said, getting out.

She walked across the tiled driveway and up the three steps to their front door.

Happy to be home.

None of them knew they had company until after Rob had dumped the last of the bags in their hallway and kicked the door shut, while his dad drove his Acura TL into the garage and remote-closed the up-and-over door.

'Please don't kick the door,' Luisa said, coming out of the kitchen.

'Thanks for schlepping the bags, son,' Rob said.

'Don't be cheeky,' Luisa said.

They didn't hear them coming.

96

Two men from the family room.

Two from the back of the house, where the bedrooms were.

Four strangers, all golden-haired, their hands black-gloved.

All holding guns.

'Oh, dear God,' Luisa said softly.

'What the fuck?' Rob said.

He started to turn toward the front door, but the men moved swiftly, blocking his way, one of them sticking a gun right up against his neck.

'Don't hurt him,' his mother said, then made a quiet, mewing sound of fear as one of the strangers took her right arm while another put his weapon against her temple. 'Please.'

'Where's the girl?' one of the men asked.

'Not here,' Luisa said. 'Please don't hurt my son.'

'Where *is* she?' the man said.

'She isn't here,' Rob said. 'She's not coming back tonight.'

The man with the gun to his mother's head seemed to shrug.

'Let's go,' he said.

He had odd-looking blue eyes, Rob noted, probably contacts, then wondered crazily how he could even *notice* that.

'Where are we going?' Luisa asked.

'Don't you want to see your hubby?' the man said.

Terror shot up into her head like mercury rising, made her dizzy.

'What have you done to him?' Rob said. 'What have you done to my dad?'

'Shut up, kid,' his gunman said.

Two of them grabbed his arms, started walking him toward the door that led to the garage.

'Dad!' Rob yelled suddenly. 'Dad, get out of there!'

Luisa's gunman glared at the teenager. 'You want me to shoot your mom?'

'No,' Rob said. 'Hell, *no*, please!'

'Then shut up and do as you're told.'

'It'll be all right, Roberto,' Luisa said quietly to her son.

'No,' said her personal gunman. 'It won't.'

June 7

Now it felt personal.

A second crime. Three victims this time, one of them a minor. A sixteen-year-old male. A teenager. A *boy*, hogtied and gassed with his parents in his father's Acura sedan in the garage of their house on Emerson Avenue in Surfside.

Another windshield message.

Same white letter-size paper, same Baskerville font. Longer than the first, but to the same addressee.

That was what made it personal.

For the Personal Attention of Detective
Samuel Becket,
Miami Beach Police Department

Observe these further repercussions, Detective.

98

Generations down from the original sin.
Let mourners grieve and rail at this punishment, but understand:
This woman's mother and *papá* bear responsibility for their loss.
If others wish to perpetuate these crimes, let them move someplace like Réunion, where *métissage* is celebrated. (I use the French word, because our own is deemed offensive, and my intention is not to offend.)
Just to punish.
And to warn.
I can't stop you all.
But I am saying my piece.

Love Virginia

No formal identification yet, but Mrs Wendy Loeb, the friend who'd found them, had named them as Dr Sergio Gomez, a dentist, his wife Luisa and their son, Roberto.

Only their daughter, Laura, age twelve, spared, having been on a sleepover at her house in Coral Gables.

Mercifully.

But a twelve-year-old, having to face up to this . . .

And if she had been with her family . . .

No limits to this wickedness, clearly. No boundaries. And though Sam knew that the first person singular wording of the messages might be trickery, it felt like the thought process of an individual, probably directing a killing team,

99

maybe a hit squad, maybe something less mercenary, more personal. The words more cold-blooded than ranting, not a note from a deranged psycho but from someone who had planned, deliberated, meticulously organized.

Wendy Loeb had discovered the horror and called 911 at ten forty-eight. The dispatcher had directed her to leave the scene and wait outside for the police, had tried to keep her on the phone, but a neighbor, seeing her weeping on the sidewalk, had taken her in, and after that it had been impossible to maintain verbal communication.

They spoke to Wendy Loeb in the neighbor's kitchen.

She was ashen-faced, trembling, her makeup smeared, her blonde hair wild, as if she'd torn at it, and they did what little they could to offer comfort, seeing in her haunted eyes that the horror would be etched in her memory forever.

'It's unbelievable,' she said. 'They were all drinking coffee in our house yesterday afternoon. It's *unbelievable*. They'd had a lovely vacation, taken the kids out of school for a family celebration in Spain, and Luisa was tanned and beautiful, and Rob looked so handsome . . .' She fought to stem tears. 'I can't believe it. I don't *want* to believe it.'

Convention and caution had it that the reporter of a crime might be a suspect, might have believed themselves to have been seen and be trying to lessen suspicion, might even be a game-playing psycho.

Not the case here, both detectives were certain.

Wendy Loeb wiped her eyes and explained that today was her daughter's eleventh birthday, which was why Dr Gomez had driven the family from MIA via Coral Gables, so that Laura and Dani could spend the night and get ready for her party together.

'Oh my God,' she said abruptly. 'We have to cancel.' Her eyes filled again. 'I haven't told the girls anything yet. I called my husband, Al, at his office – he's probably there by now. We agreed we shouldn't tell Laura anything until we're prepared.' She shook her head. 'God.'

'Do you know if Laura has other close relatives?' Sam's mind was buzzing on two fronts: concern for the twelve-year-old, but also remembering the stressing of 'mother and *papá*' in the killer's note – and were Luisa Gomez's parents living in the United States? Were they alive, period?

'I don't know, though I got the impression that any close family would have been going to Spain for that celebration.'

'Is it possible for Laura to stay with you until arrangements can be made?' Sam asked.

'Of course.' She shook her head again.

'That's good, ma'am.' Martinez felt for her. One minute, a birthday party to prepare, the next, sheer horror and her home turned into a place of mourning.

'Do you think we should tell Laura,' she asked anxiously, 'or should we leave it to someone experienced from the police, or . . .?'

'Someone will take you home, Mrs Loeb,' Sam said. 'Help you out.'

'OK,' she said. 'Thank you.'

'So how come you came here this morning, Mrs Loeb?'

'Laura tried calling home last night but got voicemail, and we all figured her family had turned in early, and Al said "Good for them", because he can never sleep after a flight from Europe.' She shook her head. '"Good for them". Dear God.'

'What time did Laura call home?' Sam asked.

'At around nine, I think.' Mrs Loeb paused. 'Did I mention that Sergio's a dentist?'

'Yes, ma'am,' Martinez said. 'Do you know where his office is?'

'No, I'm sorry. Laura will know, obviously.'

'That's OK. We'll find it,' Martinez said. 'So, this morning?'

'Laura called again at eight-thirty, and Dani came to find me, said that Laura was worried about them because her mom and Rob ought to be there, and I said maybe Luisa had gone to the supermarket, stocking up, and Rob was still sleeping.' She paused. 'So Laura waited till after nine, tried home and their cell phones, and then she called Dr Gomez's office. They said he hadn't shown up yet, and suddenly I felt concerned, too, so I waited for our housekeeper to show up, told Laura to stay with Dani and came to see if anything was wrong.'

Sam waited a beat.

'What happened when you arrived?'

'I rang the bell and knocked on the door but there was no answer, so I took out the keys – did I tell you that Laura gave me her house keys?'

'No, but that's fine,' Sam said. 'Go on.'

'I let myself in, called their names, but then I wasn't sure what to do. I felt I was intruding. I'd only been in their house a few times – once for dinner, once for a barbecue, the other times when I was picking up Dani. The girls are best friends, but Luisa and I didn't have the kind of relationship where you exchange keys.'

'You still weren't intruding, ma'am,' Martinez said. 'Just wanting to help Laura.'

'I was thinking about going back outside when I saw that their bags were still in the hallway. That was when I got really worried – and I was just telling myself I had to look around when I heard the sound.' She gave a small shudder. 'I don't know why I didn't hear it when I was standing outside – maybe a car was driving by . . .'

'What did you hear?' Sam asked.

'The motor running.' Almost a whisper.

'Take your time, Mrs Loeb,' Sam said.

She swallowed, took a breath. 'That was when I noticed the tape around the door – I was still in the entrance hall, and I was pretty sure this door led into the garage.'

'Where was the tape, ma'am?' Martinez asked.

'All around the door.' She was paler. 'I suddenly had this terrible feeling – I just knew I had to open the door, and I got hold of one part of the tape and tore at it.' She looked down at her hands, held them out, stared at the mess of sticky stuff still on her manicured nails. 'And I got it open.'

She described, as best she could, what she had seen before she ran out of the garage and called

103

911, her voice growing lower, flatter, and Sam thought she was shutting down as a kind of self-protection, could well understand that.

So, same scenario as before.

Making one thing certain. The definition was: the unlawful killing of two or more victims by the same offender(s), in separate events.

Serial murder for sure.

Arrangements in place for their family doctor to be on alert in case help was needed with Laura Gomez, Wendy Loeb returned to Coral Gables with Detectives Mary Cutter and Joe Sheldon, who would assist with the awful job of breaking Laura's heart.

'Jeez.' Martinez watched them go. 'Tough one.'

'Understatement,' Sam said.

'Hey.' Martinez saw his partner's face, knew pretty much what he had to be thinking, because Cathy had been homicide-bereaved, and he and Grace had seen her through her long nightmare, which meant that a case like this cut even deeper for Sam Becket. 'Mary's going to do good by her.'

'I know it,' Sam said.

The fact was their job this morning was not with young Laura, who was, from the investiga-tional standpoint, neither a potential witness nor suspect; their priority was applying for search warrants, getting the most effective start at and close to the scene along with the ME and Crime Scene, and conducting the first neighborhood canvas themselves.

Then back to the station. Task force to organize.

* * *

They signed the security log at the Gomez front door, donned coveralls, shoe covers and gloves and headed for the garage, ventilated and opened by Fire Rescue.

Elliot Sanders was already there, had moved fast because he'd dealt with the first case and because, in a serial situation, consistency was preferable where more than one case occurred within the same jurisdiction.

'Better make your sketches, everything else you need,' Sanders said. 'Flatbed truck's going to take the car with the deceased, same as last time.' He got out a cigar, brought it up beneath his nose, took a long sniff. 'Nothing new to tell you yet about the first case.'

'And here?' Sam kept his voice low. Too many people around – not to mention the zoo stacking up beyond the tape, hopefully being kept out of range, long-distance directional mikes probably already straining to pick up tidbits.

'The older male apparently singled out this time, torture-style, cord around his neck. First indications that they succeeded in strangling him. The female and young male both hogtied and almost certainly succumbed to CO poisoning.' The ME took another sniff of his cigar. 'I heard about the younger sister. Any decent relatives?'

'We don't know yet,' Sam said. 'Don't know how the killers arrived, either. Almost certainly not by boat this time, but it's serial, no question.'

'Robbery?' the ME asked.

'No open safe,' Martinez said. 'But the master bedroom and what looks like Dr Gomez's home office both turned over.'

'So either they did rip them off,' Sam said, 'or made it look that way.'

'And another message for you,' Sanders said. 'Didn't care much for its tone.'

'You and me both,' Martinez said.

'We're hoping I'm just a handy illustration of what our killer feels needs punishing,' Sam said lightly.

The chief medical examiner's voice was very low. 'You still sure working this case is right for you and yours, Sam?'

'I suggested Grace take Joshua to France,' Sam said. 'But Grace doesn't want to rain on Cathy's parade, and she said she's not going anyplace without me.'

'That was before today, man,' Martinez said.

Friday flew, guidelines for a task force being followed as appropriate for the jurisdiction and investigative work already undertaken. The Stillwater Drive crime had previously been entered into ViCAP, but there was more networking to be done, more information-sharing mechanisms to be utilized, more complex operational issues to be nailed down.

The Behavioral Analysis Unit-2 – the section of the FBI's National Center for the Analysis of Violent Crime that focused on serial murder, among other things – had developed a model upon which law enforcement agencies were free to act when such crimes hit their jurisdictions, and also provided support and advice where required.

At a moment like this in Miami Beach, when lines of inquiry into persons of interest, victims' relatives and colleagues, intensive searches state- and country-wide for matches of the crime combination – and the need to comprehend the true motive for these killings – threatened to shoot off like fireworks in a score of directions, multiple decisions had to be made.

A sound, functional task force, it was generally agreed, needed a lead and co-investigator, both experienced, dedicated and tenacious enough to direct all aspects of the investigation, reviewing and collating information, assigning leads and, wherever necessary, delegating responsibility to other experienced investigators and administrators.

Meantime, though, the *work* needed to continue, the things that the first twenty-four hours of a homicide investigation almost always entailed. Crime Scene and the ME's team doing their thing, witnesses sought, along with the intimate or at least personal knowledge of those close to the victims.

Sam and Martinez getting on with the job.

Next stop, Dr Gomez's office on Biscayne Boulevard, where they wanted to be the ones to break the news, see how people took it, and, in their judgment, the colleagues they encountered over the next hour were shattered. Dr Patrido Ortiz, the victim's partner, their receptionist, two nurses and a dental hygienist all seemed close to breaking point, and if their responses were to be trusted, the late Sergio Gomez Vega had been a good, kind, decent man, his wife, Luisa, known to them and well loved, and their son, Roberto, adored.

Black, black day.

'If there's a suspect in there,' Sam said later, 'I'll eat my badge.'

'Agreed,' Martinez said. 'At least we got some relatives out of Ortiz.'

An aunt in Boca Raton – Dr Gomez's sister, Mrs Carrola Rivera – already on her way to Coral Gables with her husband, so by evening, Laura might be under their roof. A massive upheaval, and who knew if the child might not find it easier to stay with her best friend, but family was family.

They had gotten more than relatives' names out of Patrido Ortiz.

'I only met Luisa's parents one time,' the dentist had told them. 'Way back at Sergio's wedding, when we were all young and starting out. They seemed like nice people, as you'd expect, knowing their daughter.'

'Are her parents still living, do you know?' Sam had asked Ortiz.

'No.'

'Were they Florida residents?'

'At the end of their lives, certainly. Before that, I don't recall.'

'How long ago did they die?' Martinez asked.

'Luisa's father passed away about ten years ago from a heart attack. And then her mother got Alzheimer's and for a while she came to live with Sergio and Luisa, but then it got too tough for them all and the lady went into a home.'

'Do you know where?' Sam asked.

Ortiz's forehead creased in puzzlement. 'Why so much interest in Luisa's parents?'

'It's routine,' Sam said. 'We track down family.'

'The living, I'd have thought,' Ortiz said, then remembered something. 'You might want to read the book Luisa wrote about them. Not a real book, as such, but it was published on the Internet a few years back.'

'Like a blog?' Martinez said.

'Not at all,' the dentist said. 'Luisa wanted to commemorate her parents' lives. Her mother's dementia affected her deeply, and Sergio once said that she was afraid of forgetting about their past, so she started writing, mostly so that Roberto and Laura . . .' He stopped there, emotion surging.

Sam and Martinez waited a few moments.

'Do you have a copy of the book?' Sam asked finally.

Ortiz shook his head. 'But I imagine you'll find it. Search Luisa Gomez – she took Sergio's name, American style – and maybe Alzheimer's, and perhaps her mother's name. Nina was her first name, and in the book, I recall that Luisa wrote her full name according to the Spanish custom of father's surname first, then mother's, but I'm ashamed to say I only remember Fuentes – Nina Fuentes.'

They had asked Ortiz more questions. Did he know if Dr Gomez had any enemies? Had he received any threats? Were there any former patients or employees with a possible grudge against him?

'No, no and no again,' Ortiz had answered. Dr Sergio Gomez Vega had been liked by everyone, to the best of his knowledge.

Ortiz had come to the question most burdening him, and they saw his mouth tremble as he asked it. 'Can you tell me how they died?'

'Not at this stage,' Sam had said. 'I'm sorry.'

'But there's no chance that it was an accident?'

They saw the last flickers of hope in his eyes, because though an accident was just as final, it might be easier to comprehend.

'I'm afraid not,' Sam had told him.

Dr Gomez had kept a floor safe in his home office, its steel cover plate hidden by a rug, its combination digital, but it had been opened, indicating either that Sergio or Luisa had been terrorized into disclosing the digits, or forced to open it themselves.

Either way, the safe was empty.

'Hey,' Martinez said, in the bedroom. 'This looks traceable, if it's real.'

A photograph on the dressing table showed Mrs Gomez wearing a substantial diamond ring and, as with the first case, none of the victims had had any jewelry on their persons when found.

'We need the doctor's insurance files,' Sam said. 'Here and at his office. We need copy valuations, more photos of jewelry, policy details.'

'I'm thinking a dentist might take cash from some patients,' Martinez said. 'Save on a little tax now and then. Could mount up.'

'Not enough to make sense of a crime like this,' Sam said.

'No,' Martinez agreed.

Both of them thinking of Laura Gomez again. Neither wanting to do anything to bring her more hurt.

Luisa Gomez's book, printed and leather-bound, clearly self-published, stood on the bookcase in the living room. Titled *Nina and Andres: a daughter's tribute*, copyright date 2007, it looked virtually untouched, more than likely intended as a keepsake for Luisa's children.

No problem locating it in the Favorites on Sergio Gomez's desktop computer.

Sam forwarded it to himself and Martinez scanned it swiftly, then searched the text for the Stillwater Drive victims.

No matches.

A guy could hope.

The obvious link, however, was apparent from the opening chapter. Nina Fuentes Garcia, born in 1925 in Madrid, Spain, had traveled to New York City in the fall of 1950 and had met a young Puerto Rican lawyer named Andres Ramos Rodriguez. A love match between a Caucasian woman from a prosperous Spanish family and a man of mixed white and African descent (who, as a returning World War Two veteran, had made use of the education benefits of the GI Bill, and was specializing in representing fellow Puerto Ricans with discrimination cases) was never going to sit easily with Nina's family, but she and Andres had weathered their storms, married

111

and had one child – their daughter, born Luisa Ramos Fuentes – moving to Florida in the early sixties.

Sam whipped through to where Luisa confirmed what Dr Ortiz had told them: Andres's death from heart disease and Nina's sad, slow, mental and, finally, physical decline and death.

'Homework for us both,' he said.

'You think Virginia knew them?'

'Probably not,' Sam said. 'But we need to be sure that nothing except the glaringly obvious might connect them to the other victims.'

'But this could be random, this scum picking mixed race couples off the fucking Internet . . .' Martinez shook his head.

'We start with crosschecks.' Sam stayed grounded. 'Nina and Andres – every damn permutation we can come up with – see how often Luisa's book shows up.'

'Then the same for the Stillwater victims,' Martinez said. 'And we're doing this ourselves, why?'

'Because we need to get into "Virginia's" head,' Sam said. 'Find out how the monster chooses victims. Pray we find something more solid to connect Stillwater and Emerson so we can do more than just hope there won't be any more.'

'But if it is just mixed marriages, man . . .' Martinez's eyes were growing more troubled by the second. 'I mean, this is the next two generations.'

'I guess that's Virginia's point.'

'You're going to need to get home some time, talk to Grace again.'

112

Sam caught his grimness, realized with shock that he'd been so deeply into the case that he'd temporarily almost forgotten the threat of the messages.

In Virginia's brain, he and Grace were presumably the guilty ones. But Joshua, their beautiful boy . . .

Sins of the parents.

Martinez was right. Hell, even Kovac was right.

Jesus.

'We have a problem,' Captain Kennedy said to Sam in his office at three p.m. 'Or at least we have an issue that needs addressing right now.'

'Do I take it that the issue is my lead?' Sam asked.

'The chief has concerns, as does Lieutenant Kovac.'

'And I'm grateful for everyone's concern, but I still believe that as investigators on the ground from June the third, along with previous experience, Al and I are the right people to continue with this case.'

'Martinez isn't the issue.' Kennedy paused. 'We believe you need to be interviewed as a potential victim, Sam.'

Sam frowned. 'To what end?'

'There's a possibility that you might, unwittingly, be burying some possibly useful sliver of information.'

'I spent most of the first night after Stillwater running over the past, Captain. If I'd come up with something, I'd have shared it.' Sam paused. 'Am I allowed to know who came up with this idea?'

113

'No need,' Tom Kennedy said.

'May I ask if it's the lieutenant?'

'It is not, and I'm not about to play Twenty Questions, Sam. Are you willing to be interviewed?'

'So long as it doesn't waste too much time. I'm keen to get this task force squared away and to move on asap. For the real victims, sir.'

'I don't think you'll have a problem with this interviewer wasting time,' Kennedy said. 'Special Agent Duval contacted us earlier, said he's available if you feel he could be helpful.'

A small sense of relief washed through Sam.

'For sure,' he said.

'Good,' Kennedy said. 'He's already on his way.'

They had cooperated in three previous major cases, and from the outset, Joe Duval of the FDLE – the Florida Department of Law Enforcement – had worked effectively alongside Sam and Martinez. Duval – early fifties, sharp-featured, slim, fit and a family man – had spent years as a Violent Crimes detective in Chicago, had once completed a criminal personality profiling program with the BSU, and, whilst being a methodical man, he tended, like Sam, to work instinctively as well as logically.

No one better to help them pull this task force together.

And maybe, Sam allowed, there was good sense behind the notion of an interview with himself as subject, ransacking his own history for something he might have forgotten.

Whatever helped.

The captain had assigned them a three-desk office near the squad room, Sam having requested that Martinez sit in, since if any links were going to crawl out of the job, their collective memories would be needed.

They started out flicking back through cases, looking for the obvious: enemies made. A heap of them, for sure, and who knew when an armed burglar or violent thug stewing in jail might have turned hatred of his arresting detective into a campaign?

'I guess we can exclude sex criminals,' Duval said.

'Though power being a major turn-on, that might still be relevant to one or more of the four suspects,' Martinez said.

'Not to "Virginia", though.' Sam shook his head. 'I've helped put away my fair share of bigots, but no one individual seems to fit this.'

'Jerome Cooper might have,' Martinez said. 'If he wasn't dead.'

'All the meanest and sickest I've known are dead,' Sam said.

Duval sighed. 'And still they keep on coming.' He took a slug of coffee. 'OK, Sam, we need to deal with you as the focal point of the messages.'

'I'm a black cop with a white wife, and we've made the news a few times. Which makes me the perfect recipient with the added bonus of shaking us up and wasting time.'

'Unless you're at the core of it,' Duval said. 'What if the killings were devised specifically to torment you?'

'That's a nightmare suggestion,' Sam said. 'And if there is someone who believes they can get to me by murdering innocent people, I have no idea who it might be.'

'Could be some random crazy who's fixated on you,' Martinez said.

'These crimes haven't been organized by some "random crazy",' Sam said.

'I agree,' Duval said.

'Yeah,' Martinez said. 'Me too.'

'We're looking at a highly organized killer, probably genuinely obsessive about interracial marriages,' Duval went on. 'What I'd like to rule out is that you could have aroused sufficient motivation in an individual or group to make them kill in Miami Beach just because it's your turf.'

'Jesus.' Sam took a breath. 'We can't rule it out. But we *can* still remember that many serial killers murder in their own cities or counties simply because they know it better than anyplace else. Because it's their comfort zone, not because of some cop who works there.'

'Hiding in plain sight,' Martinez said.

'Sometimes pillars of their goddamned community,' Duval said.

'Like that sonofabitch in Kansas who wrote messages to the media, taunting the cops,' Martinez said.

'Dennis Rader,' Duval supplied. 'Married with kids. Boy Scout leader, worked in local government.'

'Churchgoer, too,' Sam recalled. 'Guys, now we are wasting time. If anything hits me in the

116

dead of night, Joe, I'll call you, OK? Meantime, we need to get this task force organized.'

Duval leaned back in his chair. 'I'm going to recommend you two as lead and co-investigator. OK with you both?'

'What about support?' Martinez asked.

'Strength, not numbers,' Sam said.

'Agreed,' Duval said. 'Going on past cases, your data systems are pretty well set up, which they'll need to be.' He made a note. 'Who do you want as family liaison?'

'Mary Cutter started out with Laura Gomez,' Martinez said.

'She's tough enough to protect the families from the media,' Sam said. 'I think liaison with the ME's office and the lab would be perfect for Riley – and public information would suit her too.'

Beth Riley was pregnant, he told Duval. Four months and doing great, more than strong enough to deal with the media.

'Having the murders in a single jurisdiction simplifies that job a little,' Duval said.

'It's the reports and briefings that'll get me most bogged down,' Sam said.

'Afraid you guys will have to write your own reports,' Duval said, 'but I'm willing to act as lead control, if you're in agreement.' He saw Sam's relief. 'I take it that's a yes.'

'You bet,' Sam said.

'The rest's all about delegating and keeping everyone informed. We keep it tight, but flexible.' Duval shifted. 'Captain Kennedy asked me to consult with you guys first, then run our decisions past Lieutenant Kovac.'

'You deal with Kovac,' Martinez said, 'and you're my buddy for life.'

'In case we forgot to tell you' – Sam stood up, stretched – 'it's better than good to have you on board, Joe.'

Their next press conference was held out on Rocky Pomerantz Plaza at five p.m.: a major media presence there to suck up what was made available, then to try to drag out anything under wraps before making a break for their on-the-spot crews, vans and studios to get their stories and angles out there. 'Reasons to be fearful in Miami Beach' the most likely.

The air real sticky this afternoon, everyone uncomfortable.

Sergeant Beth Riley making her debut as PIO with her first press release, giving the facts – holding back key sensitive items – and Duval had suggested limiting her access to all details in case of inadvertent disclosure, but Sam had argued that Riley was smart enough and experienced enough to deflect a barrage.

The chief spoke when Riley had sat down. He began with a statement of horror, condolence and utmost commitment, then addressed the wider public beyond the plaza.

'These killers – and the brains behind them – could be among us,' Chief Hernandez said. 'They could be our neighbors, our colleagues, people we see as decent, respectable citizens. They may seem like you and me on the outside, but these people have dark souls and no conscience. If you think you may know or have any association with these people – if you know them from a distance, or if one of them is your husband or relative or friend, you have the potential to help us catch these murderers. Because they have done this twice now, in our beautiful, peaceful, fun city – in our community – and if they've done it twice, that means they could be planning to strike a third time.

'We need to stop them. We will stop them.'

A handful of miles away, the woman who had signed herself 'Virginia' on both windshield messages was watching the live press conference, listening to Chief Hector Hernandez.

'Maybe one or more of those killers may be feeling that this is spiraling out of control. If that is the case, if one of you people does have a conscience and wants to stop now, then please do something halfway decent before it's too late. Get in touch now. Call this number.'

She saw it flash up on the screen, considered her own conscience, found it untroubled and smiled at the police chief.

The woman with short red hair was taking over again.

'If you saw these four men—'

They ran the video again, the black-and-white grainy film of her Crusaders walking back to the boat after the first job, and she studied it once more, still satisfied that identification was not an issue.

'If you know these four men seen near the house where Molly and Gary Burton and Mary Ann and Pete Ventrino were robbed and savagely murdered on June the third, or maybe if you saw them yesterday, before or after the brutal killings of Dr and Mrs Sergio Gomez and their sixteen-year-old son, Roberto.' The screen flashed to a shot of the victims in happier times. 'Or if you recognize one or more of them, please call this number.'

Another man got to his feet.

Tall, broad-shouldered, black, unquestionably handsome.

Detective Samuel Becket, stooping to speak into the microphone, his voice deep and rich, speaking to the public. 'An official task force has been assembled to work on these cases, these serial killings, which means that all the power and man-time available to us – that's detectives, patrolmen, forensics, FBI and FDLE experts and systems – are being brought to bear on catching those responsible.'

The camera closed in on Becket, his eyes dark and hard.

'To the killers, we want to say that every hour that passes is bringing us closer to identifying you, to catching you, stopping you, putting you away. And to the rest of you, as Chief Hernandez said, if someone out there knows who these killers are, or if you just have a suspicion about a neighbor or a colleague or a person you've seen in a store or on the street, do not hesitate. Call the Crime Stoppers TIP line, or you can text or submit online. Your information will be handled with respect and in confidence – and who knows, your call may be the one that makes the differ-ence. Please help us. Help the families and loved ones who are in shock and grieving. Help the victims in the only way you can. Help us nail these brutal killers. Thank you.'

'Virginia' sat back in her chair, still studying him.

Nothing really galvanizing about his words, the usual public appeal, yada yada, but a sincere man, dedicated cop, loving family man.

But flawed.

The right man for her to have chosen.

More coming his way soon.

Not long to wait.

No space left on his walls now for more photographs of Catherine.

And the time for dreaming about her almost over.

Before too much longer, he would make it happen. The mind-travels and fantasies would become reality. Catherine would be with him.

Would be *his*.

He'd just frozen a shot of her father on 7 News, updating media and news junkies on the latest gruesome killings in Surfside – so close to where he'd stayed two years ago, until Sam and his sidekick had jostled him out of their precious country.

Their hostility had really hurt, especially Sam accusing him of being a stalker, because when all was said and done, he, Thomas Chauvin, had saved Sam Becket's life, and just a little gratitude was all he'd expected.

'*C'est du passé*,' he said out loud. All in the

past. *Now* was what counted. And the future. His future, with Catherine, once he'd rid her of the American waiter.

He still felt great respect for Sam. Watching him now, still tracking down real-life *assassins* – amazing guy – he felt a wave of gratitude to him and Grace for taking care of Catherine for so many years, but soon he would take over . . .

He pressed play, looked at the Breaking News caption, at prerecorded shots of the Surfside house, the crime scene behind the yellow tape, and wished he'd been there, taking his own photographs of the ugliness. Carbon monoxide poisoning, they'd said, same as the killings on June third.

'Brutal,' they'd said. Gagged and hogtied.

Chauvin flicked to another window, a set of photographs he'd already downloaded of a victim of CO poisoning, a naked man with his face hidden, his body suffused with red.

Lousy shot. Badly composed. Poor lighting. No drama. Sordid. Whoever he'd been, the poor guy deserved better photography.

He got up, went back to his bed, sat down, looked around at Catherine.

Woman of many faces, all of them beautiful.

He thought, briefly but kindly, of her mother. Grace-*mère*, as he thought of her, so astonishingly similar in appearance, considering Catherine was adopted.

He needed to hear his music again, had not played it in the last hour or more, leaned across to his remote, pressed Play.

Mica's voice again, singing 'Grace Kelly' to him alone.

He lay back and stared at the ceiling.

At *her*.

Soon.

Friday evening, and Mrs Hood's four Crusaders were celebrating again.

Another job well done.

Not that they'd all enjoyed it, CB reflected – though Leon had, for *sure*, unfazed even by the killing of the young man.

Sixteen years old. A kid, for Christ's sake.

CB thought that Jerry had hesitated briefly when the boy had cried through his gag, a wail of terror and fury at seeing what was being done to his mom, what had already been done to his dad. But still, Jerry had gone on with it.

They all had, and then they'd waited a while, in case they'd lied about the sister, in case she came back after all, but she didn't, so they'd taken care of business and left.

No problems, and no *visible* cameras this time – nothing in the news to contradict that, so far. Jerry had ditched the 2006 Subaru Outback they'd used – roomy enough for them to strip off and give their killing clothes, weapons, left-over cord and tape to Leon for disposal, and there had been a *moment* earlier when Jerry had asked how they could be certain that Leon could be trusted to do that with their things, or with the stolen cash and jewelry, and CB had said they had no real choice but to trust each other, and Leon had patted his shoulder, and CB had wanted to throw up. But he hadn't, had just gotten on with the job.

Killing almost an entire family.

Almost. One survivor.

The only redeeming feature, something CB had clung to while he'd watched the press conference, all the while torturing himself with it: what if the little girl had been there, what would they have done, what would *he* have done? Were there no depths to which he would not sink if so ordered by Mrs Hood and Leon?

The boss had asked them separately, before the job, what they wanted this time for their 'reward'. Andy had said he'd always hankered after a waterbed. Now he had it, and it was no disappointment. The only problem was that his sixty-inch TV was in his living room, so he figured that next time he might ask for a smaller flat-screen, maybe hang it right opposite his bed, so he could watch porn and jerk off in comfort, or maybe, one of these nights, he might be ready for another woman, because with another thousand bucks stashed away, he might soon be *worth* knowing. And sure, he hated what he'd had to do to earn it, but hell, how else could a no-hoper like him get ahead in this shitty world?

Jerry had asked for the same woman as last time, but Mrs H had insisted on someone new. 'We can't risk anyone asking questions,' she'd said.

'I wouldn't say anything,' Jerry had told her.

124

'No,' Mrs Hood said. 'I'm hoping you're too smart for that.'

She'd said that with her iciest smile, and so now Jerry was at a different address, in a room that had taken his breath away.

Padded walls and ceiling, so no one could hear him scream.

A torture chair, with straps and a tilt mechanism.

And here she came, with sharpened incisors and a hiss like a cornered alley cat, wheeling a cart loaded with baddies, and for a moment Jerry felt scared to death, but then the first rush hit him, and his hard-on was so huge it fucking hurt, and if this creature of the night did actually kill him, at least he'd die with his cock standing proud.

CB was back in his own chamber of horrors, at the dentist, and he supposed Mrs Hood *was* rewarding him, that this would put an end to his chronic pain and ultimately benefit his health, but with his mouth jammed open and the dentist grinding relentlessly up into another root . . .

No chance of *him* saying anything to the dentist or anyone else any time soon.

Mrs Hood was making sure of that.

Be grateful, he reminded himself, and thought about the thousand bucks he'd been able to send his mother and brother.

What about her?

The absent child, the lone survivor, the pretty child in the photographs.

An orphan now.

The dentist was using the slow drill, making his brain reverberate, which was good because it blotted out her picture for a while.

Though she'd be back again soon enough, CB knew. She'd be in his mind while he worked, ate, tried to sleep; and even then either she or her family would be there in his nightmares, he was sure of that too.

Haunting him.

Leon was eating fit for a king again.

At The Palm, on one of those fancy Bay Harbor Islands, and all he could say was that if it was good enough for Clooney, Clinton and Mike Tyson, it was good enough for Leon-the-*Man*, which was how he was starting to think of himself, because the more he'd killed, been in *charge* of it, fuck-sake, the more he knew he'd found his niche in life, and if it came to an end with Mrs Hood, he might just take this up for a living, maybe as a professional hit man or even a mercenary.

For tonight, all he'd had to worry about was what to pick from the menu. Baked Clams Casino to start, then a twenty-four-ounce bone-in rib-eye made into Surf 'n' Turf with a half-lobster, fries and onions on the side. Dessert had been a tougher call, and if he was going to be a fulltime mercenary, he'd need to be leaner, harder; but that was in the future, and this was his reward night, so he'd have the seven-layer chocolate cake and if he was going to live a high-risk, high-stakes life, he might as well let his arteries teeter on the edge too.

Screw his arteries.

God, but this cake was good.

Less than a mile from where Leon was dining, in the den at home, Sam was getting nowhere with persuading Grace to leave Miami Beach.

'Not without you,' she said.

'I don't think I can walk out on this case.'

'You don't want to walk out on it.' Grace's smile was sad. 'I'm not getting at you, Sam. I totally understand why you feel you can't, but the fact is this is probably the first time ever that everyone in the department would be behind you going.'

'Do you want me to hand it over?' Sam asked. 'Al and Joe could work it together, if the captain would wear it.'

'Except that this horrible case literally has your name all over it. Which makes you feel partly responsible for the killings – which you know isn't true, but that doesn't rub out the feeling, does it?'

'If we're talking about my feelings, I have to say I'm getting edgy about you and Joshua.'

'You want us to go into hiding,' Grace said.

He looked at her, knew she was remembering another time . . .

'I think it has to be considered,' Sam said.

'And for Joshua's sake, I get that, but where would you have us go? We're not going to endanger any other members of our family, and if you're going to suggest France again, I meant what I said about not spoiling things for Cathy.'

'I could talk to the captain,' Sam said. 'See if the chief regards this as a credible threat, in which case—'

'What? A safe house?' Grace challenged. 'And where would that be? In Miami-Dade or Broward or maybe the Gulf coast, or why stop there, why not move us interstate?'

'Hey,' Sam said gently. 'Don't get mad.'

'I'm not mad at you,' she said wearily. 'But am I supposed to drop all my patients again?'

'Only two options left then,' Sam said. 'I drop the case or—'

'Would that even guarantee our safety?'

'Only if we leave.'

'Second option?' Grace asked.

'I go on working with the team until we nail them, and meantime, we make this house even more secure and—'

'We already have the alarm.'

'Which we forget to switch on half the time,' Sam said. 'I'd have our own guys come in, upgrade the system, put in panic buttons.'

'Turn our home into a fortress,' Grace said, dismayed.

'Exactly,' Sam said emphatically. 'And I'm going to try for surveillance twenty-four-seven – not just a patrol car making the rounds, because this might not just be about protecting us; this might possibly be one way of catching these people.'

'Sam, now you're starting to scare me.'

'Then I'll walk and we'll go away.'

'Give me a minute. I need to think.'

'Take all night if you need it.'

'I hate the idea of surveillance.' Grace took a breath. 'But if it's going to keep Joshua safe . . .'

'I'll talk to Kennedy in the morning,' Sam said. 'If the department can't do this, then we'll pay a private firm.'

'I don't know.' Grace felt the situation getting away from her, and sometimes she just *hated* his job . . .

Part of him, for better or worse.

'I want you to feel in control,' he said.

'But I'm not – we're not. The author of those messages to you is the one in control.'

'Not if I have any say in it,' Sam said.

Grace sighed. 'Speak to Tom Kennedy tomorrow, see what he has to say.'

'So you're not asking me to drop the case?'

She saw his troubled face, knew that if she did ask that of him, he'd probably do it.

Tempting.

And then she thought of the seven victims and of that poor child, her world shattered, of their families. And of the two windshield messages addressed to Sam, bizarrely implying some kind of responsibility – because they had fallen in love and married, brought their own child into the world.

And part of that made her want to ask him to leave, keep them safe until it was over. But a greater part filled her with rage against the killer, the writer of messages who had laid this at their door.

'No,' she said. 'I'm not asking you to do that.'

On Saturday, Nic came to the staff lunch to tell them about the publicity plans he was setting up which would necessitate *Le Rêve* being at a pinnacle of perfection.

'Jeanne and I have been working on a new menu to be launched just under a month from now, which will coincide with press and TV interviews happening here and in the kitchen. It'll be tough, and it won't always be pretty, because it's going to be *real*, a kind of *pris sur le vif* documentary—' He grinned at Cathy. 'That's French for "fly on the wall", even though they're not welcome at *Le Rêve*.'

'Better than roaches,' Cathy said, then flushed, knowing the subject was taboo.

'It's OK.' Nic moved along. 'So chances are you're going to be on FR3 Côte d'Azur, and – if all goes well, and it must – we'll be the lead piece on Bouche, a major new food website, and there'll be photographers in and out before then, and they'll get in our way, but we'll all keep our focus, and the food – from prep to table – will look and taste superb. *Ça va, mes amis?*'

'*Ça va*, chef!' they said in unison.

'OK, so the launch date is July the fourth, so Cathy' – Nic turned to her – 'I'm thinking you and I should toss around a few American ideas that could mesh with our style.'

'I'll try to think of some,' Cathy said, already panicking.

'Do more than try, please.'

'Yes, chef,' she said.

And thought she felt, abruptly, a frisson of hostility in the air, glanced swiftly up and down the table, but couldn't tell who it was coming from.

Imagination, she told herself.

She'd begun mulling over ideas – perhaps a Provençal take on an *antipasto*-cum-American *amuse-bouche* of tiny wild boar burgers and Toulouse sausage hot dogs – when, leaving at the rear to run an errand for Aniela, she turned to check that the door had fully closed.

And saw it.

Impossible to miss.

Sprayed on the pale ocher stone wall beside the door in red large letters.

YANKEE GO HOME!

Hardly original. But still, Nic wouldn't like it.

Assuming it was directed at him. Which it probably was.

Yet knowing it had to have been recently done, that sudden sense of hostility at lunchtime came back to her. Someone at that table disliked her, she'd felt, had maybe not liked Nic singling her out because of the Fourth of July – though surely no one at *Le Rêve* could be especially anti-American, since as far as Cathy could tell they were all devoted to Nic . . .

Or maybe it was another nasty trick.

She checked her watch, remembering her errand and decided that Jeanne would want to know about the graffiti immediately. About to enter her code into the digital entry keypad, she fished for

131

her iPhone, rapidly photographed the message
and went back inside.

June 10

The Monday morning task force meeting brought
nothing but frustration.

All leads going nowhere, no breaks in the
case. Nothing noteworthy yet on Mo Li Burton's
uncle, James Lin, or his associates. Nothing
further on Sean Reardon – and even if Sam and
Martinez had *almost* ruled him out, they were
still looking. They'd spent time on Saturday
with employees at GG Fitness, had been asked
not to approach members, though Nick Gibson
had provided a list of individuals whose
memberships had been terminated for various
reasons. Everyone on that list checking out to
date; no one with a rap sheet or significant
history.

It seemed increasingly possible that 'Virginia'
might have trawled the Internet for examples of
her-his-their obsession. Luisa Gomez's book
was out there on the Web, and Gary Burton's
health club had scored some results when
Googled – all of them advertorial in nature, no
personal details mentioned other than that
Burton had been 'married'. Likewise, James
Lin's air freight company: all hits commercial,
though in a piece in a newsletter of the CCSF
– Chinese Community of South Florida – Mo
Li had been mentioned as Lin's right-hand
woman. Nothing about her husband or any other
personal information: strictly business, probably

irrelevant. As were Lin's areas of specialty: cheap Chinese jade jewelry imports and cosmetics exports, both trades apparently highly regulated, and no strikes against Lin's company found to date.

On the personal front, the Beckets' increased security measures were in hand. No twenty-four-seven surveillance deemed necessary yet – prevailing logic being that if the risk was that great, then Sam should remove himself from the case and his family from danger. Budgets being what they were, Sam was not overly surprised, and he guessed that the security upgrade ought to give them peace of mind, at least for the time being.

At around eleven, three things happened.

First, Nick Gibson called to say he thought he might have something for them.

'What kind of something?' Sam asked.

'I'm not sure,' Gibson said. 'But it might be construed as a threat against Gary.'

Sam said they'd be at his office within the hour.

Two minutes later, another call: from a Moira Lombardi, part-time clerk at the Santa Barbara Police Department, who knew that Miami Beach PD had accessed an old accident report last week, and who'd just come across something that had become separated from the file.

'Knowing a little about your investigation,' she told Sam, 'particularly that one of your victims was the daughter of the deceased couple in our accident – Zhu and Meihui Lin – I figured you'd probably want to know that someone else tried to access that old file one month before your first homicide.'

'You figured right,' Sam said.

'OK.' Moira Lombardi sounded young and vigorous. 'I'll scan the application letter and email it across.' She paused. 'The application was refused, as you'll see, but I thought that coming nine years after the accident, it seemed a stretch to call it a coincidence.'

'Right again,' Sam said, and thanked her.

'Oh, and by the way, I'm sure you'll probably realize it anyway, but the letterhead's definitely not Fairmont's, and so far as confidentiality allowed me to check, there's no student of that name at the university.'

The email and attachment arrived within minutes.

What had started as a buzz of anticipation of that elusive *something*, spun, in less than ten seconds, straight into flashing anger.

Fairmont University of Santa Barbara

City of Santa Barbara Police Department, Police Records Bureau.

May 3, 2013

To Whom It May Concern:

I am a law student at the above university, and require, for research purposes, the case files relating to the accidental deaths of Zhu and Meihui Lin on August 22, 2004.

134

I enclose twenty-five dollars, which I am told is the fee payable, and will, of course, pay any additional copying fee on collection.

I will attend in person in one week's time, in the hope that the files will be available.

Yours sincerely,
Joshua Becket

The name – *that* name.

'What the fuck?' Sam said.

'*Who* the fuck?' Martinez said.

Sam and Grace's little boy, as beloved to him as if he were his nephew.

No one messed with Joshua, not even with his name.

'OK,' Sam said. 'Couple of deep breaths.'

They examined their printout.

As the clerk had said, the letterhead was fake, probably created with a free letter graphic straight off the Internet, the kind utilized by an incalculable number of people.

'Smart woman,' Sam said, appreciative of Moira Lombardi. 'Even if this had stayed with the file, there's no guarantee anyone would have realized its full significance to our case. Certainly not its significance to me personally.'

'The letter doesn't seem to me like it was written by any law student,' Martinez said.

'Did you notice the font?'

Martinez nodded. 'Same as the windshield messages.'

'So a link, unquestionably. And as good as addressed to me.'

'Except if it weren't for this Moira, we'd never have known it existed.' Martinez paused. 'You think there's any chance this is down to James Lin?'

'Makes no sense. It was sent before Mo Li and the others were killed, and I honestly don't believe that Lin had his niece murdered.' Sam paused. 'Unless he's a total fruitcake and maybe had some obsession about her being to blame for his brother's death.'

'She was what back then, twenty-one?'

'Still studying for her CPA license.' Sam shrugged. 'Nothing's impossible, but I don't buy it. Everything we've heard about Molly Burton has her grounded, sane, decent.'

'So no reason we can think of for Lin faking this letter,' Martinez said. 'But three reasons for thinking it was written by our killer. Mo Li's parents. Baskerville font. And the signature.' He paused. 'What now?'

'I'll give Duval a heads-up, ask him to get the FBI field office in Santa Barbara to double-check that there really is no Joshua Becket at Fairmont, while we go see Gibson about this "threat" against Gary Burton.'

'Then what? Do we fly west?'

Sam leaned back in his chair. 'Even if the whole letter was fake, the name could still be a coincidence. Even if there's no such student, the writer could have plucked it out of the air – maybe he's a Dodgers fan.'

Martinez frowned. 'That's Josh – not Joshua

136

– and Beckett with two Ts. And we don't buy coincidences, do we?'

Sam shrugged again. 'Then I'm guessing that whenever and however "Virginia" chose the Burtons, they researched the whole family and figured we'd go back and check out the accident.'

'Unless it wasn't an accident.'

'That doesn't work for me,' Sam said. 'Zhu and Meihui Lin – Joe and May – were both Chinese. And they died before Mo Li even met Gary Burton, so if we're accepting mixed race as the motive for the Miami Beach killings, that rules the parents out as victims.'

'Maybe the killer was just racist, period, back then,' Martinez said.

Sam tapped the letter on his desk. 'The accident happened almost nine years ago. Let's check for other fatal accidents at that location. This could be some campaigner wanting to get the bridge fixed or closed – even a journalist wanting to write a "Ten Years On" piece.'

'And this campaigner or journo just happens to be called Joshua Becket – with one T – but decides to pretend he's a law student, or fakes his identity by misspelling the Dodgers pitcher's name. And he happens to like the same font as "Virginia".'

'Still no purpose in flying to Santa Barbara,' Sam said. 'Let's ask Duval to get the letter tested locally, though who knows how many people have handled it since it was sent.' He paused. 'We have no envelope, no postmark. If this is a real link, it could have been sent from Florida.

137

Or if it was mailed from California, even from the university, that's not exactly hard for "Virginia" to have arranged.'

The third thing happened just as Sam ended his call to Duval.

His cell phone rang. David Becket calling.

'Mildred might have something for you, son.'

Sam and his dad had spoken yesterday, and having heard about the Gomez tragedy, David had enquired about the bereaved twelve-year-old, and Sam had mentioned Luisa Gomez's book.

'What kind of something?'

Before his stepmother had become a beloved member of their family, she had been Mildred Bleeker, a homeless person respected by a number of Miami Beach cops, Sam most particularly. If Mildred – having good reason to hate illegal drugs – saw or heard anything she felt might help get pushers off the streets, it had always been Sam she wanted to share the information with.

Bottom line, even now: if Mildred said she had something for him, he'd listen.

'Luisa Gomez's story struck a chord,' David said. 'In the old days, she says she read newspapers people left lying around, but what she really enjoyed were the free newspapers, in particular a free monthly called *The Beach*. She's almost sure that's where she saw an article about Luisa Gomez.' He paused. 'Here she is now.'

'Samuel, I found it.' Mildred sounded triumphant. 'I thought I'd kept it, because the story

138

was remarkable, and the interviewer asked good questions. So I looked in my box of keepsakes and sure enough, there it was – October issue, 2007 – and I wondered if it might be of help?'

'It might. *The Beach*, right?'

'Right.'

'How often would you say you read it?'

'Most months.'

Sam searched the title, followed it with 'Miami monthly' and got a bunch of junk about hotels and parking, nothing about a newspaper.

'It was a good paper,' Mildred said, 'but I think it must have shut down.'

'Was this the only back issue you kept?'

'No. I looked, in case you asked, and I do have a few more, if you want them.'

'If you don't mind, I'll pick them up later today,' Sam said.

'They'll be waiting,' Mildred said.

They asked Joe Sheldon to search for past issues of *The Beach* featuring interviews with any of the other victims, or maybe pieces dealing with mixed race marriages, and to locate the editor and journalist responsible for the Gomez interview, and then they headed over to GG Fitness to see Nick Gibson.

He looked tired, the impact and nature of his loss perhaps still dawning.

'You mentioned a threat,' Sam said.

'It's more than that,' Gibson said. 'At least, I think it might be.'

It lay on his desk, a small black rectangular object with a handwritten label.

139

A microcassette.

'I found it in our office safe,' Gibson said. 'I took a quick look after it happened, because of the robbery at Gary's house, but our stuff was all there – five hundred bucks, for emergencies, legal papers, our lease, that kind of thing. And then yesterday I was looking for some keys and thought they might be in there, so I fished around at the back, and that's where I found it.'

Martinez leaned in, looked at the little cassette, read its label.

'February 7, 2007,' he said.

'That's Gary's writing,' Gibson continued. 'Those cassettes used to fit in an old recorder we hadn't used for years, and I don't have anything now that I could play it on. So I looked around for the recorder for a while, and then the day got away from me. But last night it was bugging me, and I remembered our junk store out back – part unclaimed lost property, part things we're not quite ready to throw out, you know?'

'And you found it.' Sam cut to it.

'I did.' Gibson opened a drawer, pulled out a small black recording device, inserted the cassette. 'It's a phone message. It's obvious why Gary kept it, but I'm guessing it made him so mad he didn't want to talk about it, even to me.'

He hit the play button.

'Listen carefully, Gary Burton.'

The voice was whispering and so muffled it was impossible to tell so much as the caller's gender.

'If you marry that girl, you will bring shame on yourself and your family.'

140

Sam met Gibson's eyes, saw intense anger in them.

'If you marry her, you will be very sorry.'

No discernible accent, hard to say more.

'Some things go against creation, Gary Burton.'

Sam felt his skin crawl and looked at Martinez.

'Call it off, or shame on you.'

A low click, and it ended.

'It is something, right?' Gibson said.

'Oh, yes,' Sam said.

'February 07,' Martinez said. 'Not long after they met.'

'We took that Vegas trip early October 06,' Gibson said. 'And you already know how hard and fast Gary fell for Molly. He was proposing within a week or two, she was here by Christmas and they were married in early March.'

'Any notifications of their engagement?' Sam asked.

'I don't remember. Not my thing, or his, I wouldn't have thought.' Gibson shrugged. 'I'm guessing it wasn't Molly's uncle's thing, either – at least, unless she'd been going to marry a nice Chinese boy.'

'We'll check back,' Sam said.

'No engagement announcement in their wedding album,' Martinez said.

'You could ask Gary's dad,' Gibson said.

'We'll do that,' Sam said.

'I saw him yesterday. He looked bad, but he won't accept help.' Gibson rubbed his forehead. 'So what, we're thinking that this could go all the way back to that message?' He looked confounded, as if it was impossible to compute.

141

'That much hate? To have it build for years and then do *that*?'

'Maybe,' Sam said. 'Or maybe this message was just an anonymous hate call.'

Gibson sighed, took the microcassette out of the machine. 'I guess you'll be taking both of these for testing? Maybe find out who that is?'

'We'll be doing our best,' Sam said.

Martinez took an evidence bag from his pocket.

'I'm sorry I didn't find it sooner,' Gibson said.

'Hey,' Sam said. 'This is something. You're helping.'

'This doesn't have to have anything to do with an engagement announcement, does it?' Gibson said. 'That message could have been left by anyone who knew they were going to get married. Someone at the club, a business supplier, *anyone*.'

'Hey,' Sam said again. 'You need to let us drive ourselves crazy, OK?'

'I don't envy you,' Gibson said.

'Not just a hate call,' Martinez said, back in the car. 'Not with those words.'

The windshield messages still under wraps. The first one etched in their memories. '*It goes against creation.*' And the words in the phone message. '*Some things go against creation, Gary Burton.*'

'Could be another coincidence, man,' Martinez said.

'Could be a lot of things,' Sam said dryly. 'Could be Nick Gibson used some old machine and made the recording himself.'

'Hey,' Martinez said. 'You really think that?'

'Nah,' Sam said.

* * *

Lunchtime, the team updated, they went to Markie's for cheeseburgers.

Emotion kept driving Sam's mind toward Santa Barbara, though assuming that no innocent law student sharing Joshua's name would be found at Fairmont University, then all that letter seemed to confirm was that 'Virginia's' issues with Sam were no recent aberration.

If the recorded message was deemed by forensic audio to be as old as the date on the micro-cassettes's label (and if that handwriting was judged to be Gary Burton's), then they had to face the real possibility that the mind behind these slayings had been simmering for years.

'If that's true,' Sam said, 'then we're looking at two alternatives. Either "Virginia" had specific reasons for selecting the Burtons and the Gomez families out of thousands of mixed-race marriages, or there could be a massive list of potential victims just waiting.'

'Including you.' Martinez spoke softly, though they were out of earshot of other customers. 'If there's a shortlist, we have to accept that you and Grace are on it.'

'Maybe it's just couples who "Virginia" perceives as having drawn attention to them-selves.' Sam pushed his plate away, his appetite gone. 'Like Luisa Gomez writing and being inter-viewed about her parents.'

'You've never deliberately drawn attention to your marriage.' Martinez was still eating. 'I mean, you've made the news, but you've never given interviews about personal stuff.'

'But we have made the news,' Sam repeated.

'Not as an interracial couple.' Martinez shook his head. 'Jesus.'

'On the plus side, we have two physical pieces of evidence.'

'For forensics, not us.' Martinez hated waiting. 'What do we do next?'

'We go check with William Burton re. engagement announcements, then we go pick up Mildred's copies of *The Beach*, see if any of our other victims figure in them, unless Joe beats us to the punch.'

Burton had no copy of any engagement announcement, nor could he remember there having been one, and early searches had thrown up nothing. A call to James Lin had brought a more exact response. There had been no public announcement, and had his niece suggested the idea, Lin would not have approved it.

'That really narrows it down,' Sam said wryly. 'Now it's only every person from San Francisco to Miami who might have been told or overheard that she and Gary were planning to marry.'

Forensics would establish whether the recording was authentic and try to enhance the quality, though that depended on what the caller had used to muffle his or her voice, but at least if it came to matching the message to a suspect, voice ID software would probably assist in that.

First, of course, they needed a damned suspect.

Having run out of time at the office, Sam brought Mildred's newspapers home to share with Grace.

144

Five of them, containing predictable publicity splashes for average-budget Miami Beach hotels and punchy reviews for new restaurants, bars and clubs. Plenty of ads to pay the rent, a book review page, and in each issue at least two, sometimes three features involving locals.

Same editor credited for each issue. Sam photographed the newspaper's contact details – all presumably out of date – and texted them to Joe Sheldon.

Mildred had stuck a Post-it noted '*Page 14*' on the front of one issue.

The page showed a nice color photo of Luisa Gomez – dark, kind eyes, warm smile – and an old picture of her parents, standing close, laughing into the camera.

No surprises in the article, Sam having read Luisa's book.

He handed it to Grace and moved on.

'Can I help you search?' she asked after reading the piece.

'Definitely.' Sam noted down all the victims' names, added James Lin and his company, Nick Gibson and GG Fitness, Sean Reardon, the other close relatives and Mo Li's parents. 'Any mention of any of them.'

'Are we allowed a glass of wine?'

'Counting on it, Gracie,' Sam said.

They found no other references, and then Joshua woke up, wanting to talk, and when their five-year-old felt like talking he could turn into a regular inquisitor, especially when it came to his daddy's job: police detective – *the* best show-and-tell – usually without the 'show', but that seldom stopped Joshua.

With their son all questioned-out and tucked sleepily back in his bed, they stir-fried shrimp with garlic, baby bok choy and noodles, and settled to eat it.

'So, you're not considering going to Santa Barbara?' Grace said after a minute.

Sam shook his head. 'For one thing, if that letter was sent by the killer, which is still a big *if*, that might be – or have been – exactly what they wanted.'

'The letter having been sent before the first killings.' Grace followed his thought. 'So if it hadn't become separated from the accident file, and assuming you'd learned about its existence immediately after the murders, you might have gone there, leaving us . . .'

She stopped.

Not just she who would have been left as a potential target.

Joshua too.

Sam put down his chopsticks, reached for her hand.

'I'm not going to California,' he said.

His cell phone rang as they were heading to bed.

'Sorry to call late,' Joe Sheldon said.

'What did you find?' Sam asked.

'A photo taken in January 07 at a party to celebrate GG Fitness's first anniversary. Six people in the photo, caption identifying them, including Gary Burton and his new fiancée, Molly Lin.' Sheldon paused. 'The issue was on the streets from February first. Which could conceivably mean that the phone whisperer saw them in *The Beach*.'

'And now we have victims from both killings getting publicity in the same paper.'

'Which went belly up two and a half years ago,' Sheldon said, 'but I tracked down the last editor, who actually had their distribution list on her PC and emailed it to me. Helpful, but not much help. Hotel foyers, doctors' waiting rooms, office buildings. No way of knowing who got to read it.'

'Is the editor available to talk?' Sam asked.

'Ready and waiting.'

Sam took down her name – Harper Benedict – maybe with parents of a literary inclination or into glossy magazines – and phone number, thanked Sheldon, then went into the kitchen and made some decaf – not that he was likely to get to sleep any time soon.

The younger detective was right about the distribution list getting them no place, at least in the short term. Still, a conversation with Ms Benedict might lead someplace.

Like the phone message in Gary Burton's safe and the letter to the Santa Barbara police bearing their son's name, this newspaper connection was *something*. It was trying to make something *solid* out of it all that was making Sam's brain feel tight as a drum, making him want to pace and think.

Because whoever was driving this wickedness, the roots came from a long way back, and the big question remained: had the victims been

147

earmarked from the start, or were they just random choices from the massive pool of possible victims that he and Martinez had touched on earlier?

'Jesus,' he said quietly.

Woody, in his bed, looked up at him and whined.

'Hey,' Sam said. 'It's OK.'

Came to something when you started lying to the dog.

June 11

Harper Benedict was interesting.

Definitely.

For one thing, she was a stunner. Mid to late thirties, blonde bobbed hair, intense blue eyes, snug-cut white dress showing off a great shape that she probably worked hard to maintain.

Tuesday morning, after their morning task force meeting, they were meeting at her Bal Harbour home, not far from where Grace consulted. A few minutes from their own home.

'You may not know anything about me, Detective Becket,' she said, having offered them seats in her gray-and-white living room. 'But I know a good deal about you.'

'Is that so?'

'Don't you want to ask what I know?' Her voice was low, cool as the room.

'Not especially,' Sam said. 'You were the editor of *The Beach* when you published an article about Luisa Gomez and her parents.'

148

'I was.' She paused. 'I heard the news, obviously.' She indicated some buff folders on the low table ahead of her. 'I assumed you were coming because of the connection, so I retrieved those files from the archive.'

'That's helpful, ma'am,' Martinez said.

'I hope so,' she said. 'Though I can't imagine why they would be. It was a straightforward enough piece resulting from the book Mrs Gomez had self-published.'

'Did you often pick up on self-published books?' Sam asked.

'Her story was interesting and she was local.'

'But how did you come to read it in the first place?' Martinez asked.

'Her husband sent it to us,' Harper Benedict said. 'My PA looked it over and gave it to me and I had to say that, for once, the guy's pride in his wife was justified. It was a good story, well-written.'

'Did it slot in with anything else you were publishing around that time?' Sam asked. 'Was it a theme that interested you?'

'The theme of interracial marriage?' Her gaze rested on him. 'We hadn't been running a series on the subject, though Luisa Gomez's story did pique my interest enough to consider that possibility.' Her smile showed small, perfect teeth. 'In which case, you might have been on my list of potential interviewees, Detective Becket.'

Sam looked back at her. 'We're not here to discuss my private life.'

'Of course not,' she said. 'Still, it isn't exactly irrelevant, surely?'

'Why isn't it?' Martinez asked quietly.

Sam knew that particular tone of his partner's voice well, felt that it was, on occasions, a little like traveling with a personal guard dog – not big, but tough and tenacious.

A good feeling.

'Detective Becket and his wife have hit the headlines more than once,' Ms Benedict answered Martinez's question. 'Making them a pretty significant interracial couple, I'd say, and therefore relevant.'

'To what, exactly?' Sam said.

'To the "theme" – your word.' She paused. 'From what we outsiders have learned about the victims, that does seem to be a possible link?'

Sam regarded her with open curiosity, saw a glacial quality in the blue eyes, felt at once uneasy and excited.

'How long did you edit the paper, Ms Benedict?'

'From August 2006 until December 2010. I was its last editor.'

'So you're probably aware that a photograph of two of the victims in the June third murders appeared in one of your issues?'

'I've become aware of that.'

'Quite a coincidence,' Martinez said.

'Not really.' Her tone was matter of fact. 'The gym wanted publicity, we obliged. Dr Gomez wanted coverage for his wife and her book, we obliged. Miami Beach citizens with something to sell. I can't tell you how many individuals and local firms wanted to get inside our covers. They just got lucky. Or thought they had at the time.'

'Aside from your having been editor,' Sam said,

'did the two items have any personnel in common? Photographers, for instance.'

'No. I did check.' She paused. 'I'm somewhat confused. You seem to be standing this "coincidence" on its head.'

'Meaning what?' Sam asked.

'Surely it's not the fact that these poor people were included in *The Beach* that might be flagging some kind of clue? Isn't this more about the readers of those issues, the people who learned about Luisa Gomez and saw the shots of Gary Burton and his fiancée?'

'They'd be of great interest,' Sam agreed. 'But the way your paper was distributed, they'd be impossible to track, surely?'

'You're forgetting the readers who make contact with newspapers,' Harper Benedict said. 'We had a number of regulars who enjoyed corresponding with us. Some who liked expressing strong opinions – sometimes one-offs, sometimes not – about items we'd published.'

'You kept those on file?' Martinez asked.

'Sure.' She smiled at him. 'In fact, I've already trawled through the 2007 files and extracted anything that might possibly be relevant.'

'That's great,' Sam said. 'Though I'd be grateful if we could take a look at those files ourselves.'

'In case I've omitted something,' Harper Benedict said coolly.

'You might inadvertently have overlooked something relevant,' Sam said.

'Inadvertently or deliberately,' she said. 'Or I could have found something "relevant" and destroyed it.'

151

'Why would you do that?' Sam asked evenly.

'A whim, perhaps,' she said. 'Who knows? You're the detective.'

'Ms Benedict, this is not a game,' Sam said. 'Do you have an objection to showing us the 2007 correspondence files? And perhaps the previous year's too?'

Her eyes grew colder. 'Am I a suspect, Detective?'

'Do you think you should be?'

She laughed, lightening up again. 'You'll have the files before you leave.'

'Thank you,' Sam said.

'You know, you're starting to make me regret that I never did approach you and your wife for an interview.'

Sam took a moment. 'When were you considering that?'

'Just after the two of you almost bought it – in the "Couples" case. Spring of 2009, I think.' She paused. 'Not the first time I'd heard of you, obviously. You and your family having been in the news previously.'

'And what would your angle for such an interview have been?'

She smiled again. 'So many possible angles, I'd have been spoiled for choice. Interracial marriage, naturally. Homicide detective and child psychologist. Both sailing dangerously close to the wind more than once.'

If they'd been out in the open, say, at a press conference, Sam would have slapped her politely down, but this was starting to feel rather different.

'So why didn't you make the approach?' he asked.

'Are you saying you would have considered it?'

'Not for a second.'

'Ah, well. In the event, something else took precedence during the month in question, and after that, you and Mrs Becket were old news.' She paused. 'Still, since you'd have turned me down, it's as well I didn't ask. I'm not good with rejection.'

'So, Ms Benedict,' Martinez said, 'what are you doing now?'

'I'm tempted to say it's none of your concern, but cops tend to think everyone's business is theirs.'

'Pots and kettles come to mind,' Sam said lightly.

Her smile this time seemed more genuine. 'I'm writing.'

'For another newspaper?' Martinez said.

'I'm working on a book,' she said.

'Fiction?' Sam said.

'Non,' she said.

'Mind if I ask what it's about?' Martinez said.

'I don't mind you asking,' she said, 'so long as you don't mind if I don't tell you.'

'No problem,' Martinez said easily.

'So.' Sam steered them back. 'You've found no other details in common between the Gomez feature and the issue that ran the photos of Mr Burton and his wife-to-be?'

'None,' Harper Benedict said.

'Can you think of any other articles in *The*

153

Beach during your editorship that shared commonalities with those items?'

Her chin went up. 'You're expecting more killings?'

'I sincerely hope not,' Sam said. 'On the contrary, if you had run, say, a number of stories featuring the subject of interracial relationships—'

Benedict shook her head. 'I can't recall any features concerning that subject, but I'm betting there were any number of photos of interracial couples or mixed race individuals.' She shrugged. 'You'll be welcome to read through as many issues as you like, and all the correspondence files too.'

'That would be good, ma'am,' Martinez said.

'I imagine you've already checked to see if any local news stations or magazine programs ran anything about the victims.'

'Ongoing, ma'am,' Sam said.

'I wasn't trying to tell you your job,' Harper Benedict said.

'All help gratefully accepted,' Sam said.

'So,' Martinez said outside, heading back to the car, a dozen more back issues of *The Beach* under one arm, the promised correspondence files to be sent to the station by day's end. 'What did you make of her?'

'Jury's out,' Sam said.

'The cool, untouchable type.' Martinez opened the doors, dumped the papers on the back seat, got in with a grunt.

'You don't trust her.'

'Not one bit.'

'Me neither.'

154

'The eyes had a lot to do with it. Warm and friendly to icicles in a blink.'

'Just playing us,' Sam said.

'Like this is amusing?' Martinez was grim. 'She knows we're looking at seven dead people and she wants to mess around?' He started the engine, checked the mirror, hesitated. 'We got five minutes to visit with Grace?'

'She'll have patients and we don't have time.'

'Nah, we got old newspapers to read,' Martinez said.

'And their editor to check up on,' Sam said.

And forensics and voice ID to chase regarding Nick Gibson's recorded message.

And their own brains to rack as to how to trace the writer of the letter to Santa Barbara PD.

Enough to be getting on with.

Tuesday evening, Cathy and Gabe had worked the same shift, had a late pizza with Luc, then gone back to her place for the night.

'I'm heading up to my uncle's tomorrow for a few days,' Gabe said, about a minute after they'd finished making love.

Surprise, followed by irritation, hit Cathy.

'What's up?' Gabe asked.

'You hadn't mentioned it.'

'I didn't know until today.'

'We've spent hours together and you still didn't mention it.'

'I'm telling you now.'

'Maybe I could ask for time off,' she said lightly. 'Come with you.'

155

'Not a good idea.'

'Why not?'

'For one thing, Nic wouldn't appreciate the lack of notice.'

'You didn't give any.'

'I made sure Michel could work my shifts,' Gabe said. 'Easier for a waiter.'

'What's the other thing?' She shifted onto her right elbow, waited.

'It's not a good time for my uncle,' he said.

'Why not? Is he sick?'

'Not sick. Just busy. Preoccupied.'

'Not too preoccupied for you to visit.'

'I'm going to my *lopin*,' Gabe said. 'I won't see much of him.'

'So why can't I come there with you? To your *lopin*, I mean.'

'It's still on my uncle's land.' Gabe sighed. 'You need to understand, Cathy. Yves isn't the most sociable of men.'

'And you don't want him to meet me,' Cathy said.

'More the other way around, I'd say. If that were the reason.' Gabe sat up. 'Why does it bug you so much, my not taking you there?'

'I guess I feel it's a missing piece.'

'So I'm a jigsaw?'

'I think we all are,' Cathy said.

'I haven't met your family,' Gabe said. 'But I don't feel as though you're keeping something from me.'

'They're thousands of miles away. If we were home, you'd have met them.'

'If I wanted to.'

156

Annoyance returned. 'Why wouldn't you want to?'

'I probably would.' Gabe shrugged. 'Though sometimes you make them sound a little too perfect. I might feel inadequate.'

'Hardly.'

'Why? Because they're too perfect to let me feel bad?'

'Jesus,' she said.

Gabe was silent for several seconds. 'If you really want to go there, I'll take you. Not tomorrow, but soon.'

'I don't even know exactly where "there" is. Somewhere in the Var. I know your uncle's name and that he has a farm, and I know he grows olives and maybe lavender because you brought both once when you'd just come back from there. If that was where you'd been.'

'Where else would I have been? If that's where I'd told you I was going.'

'I don't know.' Insecurity made her mad at herself. 'I still don't even know what you grow on your *lopin*. If you grow anything.'

'Marijuana,' he said.

'Uh-huh,' she said, unsure if he was joking.

'Maybe that's what I grow,' he said. 'Maybe that's why I haven't taken you there yet, because I'm not sure how you'd react.'

She felt tired abruptly, disliked sparring. 'So you'll take me some day.'

'Sure.'

'But not yet.'

'Not unless you insist.'

'I wouldn't do that.'

157

'Maybe I have another girlfriend there.'

'Maybe you do.'

He rolled closer, put his arms around her. 'I don't. I'm just being an ass. No other girlfriend, there or anyplace else.' He paused. 'And on my land, I grow—'

'No.' She cut him off. 'Please don't tell me.'

'But you want to know.'

'Not till you want to tell me.'

'OK,' Gabe said.

Late on Tuesday, the back issues of *The Beach* and folders of correspondence having yielded nothing of obvious significance, Sam's researches into Harper Benedict's family history raised some interesting information.

Harper had been born in 1975 in upstate New York to George Benedict and his wife, Hildegard, known as Hildy. George, a modern language teacher born György Benedek in Hungary in 1940 to Edvard Benedek, heir to an old paper manufacturing business, who had emigrated to the United States after World War Two with a considerable fortune intact.

Mildly interesting as that was, what had perked Sam and Martinez right up was the small detail that George's mother, Alida Benedek, had written a book published by an insignificant Budapest house in 1933: a rant in support of Nordicism, the ideology that claimed Nordic people to be racially superior to all others.

'So Harper's grandma was a white supremacist,' Martinez said.

'For sure,' Sam said. 'And the name, Alida, by the way, means "noble".'

'Which takes us where?'

'I guess that depends on what Harper thinks about her grandma,' Sam said. 'Though even if she keeps a shrine to Alida in her bedroom, it still doesn't give us much more than a bad smell.'

They sat in the office, mulling it over. Florida had more than its share of neo-Nazi groups, particularly active in its prisons, but the City of Miami Beach itself was never going to lay down any kind of welcome mat for residents or outsiders trying to ram those kinds of sentiments down people's throats.

'There's no way that paper had a white supremacist following,' Martinez said. 'I checked through the 2007 issues three times and I didn't see a spark of bias.'

'This still feels like something,' Sam said. 'Three victims in a paper edited by a woman with a bigot for a grandmother.'

'Maybe Harper hates what her grandma stood for,' Martinez said.

'What if she doesn't?' Sam said.

'Do we know how come Harper moved to Florida?'

'Came with mom and dad. George passed away in 2000. Guess they got tired of cold winters.'

'Hildy still alive?'

'No mention of her death. No mention of anything much about Hildy, other than that she married George and gave birth to Harper. No other kids.'

'So Harper's probably rich.' Martinez paused. '"Virginia" has to be rich too.'

'Wow,' Sam said wryly. 'Conclusive or what?' He looked at the back page of the July edition. 'Published by HBP Press, so probably her own company, or her mother's – or maybe George bought a publishing house for them, put it in their names.'

'I thought George was a teacher.'

'With a possibly sizable inheritance.' Sam paused. 'It's not the McClatchy Company, but I guess it signifies a certain amount of power.'

HBP Press, it turned out, had published a free weekly paper called *Hudson*, circulated in the north-east in the late eighties, surviving just two years. Then the firm had moved to South Carolina, where *Santee Weekly* had been born, its distribution from Columbia to Charleston, this paper still in existence, though no longer owned by HBP. The move to Florida appeared to have happened in the mid-nineties, and here the publishers had quit naming newspapers after rivers and had plumped for *The Beach*, which had apparently brought HBP's newspaper publishing history to an end.

'Going into book publishing now, you think?' Martinez said. 'In time for Harper's book, maybe?'

'I don't know that Ms Benedict strikes me as the self-publishing type,' Sam said, scanning something on his iPad. 'Now here's a thing. HBP stands for Hildegard Bened*ek* Publishing – not Benedict. Which suggests – big maybe – that

160

Harper's mom might have admired her husband's old world.'

'Maybe it was her world too,' Martinez said.

Sam nodded. 'Time to go ask her daughter if Hildy Benedict is dead or living, and if so, where we can find her.'

Back in Bal Harbour, in the same serene living room, the kind, Sam thought, that smacked of confidence and, perhaps, a cool, clear conscience. Or maybe it was the type of complacency sometimes brought about by inherited wealth and a feeling of being somehow above the rules.

Or maybe he was letting his own prejudices run away with him.

'That was quick.' Harper Benedict had welcomed them without concern or annoyance, had brought them Nespresso coffee and told them that she was glad to be disturbed again, since her work was going badly.

'Is your mother still living, Ms Benedict?' Sam asked.

'Please,' she said, 'call me Harper. And no, she is not. She passed away several years ago. Why do you ask?'

'We did a little reading about you and your company,' Sam said. 'That fact was missing.'

'I asked you earlier if I was a suspect.' Still amused.

'Something funny about that?' Martinez said.

'I think so,' she said.

'Your family history is interesting,' Sam said.

'That's one word for it,' Benedict said.

'The history of your publishing firm too, ma'am,' Martinez said.

'Is HBP your own firm?' Sam asked.

Harper Benedict smiled again. 'You found Alida's book. My redoubtable grandmother's life's work. And now, what you really want to know is if her opinions swam down the line to me, her one and only grandchild.'

'Did they?' Sam asked.

The smile left her face and her blue eyes grew darker with anger. 'They did not, Detective Becket. As a matter of fact, they did not even make it as far as her son, my father. Though they did seem to leap the marital bridge into my mother's misguided soul.' She paused. 'Assuming she had one.'

The room was very quiet for a moment.

'I apologize,' Sam said.

'You don't know me,' she said. 'I guess you had to ask.'

'I felt I did,' Sam said.

'So.' Benedict shook her hair and the darkness lifted. 'Did anything leap out of our back issues or files?'

'Not immediately,' Sam said.

'Though we would like to hold on to them, if you don't object,' Martinez said.

'So long as you return them when you're done.'

'Of course,' Martinez said.

Sam drained the last of his coffee. 'Just to clarify,' he said. 'When your mother died, did HBP Press pass to you?'

'It had already passed to me,' Benedict said.

'So in the period of your editorship, you were also the proprietor?'

'I was.'

'Is the firm still in existence?' Martinez asked.

'No.' Affability draining away again. 'Anything else I can help you with?'

Sam stood up. 'Can't think of a thing, ma'am.'

Martinez rose too. 'So the book not coming along so well?'

'Too many interruptions, perhaps.'

'Sorry for that,' Sam said. 'Multiple homicides tend to have that kind of ripple effect.'

She got up, walked ahead of them toward the door.

'You never told us when your mother passed away,' Sam said.

'No,' Harper Benedict said. 'I didn't.'

'So, something to hide?' Martinez said outside. 'Or just being a bitch?'

Traffic on Collins thrummed between them and the high-price buildings partially obscuring the ocean.

'Maybe she just feels her deceased family are none of our business,' Sam said. 'She certainly gave the impression she rejected Grandma Alida's beliefs.'

'Called her mother "misguided" too.' Martinez took out a stick of gum. 'Could have been play-acting.'

Sam looked down the road. Make a right and he could be home, which was tempting.

Not yet.

'Back to base,' he said. 'Let's give that family tree a good shake, see what falls.'

* * *

163

The list was long.

Had been much longer, necessitating classification and sifting, and as time had passed, her top one hundred had reduced to fifty, after which she'd created fresh stipulations and qualifications in a process resembling that of a fussy employment agency. If she could have, she thought she might have enjoyed inviting candidates for interview.

'What makes you feel you're the right person for this execution?'

She had, for a time, done almost that, silently addressing each applicant or family of applicants, though after a while, it had transmuted more into a courtroom scenario. Guilt a foregone conclusion, albeit sometimes not the individual's *personal* guilt, but she had decided on a biblical bent, King James edition: 'visiting the iniquities of the fathers upon the children unto the third and fourth generation'. And who was she to argue with that?

Not that it had helped a damn when it came to carving a shortlist. Still twenty family names on there, still unviable. And she was, she thought, a pragmatic person.

So she had taken the only sensible course of action. Had taken her shortlist, closed her eyes, held a pin tightly, made a circle, twirled her hand around a few times – and then stabbed it down onto the list.

Twice it had pierced a hole in a margin, once it had landed between two names, and so she'd extracted the pin and begun again.

Bringing it down to the final five families.

Five plus one, of course.

Two already finalized and dealt with.

Three to go.

And her 'Plus One' – husband, wife and their progeny; sparing the adopted daughter who was, in any event, overseas. So, just the guilty pair and the next generation.

Planning for Number Three was already complete. A meeting set tomorrow with her Crusaders.

Her sorry, pathetic little mercenary quartet.

And then, the deed. To be topped off with the next message.

For Becket. With Love. From Virginia.

June 12

No record had yet been found of the death of Hildegard Benedict – possibly aka Benedek. She had not died in Florida or South Carolina, and all of late Tuesday's checks, including those made via the Social Security Death Index, had come up empty. Which did not mean that she had definitely *not* passed away, might feasibly mean that an incorrect record had been entered – might mean all manner of innocent things.

Sam and Martinez would, in due course, be asking her daughter about this, but before that they intended to learn as much as they could about Harper Benedict herself.

Harper had never published a book before, and all examples of her own writing appeared to have been varied; no specialist subject, no pet loves or gripes, no obvious axes to grind. So far as they'd been able to ascertain, she had never married, had committed neither felonies nor misdemeanors. Records regarding the family were minimal; the Benedicts had valued their privacy, paid their taxes, raised no hackles in any of the communities where they had resided.

Harper Benedict had attended the Academic Magnet High School (motto: Seriously Smart) in North Charleston (excelling at lacrosse and golf), and University of Miami, where she'd majored in English Literature.

They'd tried summing up late Tuesday.

'Good student, good brain, physically tough, brave enough to play lacrosse.' Sam had sighed. 'I don't know what we were hoping for, but we sure haven't found it.'

'Haven't found her mom either,' Martinez had pointed out.

'No real grounds for pestering Harper about that.'

'None for saying that Harper's a suspect, either.'

'She's barely a person of interest,' Sam had said.

'Except she is.'

'Agreed.'

Martinez had yawned. 'We need sleep.'

'Not arguing,' Sam had said.

Another distraction came right after lunch on Wednesday. One they couldn't turn down.

Mary Cutter said Laura Gomez wanted to see them.

'Maybe I'm not doing a good enough job,'

166

Cutter said, 'but her aunt feels that nothing but a face-to-face with you two is going to satisfy Laura. Mrs Rivera says she knows how tough your schedule is, but reassurance just isn't helping. Laura wants a progress report.'

'Jeez,' Martinez said. 'That's one I'd like to wriggle out of.'

Interrogation by a twelve-year-old orphan-by-homicide.

'Can't think of anyone with a greater right to insist,' Sam said.

Laura's Aunt Carrie lived with her husband in a white single family detached home close to one of Boca's numerous country clubs. An elegant, comfortable house with a pool and barbecue at the rear, but designed primarily for adults in their forties. The kids had grown and gone, and aside from her aunt and uncle's kindness and love, there was little there for a massively bereaved youngster. Except, that was, for Lola, a large, amiable, champagne-colored dog with soft eyes and a curly coat.

'She's a Goldendoodle,' Laura told the detectives.

'That's a cross between—'

'Don't tell them, Aunt Carrie,' Laura cut in. 'I want to see if they know.'

A test, Sam presumed. And in other circumstances, he might have feigned ignorance and let the child tell him, but Laura Gomez probably needed to think that the detectives looking for her family's killers were smart enough to know stuff like this.

'Golden retriever crossed with poodle?' He made it a question.

'Uh-huh.' Laura stroked Lola's head, presently resting on her lap.

'Great dog,' Martinez said. 'Though they should give them better names.'

'Goldendoodle's better than Cockapoo,' Laura said.

'Dogs deserve more respect,' Sam agreed.

'Do you have one?' Laura asked him.

'Sure. Woody's a cross between a schnauzer and a dachshund.'

'We never had a dog at home.' Laura fondled the dog's ears. 'My brother had allergies.'

Sam felt a pricking behind his eyes. He had been five years younger than this girl when he'd lost his family, and he still remembered the first weeks of shattering shock and grief, yet he knew that his accidental loss could never compare to what Laura Gomez was enduring.

'You haven't caught them yet,' she said suddenly, softly.

'Not yet,' he answered her. 'But we will.'

'How do you know?' Laura asked.

'He knows,' Martinez said, 'because we're good detectives, and because we're both mad as hell about what they did, and we won't stop till we get them.'

'Really?' Laura's voice was still soft, but touched by hope. 'Even if it takes a long, long time, you won't give up?'

'No way,' Sam said.

'Do you promise?' she said.

Oh, man.

Sam never made promises he couldn't keep.
Careful.
'I promise,' he said.
Laura Gomez's hands kept on fondling the big dog, but her brown eyes lifted and gazed right into Sam Becket's own eyes.
'I believe you,' she said.
Oh, man.

June 13

Jay Sandhu and his girlfriend, Lorna Munro, sat motionless in the hushed moments before they began, and for the briefest of instants their eyes met.

They had been playing together as part of Surfside Strings – Surfside being where they lived, in a small white one-story single family house on Dickens Avenue – for three years.

They'd been a couple for four. Had been happy for all that time, their sense of union, of moving forward together, of their great good fortune in loving so many of the same things, growing with each passing year.

Jay had played violin since he was five. Lorna had fallen in love with the cello at seven. Jay was a lawyer by profession, Lorna a kindergarten teacher; those aspects of their lives still bringing satisfaction, but nothing making them happier than *this*.

Surfside Strings were making a name, their agents getting them more quality gigs, though the wedding and party circuit was still their bread and butter.

Tonight was very special.

Playing Grieg, Mendelssohn and Borodin at the Historic Asolo Theater – a gorgeous eighteenth-century Italian playhouse dismantled in the nineteen forties and transported to the Ringling Estate in Sarasota, now wonderfully restored and housing theater, dance, music, movies and lectures.

Jay and Lorna had never experienced such *atmosphere*.

Except, perhaps, for the very different atmosphere – polar, in every sense – of the family meeting back in April when they'd broken the news to their parents.

A rare opportunity to get both sets of mothers and fathers together, Jay's parents now living in Fort Lauderdale, Lorna's residing in Vermont, where they had for two generations.

Both families wholly unsupportive of the relationship.

And as for the news of a child on the way . . .

'I never imagined I could be so glad to see the back of people I love,' Lorna had said after they'd gone, and then she'd burst into tears and Jay had tried to comfort her, his own emotions translating into anger. And later that night, unable to sleep, they'd played their own version of Lloyd Webber's *Variations*, and afterwards, as always, they'd felt better, ready to go on with their own lives.

Their way. Marrying before the baby was born – parents excluded seeming by far the most sanity-saving course of action for now.

But first, there was this amazing Thursday night. Gig of a lifetime.

* * *

170

The forensic audio experts were confident that the message passed to them by Nick Gibson had been recorded via a telephone, but that was about all that could be concluded until they had a human suspect with whom they could run comparisons.

More likely male than female.

Riley was drip-feeding the media as much 'frank disclosure' as she could, but the sharks' circling was relentless. Not unlike their beloved lieutenant, Martinez remarked, with Kovac riding them harder each day.

Sam's personal hunch scale (which he tended to parallel with the Richter) with regard to the *maybe* late Hildegard Benedict was running somewhere around the 4.00 mark. Nothing big enough to act on in any significant way, but still something that needed following up.

And a 4.00 was pretty high considering it was centered on a *dead* woman.

A woman who, if she were still living, would be sixty-seven years old.

Not that old. Plenty of women ten years older than that who still swam in the ocean on winter mornings and solved the Saturday *New York Times* crossword puzzle.

So not necessarily past criminal master-planning if she was alive.

Definitely past it if she was dead – as her daughter claimed.

'We ready to go talk to Harper again?' Martinez asked Thursday afternoon.

'Not yet,' Sam said.

Better she thought she'd been forgotten, if there was anything to this.

And there was just *something* about learning of an old woman who'd admired her racist mother-in-law that would not let Sam forget about Harper Benedict or her family.

Not just yet, at least.

June 14

With planning well underway for the new menu and publicity blitz, *Le Rêve* was buzzing. Visitors in and out of Nic's office and the kitchen, some at the boss's table in and outside opening hours, eating, drinking, conversing, sometimes intensely.

Gabe was still at his uncle's and Cathy was feeling restless, unsure of him, her impulse to get out of the confines of the kitchen and go running.

Job to do, she kept reminding herself.

Too old now to go mooning around after a guy.

Even if that guy was the best, the most relaxed, the most consistently interesting and fun and, for *sure*, the sexiest man she'd ever encountered.

Work.

'Photographers coming at lunchtime,' Jeanne told the Friday morning shift. 'Just looking around, maybe taking a few test shots.'

'*Dieu*,' Jacques Carnot said, irritated.

'If I'd known,' Aniela said, 'I'd have worn makeup.'

Jeanne ignored them. 'Just test shots, as I said, but everyone please make sure that you and the kitchen are immaculate at all times.'

Minutes later, while scrubbing Carnot's prep table, an unpleasant memory crawled suddenly into Cathy's mind.

Of Thomas Chauvin, the day he'd come uninvited to her home and taken picture after picture of her, not stopping when she'd asked him to . . .

And later, Sam had discovered the photos of her and Grace covering the walls of his vacation apartment.

Weirdo.

Arrested for stalking in the past.

What if . . .?

Her parents had been troubled when she'd told them she was coming to France, but then Sam had learned that Chauvin was living in England, and they'd both relaxed.

Cathy knew she was being absurd.

There were *thousands* of infinitely more experienced professional photographers in France, so the probability of Nic considering employing that jerk was zero.

Yet still, for just a few moments there, it had creeped her out.

Lunchtime came and went.

The photographers too.

Three of them.

Not Chauvin.

Of *course* not.

'You OK, Cath?' Luc asked a little later.

She told him she was fine.

'You seem distracted,' he said. 'Is it Gabe?'

'Maybe,' Cathy said. 'I guess I wish he was here.'

Luc put his arm around her. 'He'll be back soon, and it'll be fine.'

'I hope so,' Cathy said.

And wondered why that creepy feeling had not entirely gone away.

Lorna and Jay had spent most of Friday in Sarasota, setting off on those parts of the tourist trail that most interested them. They visited the opera house, vowed to be in the audience on their next trip, then made their way around *Ca' d'Zan*, John and Mable Ringling's Venetian Gothic mansion, and Mable's famous rose garden, before taking a cab to Siesta Key and eating seafood tacos at the Oyster Bar, finishing up with a barefoot stroll through the pure quartz sandy beach.

After that, it was back to collect their instruments from the hotel in time to catch the shuttle bus to Tampa and their flight back to Miami.

'Back to reality,' Jay said, on the plane. 'That brief to prepare.'

'Not for me.' Lorna snuggled against his shoulder. 'I'm just going to laze.'

'You're allowed.' Jay kissed his fingertips, touched them to her belly.

'Best twenty-four hours ever,' she said.

'Plenty more to come,' he said.

'Will we take her travelling, do you think?' Lorna asked.

'Sure we will, when we have bookings all over the world.'

'Not too many bookings,' she said. 'I want her to love home, have friends.'

174

'Love,' Jay said. 'The biggest thing.'

'And good health,' Lorna said.

'And a great sense of humor,' Jay said. 'She'll need it with her grandparents.'

'Oh,' Lorna said, and her hand went to her bump.

'You OK?'

'I think she's laughing.'

They were home and sleeping when they came.

Out of the dark.

Rubber soles almost silent on the hardwood floor.

Moonlight coming through the open windows, tree branches rustling in the breeze.

The couple cuddled up. Cute-looking.

Leon spoke first. Line from *Kill Bill*, as he recalled, and he'd have preferred to be more original, but using Tarantino just felt so *right*.

He bent over the guy. 'Wakey wakey, eggs and bakey,' he called.

Jay groaned softly and opened his eyes.

'Lights,' Jerry said.

Jay blinked in the glare of four flashlights, put a hand up to shield his eyes.

Saw the guns before he took in the men.

Four of them.

'Jesus,' he said.

He felt Lorna stirring beside him, pulled her closer.

'What's—?' She saw them, opened her mouth to scream, no sound emerging.

'Hi, guys,' Leon said. 'Real sorry to disturb you.'

'Where's your safe?' Andy asked.

'I hit the panic button,' Jay said, his mind fumbling.

'You don't have one,' Leon said.

'Where's your safe?' Andy said again.

'We don't have one of those either,' Jay said.

'But we'll give you what we have.' Lorna's voice was thready, stunned. 'Just please don't hurt us.'

'Right you are,' said Leon. 'Let's move this thing along.'

Jerry edged away, gun still raised, moved over to the windows and closed them, pulled down the blinds, then hit the light switch.

Jay and Lorna stared at the gunmen. All weirdly golden-haired and blue-eyed, all black-gloved, their weapons fat, solid, hideously *real*.

'Let me show you where we keep our money,' Jay said.

'Not necessary,' Leon said.

'What does that mean?' Lorna asked.

'It means we can help ourselves,' Jerry said.

'Sure you can,' Jay said. 'Just—'

'Shut up,' Andy said.

'Let's do it,' Leon said.

One of the men reached into a duffel bag, pulled out cut lengths of cord, handed them to the others.

'Oh, dear God,' Lorna said.

'Please,' Jay said. 'Don't hurt my wife. She's pregnant.'

'Get up,' Leon told him.

'Oh, sweet Jesus,' Lorna said.

'Get the fuck *up*.' Jerry bent over, grabbed Jay's left arm and yanked him out from under the covers. 'Come on, man,' he said to CB. 'Give me a hand.'

Andy moved around to Lorna's side and, as she cried out, he took a roll of tape from a pocket, ripped off a length and silenced her.

'Bastard,' Jay spat.

CB, his own jaw aching, did the same for him.

'Arms,' Leon ordered.

Jay saw the dark muzzle of the gun pointed against Lorna's temple and knew that any attempt at a struggle was pointless.

They looked at each other while their wrists were tied behind their backs.

All they could do now, as they were dragged out of the bedroom. And it was only when they saw where they were being taken that they both realized who these men were. They'd seen the black-and-white shots of the four men sought in connection with the murder of those poor people just a few miles from here; and then, a week ago, there'd been the dentist and his family on Emerson Avenue – just around the corner . . .

Their eyes filled, weeping for their unborn child.

'Wait,' one of the men said suddenly.

The one who'd been silent until now, the one who'd taped Jay's mouth.

They were inside the garage, the air cooler, their old Dodge Magnum – the vehicle they'd both chosen partly because it was easy to get the cello into – standing silent; and if they were right, then before long its motor would be started and their trusty station wagon would become their coffin.

177

'I don't think I can do this,' CB said.

'Why the fuck not?' Jerry said.

'Look at her,' CB said. 'There's a baby.'

Hope reached up through Lorna and Jay, grabbed their hearts.

'Doesn't matter if there's fucking triplets,' Leon said.

'It's too much,' CB said. 'It's too wicked.'

'Wicked is what she wants,' Andy said.

'But it isn't her doing it,' CB said.

'Just grow a pair, man,' Jerry said.

The hope let go, flew away, and despair took its place again.

Another Tarantino quote hovered on Leon-the-*Man's* lips. One about quitting barking and starting biting. Except this wasn't a movie. This was the real thing.

'We're doing it,' he said instead. 'Now.'

June 15

Just after ten on Saturday morning, as Joshua was pedaling his tricycle on the sidewalk, Sam and Woody moseying alongside, father and son singing 'The Wheels on the Bus', Sam's phone rang.

Martinez.

'We got another one.'

Sam got the details, arranged to meet, kept his voice flat.

Joshua had stopped singing and pedaling, was looking up at him. 'What's up, Daddy?'

Sam hunched down beside the tricycle, looked into his son's beautiful, enquiring dark eyes and wanted to scream.

178

Such obscenity, less than a mile away.

Surfside again. Dickens Avenue. One block away from Emerson.

'Do you have to go to work?'

No reproach, no complaint, no '*again*', this child all too accustomed to his father's lousy work schedule.

'I'm really sorry, sweet cheeks.' He ruffled his boy's hair, kissed him, straightened up.

'That's OK,' Joshua said, then laughed. 'Woody pooped.'

Sam sighed, took a bag and wipe out of his pocket, did the necessary.

'Good boy,' Joshua said.

'Yes, he is,' Sam said, turning back. 'I got two good boys.'

Joshua chuckled again.

Best sound his father was likely to hear for the rest of that day.

'Oh, dear Christ,' Sam said when he heard.

And when he saw, he choked up – couldn't help himself.

The woman was pregnant.

Not sufficiently far on to have made a post-mortem C-section viable. And the thought of the possible effects on an unborn of carbon monoxide poisoning was too hideous to bear.

The young couple had been unofficially identified by their friend, Susan Cohen – friend and agent, she'd told the patrol officers, because the murdered couple were musicians, *wonderful* musicians, beautiful people, and she couldn't believe it, couldn't bear it, and she'd come for

179

breakfast, eager to hear about their gig in Sarasota . . .

Jay Sandhu and Lorna Munro.

Five months pregnant.

'Oh, dear Jesus,' Sam said.

He saw it reflected in the faces of others around him as the machinery ground into action. Martinez looking mad enough to kill, given half a chance. Duval deeply saddened. Doc Sanders's face implacably set.

'Virginia' at work again.

'Her' message once again addressed to Sam.

For the Personal Attention of Detective
Samuel Becket,
Miami Beach Police Department

You are a reasonably educated man, Detective Becket. If you were to sit with me and debate, say, polygenesis v monogenesis, you would probably be equipped to argue your personal case, or perhaps you're a preadamite or . . .

But I've digressed. If you and I do ever sit down together, it will likely be in an ugly room with a table between us and a recording device, and the questions you pose won't be about theories of human origins, but on the manner in which I have chosen to play my paltry part in the uprooting and exterminating that a great American offered up to our country's House of Representatives one hundred years ago.

180

Better job this time, I feel. Removing
the spawn in time.
I can't stop you all.
But my piece still has a way to go.

Love Virginia

'Something's changed,' Sam said as they sat in
his old Saab with Martinez and Duval, coffees
and Danish to fortify them. 'Not as crisp.'
'Almost rambling,' Duval said.
'On something, maybe?' Martinez suggested.
'Or off something,' Sam said. 'Like medication,
maybe.'
'Sounds more like it's come from a disordered
mind than the others,' Duval said.
'Maybe an age thing?' Martinez said.
'You're thinking Hildegard,' Sam said.
'I am and I'm not,' his partner said. 'Because
it's nuts, right?'
'Our first demented serial killer, maybe,' Duval
said, and shrugged.
'We need to recheck the final year's copies of
The Beach for mentions of the new victims,' Sam
said. 'Harper edited till the final edition. December
2010.'
'How long did the agent say they'd been
playing together?' Duval asked.
'Three years,' Martinez said.
'Get Sheldon on it,' Sam said. 'And the
agent'll know about any publicity they've had.
I'll talk to her.' He paused. 'Then we go see
Harper again.'

* * *

Harper Benedict was eating eggs Florentine at the News Café, had been on her way out when they'd called, and she hadn't been willing to stay home, but had said they were welcome to come join her for brunch.

'Not what it used to be,' she told them, 'but I still like it here.'

Sam and Martinez both ordered espressos.

'We have some questions,' Sam said.

'I saw the news,' she said. 'How can I help?'

'Did you ever publish anything about Jay Sandhu and Lorna Munro or their quartet, *Surfside Strings*? Either in *The Beach* or any other publication you or your company were connected with?'

'Not to my recollection, and I'm sure you're checking, but if it helps, I'll take a careful look. I might have forgotten an ad for a performance, something minor. Definitely no interviews or features.' She paused. 'And I've never edited any other publications.'

'OK, thanks,' Sam said. 'Second question.'

'Shoot.' She dipped a piece of bagel into yolk, ate it.

The music and constant buzz of the place was incongruous with the question, but Sam asked it anyway.

'When did your mother pass away?'

'I told you. Several years ago.'

'When exactly, ma'am?' Martinez said.

'Why the interest?'

'We can't find any record of her death,' Sam said.

'How odd.'

182

'Can you give us the date, please,' Martinez said.

She shook her head. 'I can't imagine how it could be relevant.'

'Would you rather come to the station?' Sam asked. 'Answer more questions. Start accounting for your whereabouts during the weeks of the recent killings?'

She laid down her fork, her appetite apparently gone. 'This is becoming absurd, gentlemen. Do I need a lawyer?'

'It's your prerogative, ma'am,' Martinez said.

'You're not under arrest,' Sam clarified. 'You can refuse to speak to us. But you did ask how you could help, and the most helpful thing you could do now would be to talk to us about your mother.'

Harper muttered something, then shrugged assent.

'Is your mother alive?' Sam asked.

'I don't know.'

'OK,' Sam said. 'Ms Benedict, might you be more comfortable talking about this someplace more quiet?'

'No,' she said. 'I'm perfectly comfortable right here. No one's listening, and there isn't too much for me to tell you. My relationship with my mother was at rock bottom for a while a few years back. Then we cut off altogether. When you asked about her, it just seemed easier to say she'd died. She'd told me I was dead to her, so I guess I was just returning the compliment.'

'Where was she, when you were last in touch?' Martinez asked.

'Living in our family house on La Gorce Island.' Harper paused. 'Which has been sold. I don't have any information to give you on that, but I can let you have the address.'

Martinez said it would be helpful and wrote it down.

'I have to say I'm baffled as to your interest in Hildy.' Harper smiled. 'Now, if my grandmother were still living, that might be a different story, but she's long gone, and though my mother was a bitch to me, she was quite a philanthropist and pretty modest about it.'

'Did she ever talk to you much about her past?' Sam asked.

'Especially about her mother-in-law?' Martinez added.

Harper shook her head. 'You're on the wrong track, and I'm about ready to leave.'

'Just a couple more questions,' Sam said. 'How did you learn that the house had been sold?'

'On the grapevine.'

'And was it your mother who sold it?'

'As far as I know.'

'So she was still living at that time?' Sam persisted.

'As far as I know,' she repeated.

'If she had passed away before that,' Martinez said, 'who would have owned the house?'

'Not me.' Harper's impatience was starting to show. 'If you're wanting to know if I'd have benefited if she had died, then the answer is I doubt that very much.'

'But you seem comfortably off, if you don't mind the observation,' Martinez said.

'My father left me well provided for. I have no worries on that score.'

'Did your mother object to that?' Sam asked.

'Perhaps,' Harper said.

'Just one more question,' Sam said. 'What is it that you're writing about now?'

'I'm not prepared to tell you that.' Colder now, as at their last meeting. 'Except to assure you that it could not possibly have the slightest bearing on your investigation.' She paused. 'As I said before, you're on the wrong track with my family.'

Sam put down ten bucks for their espressos and stood up. 'Thank you for your time, Ms Benedict.'

Martinez drained his cup and got up too. 'You have a nice day.'

'We're going to need legal on this before we start investigating the mother,' Duval said back at the station, getting ready for another tough press conference. 'Need to be real careful about harassing a family like that.'

'If Hildegard Benedict is still alive,' Sam said, 'she might be rich enough to be bankrolling the killings.'

'No mention of the latest victims in *The Beach*,' Duval said.

'OK,' Sam said.

Martinez looked at him. 'What's your gut telling you about Hildy?'

'What's yours telling you?' Sam asked.

'Something crazy, like Hildy's sitting in some wheelchair, her brain maybe on the fritz, spending all her dough on hitmen.' Martinez looked at Duval. 'I told you it was crazy.'

'Not necessarily,' Sam said.

Things were starting to get almost as interesting in Miami as they were on this side of the pond, Chauvin thought, watching Sam on his laptop.

So impressive.

More deaths. Another *mariage mixte*.

Not actually married, but a child on the way, making it the most wicked crime in the series to date. The male victim – Jay Sandhu – had been hogtied, torture-style. His partner, Lorna Munro, pregnant, also hogtied, then gassed with CO with Sandhu in their car.

Too ghastly to think about.

Though he did see it in his mind, the way any photojournalist would.

He froze the video on Sam for a moment and tried to penetrate his expression, wondered if he felt vulnerable. It was only now, after this third outrage, that Chauvin understood that Sam and Grace might actually be in danger, and it was hard to contemplate that, the idea of something bad happening to them.

He unfroze the video. Saw that they were all there, the whole gang from two years back – he *knew* them, for Christ's sake. The slim FDLE guy, Duval, who'd come in on their very own murder scene, gun ready to blaze. And Martinez, of course, Sam's sidekick, so gratuitously nasty to him in Miami.

Sam looked magnificent. Catherine's beloved *père-noir*.

Catherine.

He froze the action again, lay back on his pillows.

Mostly, these days, he thought about her from his bed.

Here, and in the other place, the secret one almost ready now.

He rarely thought about her with her so-called boyfriend. Gabriel Ryan, a waiter with a part-interest in a market stall. A nobody, and Catherine would soon see that he was of no greater significance to her future than Luc Meyer, the round-faced cook.

Almost ready now, his web of strategies for all eventualities, for he was, he had come to realize, an imaginative, self-sufficient man.

Almost ready.

He looked up at the blow-up on his ceiling, felt love expand within him.

It was impossible for him to express his innermost feelings to anyone – his parents least of all, however often they claimed to want to understand him.

He locked this room now whenever he went out, in case they managed to enter the apartment. He'd changed the locks, but his father was a clever man and his mother incurably nosy, so he couldn't be certain they might not have stolen a key and had it copied.

He was sorry if he disappointed them, but it wasn't his fault he wasn't more like them; rather it was their fault for being so stifling, so *unim-*aginative . . .

He stared up at Catherine, at her amazing, seductive pose, leaning toward him.

He was hard – she *made* him hard – and he reached down, began to masturbate, his eyes never leaving Catherine, her mouth, and oh, Christ, but he longed for the time he would be able to put himself into her, into that mouth, and she would want him to, she would want him as much as he did her, and he could feel her now, he could *feel* her . . .

He climaxed into his hand, then spread it onto his flat stomach.

If she were here, she would probably want to lick it off him.

He sighed, started to drift off.

When he woke, he could unfreeze Papa Sam, then concentrate again on his own plans, and maybe his mind would feel clearer after a sleep, because he sometimes felt it was tearing in two, his need for Sam's approval almost as strong as his need for Catherine.

Though of course once he had her, he realized, sleepily, he would have Sam too, and Grace, and all the Beckets would become his family, and his heart contracted with the joy of that thought.

Not long now. Not long at *all*.

He slept.

She was satisfied with the way Number Three had been executed.

Her boys had done well. Her Virginians. Her Crusaders. Her Knights.

They were getting edgier, she felt. She was no psychologist – though some might think her psychotic, were probably already calling her a psycho.

Which she was not. She was just making a stand, a tiny attempt to restore order.

Not that they would understand.

Number Two had seemed easier for the boys, after the success – security camera notwithstanding – of the first act. She'd told them the second would be easier, and it had been – except, of course, for CB, her little wimp.

Not a total wimp, to be fair, given that he'd now participated in the murders of nine people. Ten, including the fetus – in some ways the most important of her victims. She had known that CB would find that very hard, that it might even have created a problem – in which case, Leon had known what to do.

Leon had what it took, though there was too much braggart in him for her to trust him for the long term. Jerry was a true psycho. Andy was an avaricious, untrustworthy man who would agree to anything. She would never put her faith in any of them except, perhaps, CB, who feared her more deeply than the others and had scruples; he'd taken payment from her, would soon be taking a larger sum, had made an agreement with her, and was, she thought, probably a wimp of honor.

She pondered again the aliases she'd allocated them, each representing a man she had admired. Leon M. Bazile, the trial judge in the *Loving v. Virginia* case in Caroline County Court in 1958, who had declared that the Almighty, having

189

placed the differently colored races on separate continents, showed that He had not intended for the races to mix. Jerry Falwell, who'd passed away in 2007, and who had once stated: 'When God has drawn a line of distinction, we should not attempt to cross that line.' Andy named for Andrew King, the first congressman, in 1871, to propose a constitutional amendment to ban inter-racial marriage nationwide. And CB had come from Seaborn Roddenbery, a man who had once said that he found intermarriage between whites and blacks repulsive, abhorrent and repugnant. 'Seaborn' too unwieldy for any of her Crusaders, so she'd dumbed it down to a phonetic CB.

He'd accepted the alias, as they all had, along with her directions and rewards, but still, she could see problems ahead. Not everyone could kill with impunity. Causing terror and suffering could have repercussions, psychological and physical, especially if children were among the victims.

And she was seeing signs. Andy had jumped at a backfire the other day. Jerry was hyper too much of the time. Leon was putting on weight and beginning to strut. And CB had fear in his eyes, constantly.

She'd felt reasonably confident about them until now. None had a record, none were in the system, and at this point they needed her more than she needed them.

It had occurred to her, of course, that she might, in time, need to replace them. Though in order to do that, she would have to have them termi-nated too. Which made her a little sad.

But only a little.

Later this evening, she would give them what she owed, and then she would pause. No need to rush. The list was long, but there was time.

'*Ceteris paribus*,' she said out loud. All other things being equal.

'*Mutatis mutandis*.' Another Latin phrase, translating roughly as 'changing what needed to be changed', or, as her English dictionary informed her, 'the necessary changes having been made'.

She might enjoy that as her epitaph.

'Gone to her rest, the necessary changes having been made'.

The list was long, and she might never reach the end, but she was, at least, getting the ball rolling, and she hoped with all her might that it would gather momentum, as all the finest snowballs did.

The purest, whitest snowballs.

June 16

Sunday evening at *Le Rêve*, the restaurant full, service smooth, good spirits in the kitchen. Nic not working tonight, but eating at his table with a TV producer. Jeanne, walking by, nodding at the boss, letting him know all was fine. And then . . .

First, a woman at table five on the ground floor, where coffee was being served, gave a sudden cry and passed out, falling sideways from her chair, her husband unable to catch her before she hit the floor.

Ten seconds later, a man on the far side of the room clutched at his head, let out a curious, high-pitched sound, and began to laugh.

Crazy laughter. Not a good sound.

Jeanne and Gabe were already attending to the fallen woman, an emergency call to SAMU made, and Nic was on his feet, moving toward the second diner, a bad feeling gripping him.

From upstairs, he heard another commotion.

A woman's voice, high and uncontrolled.

Then a man yelling.

Nic's eyes met Jeanne's across the room.

What the *hell*?

'It's a disaster,' Aniela said later in the upper dining room, where all staff had been instructed to wait until further notice. A crowded, depressing scene: waiters, chefs and kitchen staff, some sitting, others pacing, everyone restless.

'It's far worse than that,' Jacques Carnot said.

'Hey,' Gabe said. 'It won't be that bad.'

'I think Jacques is right,' Sadi said bleakly. 'Lord knows when they'll let us reopen.'

'Maybe never,' Aniela said.

'Never for sure,' Carnot said.

'Don't even think that,' Cathy said.

And then she realized that Luc was alone at a corner table, his head in his hands.

She got up, went over. 'You OK?'

'No,' he said.

'It'll be all right. Nic and Jeanne will take care of this and things will be fine.'

'Not for me,' Luc said from behind his hands.

'Why not?' Cathy said.

'Trust me.' Luc removed his glasses, revealing damp eyes. 'I'm finished here.'

Cathy sat down beside him. 'Luc, why?' She kept her voice low. 'Tell me.'

His mouth trembled. 'Because everyone who got sick ate my *fondant au chocolat*.'

'Are you sure?' She saw his nod. 'But they'll have eaten other dishes first. It might not even have been food, it might have been wine, or . . .'

Gabe joined them. 'What's up? Apart from the obvious.'

'Just my career,' Luc said.

'He thinks the people who got sick ate his chocolate fondant.'

Gabe drew up a chair on Luc's other side. 'Did you put drugs in it?'

Luc's eyes widened. 'Of course not.'

'Then it has nothing to do with you.'

'Why?' Cathy asked. 'Gabe, what do you know?'

'Not much.' Gabe shrugged. 'But I'm thinking it could have been something like acid.'

'God,' Cathy said.

'They'll still think it was me,' Luc said.

'Why should they?' Gabe asked.

'Because I always screw up,' Luc said softly.

Gabe smiled wryly. 'Don't we all?'

Sunday evening, and Mrs Hood had summoned her Crusaders for another limo get-together.

Different pickup points.

Different parking lot for the conversation, near another Domino's.

The mood inside the stretch intense.

Leon's answers to the boss's questions about the Dickens Avenue mission appeared satisfactory. They'd left the kill house separately, had walked different routes to get back to the 2009 Chevy Traverse that Mrs Hood had provided for the job. No one had been seen peering through a window or from a passing car. Leon had taken the guns, pitiful jewelry and cash and equipment, Jerry had ditched the SUV. All to plan.

Two dead.

'Two and a half,' Jerry had put it.

CB had wanted to kill him then. After all, he'd told himself, he knew now that he was capable of it. Had aided and abetted in the murder of nine human beings.

He couldn't stand to *think* about the unborn baby. Not coping real well all in all, wondering if the others could tell.

If Mrs H could see it in his eyes.

'So, Boss?' Leon said now.

'Yes, Leon.' She smiled at him. 'You'll be wanting your rewards.'

'We've done three jobs now,' Leon said.

'And?' Mrs Hood said.

'You said that after three, we'd get our first real payment,' Leon said.

A ripple of relief rolled through the others, because he'd said it for them.

'So what do you think we're doing here now?' Mrs H said.

Her right hand delved inside her large brown bag – which Leon had identified on his PC as a

Monogram Louis Vuitton tote, liked their cash coming out of that – and withdrew one fat, cream-colored envelope.

'One for you.' She gave it to Leon, dipped back into the bag, brought out another. 'One for you.' She handed it to Jerry. 'Look if you must, but please don't count it now. In the first place, it isn't polite. In the second, you all know where to find me.'

Two more envelopes. One for Andy and the last for CB, who felt glad to be last, wished it meant he was less wicked, knew it did not.

'So, everyone satisfied?' Mrs Hood asked.

'Yes, ma'am,' Leon said.

'Very,' Jerry said.

'Thank you,' Andy said.

CB echoed him.

'Is that it?' Jerry asked.

'For today,' Mrs Hood replied.

'No treats?' Andy felt emboldened by his envelope, though any second the boss or Leon might take out a gun and kill him and take back the cash, but the question was out of his mouth now, too late to take it back.

'You've got your pay,' Mrs Hood said equably.

'Yes, we have.' Leon shot Andy a look.

'What about the next time, ma'am?' Jerry asked.

'You'll hear from me,' she said. 'In the meantime, you know the rules. Numero uno: keep it zipped.'

'We do,' Leon said.

CB, whose jaw was throbbing worse than ever, was tempted to ask about the dentist, because the work hadn't been finished, but for one thing, he didn't dare ask, and for another, he was beginning to think that if there was a next time, if another gun was placed in his hand, he might just shoot himself through his diseased mouth, which would hurt a whole lot less than another visit to the dentist.

Mrs Hood smiled at him.

A little pity in the smile, he thought, but a lot more contempt.

She'd told them that so long as they kept their part of their deal, she'd always take care of them, but CB thought that if and when it suited her, she'd probably hang them out to dry without lifting so much as a manicured finger to help them.

Mrs Hood swiveled in her seat, tapped on the dividing window.

The limo began to move again.

June 17

It had gone on until the early hours of Monday, Nic asking everyone to stay until he and Jeanne had spoken with them privately. The upper floor slowly emptying out. No indication yet that the police had been notified, though since all three diners had been taken to the Hopital de Brousailles, it seemed unlikely now that they would not ultimately become involved.

Nothing in the kitchen or restaurant was to be disposed of, nothing more washed up, all receptacles containing traces of food or drink secured until they could be tested at a laboratory. And as soon as he'd arrived just after midnight, Nic's *détective privé*, Jac Noël, had requested that all gloves, uniforms and footwear be given to him for sealing, labeling and possible testing.

'They're treating us like suspects,' Michel Mont, collecting his jacket after his interview, said to Gabe. 'Not nice. Not cool.'

'I don't see why the police aren't here,' Carnot complained, 'rather than the boss's *privé*, and how long have I worked for Nic?'

'I guess they can't make exceptions,' Sadi said.

'Do we know yet?' Luc asked Michel, his voice low. 'Did they all eat my fondant?'

'They all ate the mushroom *velouté* and the *fondant au chocolat*, and they all drank coffee.'

'See?' Cathy said to Luc. 'Not just your dessert.'

'But they all ate it,' he said.

'Gabe?' Jeanne appeared in the doorway. 'Nic and Joe would like to see you.'

When he returned, almost an hour later, he was pale and angry.

'Seems I'm prime suspect,' he told Cathy and nodded at Luc. 'So I guess you're off the hook.'

'We did ask that you not discuss our conversation.' Jeanne had come up behind him.

'After what I've just been put through, *screw* what you asked.' He looked at Cathy's stunned face. 'Jeanne knows *things* about us. She certainly knows things about me. Private stuff, like what I grow at my *lopin*. From which she and Nic seem to have deduced a whole load of what I can only call shit.'

197

'Gabe, you need to calm down,' Jeanne told him.

'You need to tell Nic and his fucking private eye to go to hell.'

'Gabe.' Cathy reached out to touch him, but he shook her off.

'I don't understand,' Luc said.

'That makes two of us.' Gabe looked at Cathy. 'I'm leaving. Do you want to come with me or stay here?'

'I thought they said we have to stay,' Cathy said.

'Do you see any cops? Locked doors?' He laughed harshly. 'Not yet.'

'Gabe, I think it's better if we do stay, see this through.'

'Maybe you're right,' he said. 'You maybe do need to stay, find out what Jeanne has on you – you might be surprised.'

'Gabe,' Luc said. 'Why don't we sit, have a drink, talk?'

'I'm not staying here one second longer.' Gabe looked at Cathy. 'Are you coming?'

'We need Cathy to stay,' Jeanne said.

'Cathy?' Gabe ignored Jeanne.

'Gabe, I don't want to just walk out.'

'OK,' he said. 'Got it.'

And left.

Bad feeling ran on through the night, spreading through the slowly dwindling employees like a virus. Almost five a.m. when they were done. Luc and Cathy both interviewed, neither experiencing the sense of accusation that Gabe had felt, but still Cathy had stuck around, hoping to find some cast-iron way of clearing his name.

It was crazy for anyone to think that Gabe would do such a thing.

Le Rêve was closed until further notice. Nic was still behind closed doors with Jac Noël, the private detective. No police yet, but Jeanne was more grim-faced than Cathy had ever seen her.

'What can I do to help?' Cathy asked her.

'Just what we've asked everyone,' Jeanne said. 'Keep your phone switched on in case we need you.' She paused. 'I'll give you the new code for the back door in case you want to visit with Luc.'

'Do you have an idea who might have done this?'

'If you're asking about your boyfriend, I have nothing to tell you.'

'You surely can't think for a second that Gabe would do something like this.'

'Your conviction is touching,' Jeanne said. 'I hope you're right.'

'I am,' Cathy said, feeling angry too now, realizing suddenly how it must have been for Gabe, how insulting or worse. Her own guilt growing.

She should have jumped all over Jeanne while Gabe was still there, should have told them all they ought to know better than accusing a loyal employee.

She should have left with him.

Half an hour later, just after Luc had gone to bed and Cathy was stressing about what to do next,

Gabe called her cell phone to say he was at the rear entrance.

'Would you come open the door, please?'

He was outside, leaning against his Ducati, arms folded.

'Coming in?' she asked.

'Am I allowed on the premises?'

'Oh, Gabe,' she said. 'Come on.'

'Who else is here?'

'No one except Luc, and he's upstairs. Please come in so we can talk.'

She walked ahead of him back through the kitchen and bar into the dining room, feeling suddenly intensely weary, the events and the long night bearing down on her.

'Hey,' Gabe said. 'You should sit down.'

He pulled out a chair from the closest table, pressed her down onto it, and just his touch on her shoulders brought relief, showed he still cared.

'You didn't trust me.' He sat down opposite her. 'How could that be, Cathy?'

'Of course I trust you, though you sometimes make it hard.'

'How's that?'

'By not being open with me,' she said.

'Oh my God,' he said. 'This again.'

'Of course this again. Everything's such a mystery: your uncle and his farm, your *lopin*, your joke – maybe not – about growing marijuana there. How am I supposed to know why or what you're keeping from me?'

'I did not put drugs into anyone's food.' His eyes were cool. 'I wouldn't conceal dope in a

200

brownie, let alone play that kind of insane trick.'

'You were the one who brought drugs up last night.' Cathy rubbed her face, recalling. 'Acid, you said.'

'You're still doubting me. I'd never doubt you.'

'Perhaps that's because I've always told you everything about myself.'

Gabe leaned back. 'So let's say it's OK for my girlfriend to doubt me. Now tell me why I would do such a thing?'

'I'm not doubting you,' Cathy said tiredly. 'I just said you were the one who'd brought up drugs.'

'Because I've seen that kind of reaction, and it's not a good thing to behold, and I'm sure it's fucking awful to experience. And I can damned well promise you that I would never do such a thing to anyone.'

'I know,' Cathy said. 'I *know*.'

'Unless . . .' He stared at her. 'Were you thinking that everything – all the mean tricks – might have been down to me?' He stood up. 'Jesus.'

'Gabe, of course I didn't—'

'The roaches, the ants, the verdigris – why not?'

'Gabe, you're being crazy.'

'I'm feeling pretty crazy right now, because that's what this whole thing is. Because my girl-friend hasn't gotten to share every last *piece* of me, she thinks . . . Jesus, I don't know what she thinks—'

Cathy was silent, staggered.

'Nothing to say?'

201

'Plenty, if you'll let me get a word in.'

'Maybe,' Gabe said. 'Some day. Not now.'

Cathy stood up. 'For God's sake, Gabe, this isn't fair.'

He was breathing hard as he started back toward the kitchen. 'Make sure you don't give me the new entry code,' he said over his shoulder. 'I wouldn't want to get accused of anything else.'

'You're being a complete horse's ass!' Cathy shouted.

'Better than a traitor!' Gabe yelled back.

She heard the back door close, then, seconds later, the roar of the Ducati.

'Bastard,' Cathy said under her breath.

And burst into tears.

Don't move, Chauvin told himself.

Don't even *breathe* unless you have to.

He was keeping his breathing shallow and relaxed, his training helping, but it was dusty up here and he couldn't risk sneezing or coughing, and no matter what else happened below, no matter who else came, how upset *she* got, he could not afford to move a muscle.

Because if he did, everything would be spoiled.

All those preparations, all the waiting.

If she heard so much as a creak, she'd tell someone, her plump friend upstairs, or maybe she'd phone her boss or the manager, or maybe she'd come check it out herself, and as exciting as that prospect was, he was not quite ready for that yet. It wouldn't be perfect.

It had to be perfect.
And it would be.

He'd only learned about this ceiling cavity because Jones had shown him and some other journalists and photographers around the restaurant as part of his plans for his big publicity drive – and Jones had seemed impressed by his portfolio, and he *was* gifted, no matter how often his father tried to discourage him. Jones and Mme Darroze had been demonstrating the stringent precautions constantly taken for hygiene: every microscopic insect put to death, everything repeatedly swept and disinfected – and Jones had pointed to the ceiling above the bar area, had shown his visitors the small trapdoor where the pest control company accessed the ceiling space, had noted a small crack and asked the manager to have it sealed, but when Chauvin had arrived yesterday, the crack had still been there – so not *so* perfectly efficient, madame – and it had made a wonderful spy hole for him.

He'd come for lunch yesterday as a customer, knew Catherine's shifts by now, and there'd been no way to be positive that she wouldn't see him, but she was stationed in the kitchen, not in the dining area, so he'd felt reasonably secure. He'd paid his check, then gone to the men's room, fairly confident that no one would check for staybehind intruders (and if they did, he could invent an upset stomach, leave and regroup); and no one *had* checked, so he'd had enough time to find the quiet ten minutes needed to access the ceiling space and make himself at home.

As it had turned out, he'd certainly had more than his money's worth.

All that drama last night, and he'd been OK with the long haul, had come prepared for most eventualities: a small pillow, Evian for hydration, the empty bottles to pee in, glucose tablets for energy, and it wasn't safe to use a torch or even his phone while the place was occupied, so he'd made do with thinking of Catherine rather than looking at her photos.

The last half-hour had been *really* special. Listening to her fight with Gabe Ryan.

They'd passed right below his spy-hole, and he'd observed their body language, had seen how altered it was, and as the conversation had continued, it had become patently clear that the trust between them was almost gone.

And once Catherine's tears for the waiter dried, she'd be able to see what *real* love looked like.

And learn to love him back.

For now, he had to wait, watch and listen until she left, finally, and locked up.

So he could move again.

Go on preparing.

Getting ready.

The squad room on Monday morning felt like a war room. Combat to prepare for, enemy and battlefield still unknown. Calls and tips – including abundant 'sightings' of the four wanted men – flowing steadily in, followed up where they seemed of possible interest, as yet leading nowhere.

In a rare quiet moment, Sam took another look at the victims up on the whiteboards. Photos taken in the lives and after the deaths of nine people. Plus a monochrome enlargement of an ultrasound scan performed on June 8 of a female fetus, perfectly developed at that point, no anomalies visible.

Baby Munro. The tenth victim. A little girl deprived of her first breath by a loathsome creature calling itself 'Virginia'.

Two big differences in this latest case. Wedding rings and watches the only things apparently stolen – and agent Susan Cohen had said that, so far as she knew, the kids' most valuable possessions had been their musical instruments, not taken. And neither Lorna Munro nor Jay Sandhu had appeared, in words or photographs, in *The Beach*. No connection, therefore, to the Benedict family.

They had, however, received publicity: two mentions in the *Biscayne Times* and one in the *Miami Sun Post*, and in fall of 2011 they'd had a tiny piece in *Ocean Drive Magazine*, and Susan Cohen had told them, weeping, how proud she'd been to help achieve that for them. Sam hated to think that she might come to realize that the publicity might have flung them into the killer's radar.

Hildegard Benedict now had a whiteboard of her own as a person of interest – though it was mostly the continuing absence of any trace of her, dead or alive, which was compounding their continuing curiosity.

Nothing from the Clear database search. Nothing from the Florida court clerks' office checks. Nothing from drivers license checks or FBI fingerprint inquiry. No recent documented travel from ICE; same from Transport Security Administration. And still no death certificates.

Maybe she'd gone overseas with an altered identity; maybe Hildy was in Europe, maybe in Hungary in celebration of the past, or perhaps she'd settled in some tax haven, set up for a contented old age.

Or *maybe* she was holed up someplace geographically much closer, enjoying their lack of progress. Perhaps even now she was with her gang of four – unless she used different teams for each kill – planning with them, giving new orders.

'Maybe,' Sam said, 'she's raising a glass to Alida, her muse.'

'Or maybe we're on the wrong track altogether,' Martinez said.

'Maybe,' Sam said, feeling depressed as hell. 'Who knows?'

'Who the fuck?' Martinez agreed.

The relatives were in town. Jay Sandhu's parents and brothers driving restlessly back and forth from Fort Lauderdale; Lorna Munro's mother, father and younger sister from Vermont staying in a hotel while they struggled to deal with the unbearable.

Clearly no love lost between the two sets of parents. Everyone distraught, but aloof, even

206

hostile, when they came together. Awful vibes all around, racial divide plainly driving that, yet nothing more, Sam and Martinez both felt, than the old story of *differences*. Not the stuff that homicide was made of – certainly not serial murder.

'I think we pushed them together,' Rita Sandhu had said quietly during their initial meeting. 'If we'd been less opposed, less angry, perhaps they mightn't have felt they had anything to prove, and we might still have them.'

Sam felt only pity for the bereaved mother, however warped her logic, wished that she had reached that conclusion long ago, if only so that Jay and Lorna could have had their happiness unspoiled.

The outcome, he suspected, would have been no different.

Because their children would probably have stayed together.

Would, more than likely, still have been *chosen*.

Not karma, exactly. But perhaps their destiny from the moment they had met.

Who knew?

Monday was the worst day ever for CB.

The pain, he became more convinced by the hour, was divine wrath – maybe only a small taster of what was to come – but his jaw, his gums, his whole wicked *head* was on fire now.

He'd loaded up with painkillers at Walgreens and CVS, but nothing was working, and he knew he ought to simply accept the pain, but he was a weak, spineless creature, so he would take the pills he'd bought. And he'd already swallowed way more than the recommended dose, and he'd mixed them too, which was unhealthy, maybe even dangerous, but he didn't care.

He'd seen Mrs H once today, had averted his eyes and scurried away. He'd seen Jerry once, too, and he'd looked OK, at least on the surface, like some satisfied big cat who'd landed himself a tasty kill.

Maybe, if it weren't for the pain, CB might look that way too, but he doubted it. Because some people were made to be killers, and he was just made to do other people's bidding and do his best for his mother and brother, no matter how high the cost. *Way* too high.

And oh, Lord, but it hurt.

Joe Sheldon had finally found them an old but usable photograph of the lady.

Still the only game in town, but no one feeling real confident about the move they had, nonetheless, agreed on.

The latest press release being issued late Monday by Beth Riley showed a photo of a woman taken in her late forties at a party: a handsome woman with strong features, clear blue eyes and fair, wavy hair, smiling at the camera. Alongside that, a computer-enhanced version showing the same person approximately twenty years on.

Person of Interest in Miami Beach Murders
Wanted for Questioning
**HILDEGARD BENEDICT aka
BENEDEK**
This person is <u>not</u> a suspect, but Miami
Beach Police urgently need to speak to her.
If you are Hildegard Benedict, or if you
know of her whereabouts, please call the
Homicide Hotline

Joe Duval and Captain Kennedy were going
with Sam's gut feeling.

A whole lot riding on it.

'If the department gets sued, Becket,' Kovac
said after the conference, 'it'll be your ass.' The
lieutenant smiling as he said it.

'Don't remember the last time I saw Kovac
smile at you,' Martinez said.

'I know,' Sam said. 'Makes you feel kind of
queasy.'

Hard liquor was the best thing for a real bad
toothache, one of the guys at work had told him.

Not that CB had been managing to work prop-
erly, barely going through the motions until
finally he'd been sent home.

'Via the dentist,' he'd been instructed. 'And
don't come back till you're fit.'

He'd settled for a bar instead.

No drinker, but despair and agony could make
a man do things he ordinarily wouldn't.

'Shut up,' he told his thoughts. 'Shut the fuck
up.'

It was going OK until another customer looked at him once too often. The booze was mixing with the drugs, making him feel weird and spacey, and it was obvious this guy was a racist, which struck him as ironic.

There it was again, that look.

'What you looking at?'

CB heard his own aggressive tone, felt surprised by it because he never spoke to anyone that way, and his sister had once said he wouldn't say boo to a goose, but that was then and this was now.

'I asked what you're looking at.'

The other man was big, looked like he worked out, tougher-looking than even CB's fellow monsters, and he wondered if any of them would stand up for him in any kind of a *situation*, knew that they would not, that he was alone now in this ugly new world.

The other man laughed.

'Don't you laugh at me,' CB said.

He knew what he was doing. He was trying to provoke a fight, which he'd never done before, had always believed himself to be gentle, slow to anger and, whenever possible, kind.

The derisive sound that emerged from him was self-directed, but the other man wasn't going to know that, and the guy was saying something, maybe trying to placate him, and the bartender was talking too. But something was happening now in CB's head, like a loud clamor, almost like screaming, mixing with the pain in his jaw, in his *soul*, and suddenly he was screaming, getting off his bar stool, and the world tilted but he didn't care, and he stumbled toward the stranger, felt their bodies collide.

'Hey!' he thought the other man said.

CB took a swing.

First time he'd punched another person.

Killed, yes. Oh, Lord, yes. But never punched.

It felt good, *real* good, like if he went on doing that maybe the poison would siphon out into the air, or maybe he could smash his way into this stranger, pass it on to him.

He wanted rid of it.

He wanted it *gone*.

The siren became part of the noise in his head.

The uniforms grabbing at his arms a part of the battle.

So he swung at them too.

Anything to have it gone.

June 18

Jeanne called Cathy at five minutes after ten on Tuesday morning.

'Nic wants you to know that the situation has been resolved.'

'Resolved?' Cathy was half asleep, and it seemed like only minutes since she'd gotten home, locked the door, pulled off her clothes and crawled into bed.

'We have the person responsible,' Jeanne said.

Cathy sat up, rubbed the side of her face, tried to focus. 'Who?'

'I can't tell you that.'

'Why not?' Fear gripped her, because what she

was most afraid of was that it might be Gabe.
'Jeanne, you can't put everyone through all that
and make accusations and then not tell us.'

'First, we made no accusations, even though
Gabe seemed to think we had.'

'He was understandably upset.'

'He's over-sensitive,' Jeanne said.

'Are you admitting it wasn't him?'

'No one said that it was,' Jeanne said. 'But OK,
that I can tell you. We know it was not Gabe.'

'Have you told him?' She was angry now. 'Have
you apologized?'

'He's not answering his phone. I hoped he
might be with you.'

'He isn't,' Cathy said. 'He was too upset.'

'Do you know where he is?' Jeanne asked.

'No,' Cathy said. 'But I'll find him.'

'Please. And ask him to call me.'

'I can ask.' Curiosity resurfaced. 'Jeanne, why
can't you tell me who it is?'

'There are legal considerations. I'm sure you
understand.'

Not Gabe. All that really mattered.

'You said "the person responsible". Does that
mean for all the tricks?'

'It seems likely,' Jeanne said. 'Though I don't
think that "tricks" is the right word now. What
happened on Sunday evening was criminal.'

Cathy felt sudden guilt. 'I haven't asked how
those poor people are.'

'My understanding is that they are all much
better. The culprit is luckier than he deserves.
Someone might have died.'

'He,' Cathy repeated.

'So I can leave you to find Gabe?' Jeanne said.

'I'll do my best.' Cathy paused. 'Any news on reopening?'

'Not yet,' Jeanne said. 'As soon as we know more, we'll contact you all.'

The line went dead.

Cathy took a moment, absorbing, feeling one thing above all else. Shame.

She looked at her phone, reflected briefly how tired she felt, then called Gabe, got no answer. About to leave a voicemail, she decided against it, because this had to be done direct.

She called Rafael's apartment. No answer there either, which made sense, because Tuesday was one of Rafi's mornings at Forville. Which meant that either Gabe was at Rafi's and not answering, or maybe he was in Golfe-Juan, in which case she'd have to go there because there was no landline.

'Oh, Gabe,' she said, trying his cell again.

Jeanne had called him 'over-sensitive'.

True enough, thinking back to how he'd yelled at her earlier, and maybe all this had done was highlight fundamental trust issues between them. So rather than rush out now, when she was physically and emotionally drained and more likely to trigger another argument . . .

Voicemail.

Then sleep.

Sam heard about the break in the case at six a.m.

'Some drunk picked up last night for disorderly

conduct in Dewey's,' Martinez told him. 'Real messed up on booze and meds and whining about toothache.'

'And?' Sam had just gotten in the Saab with honorable intentions vis-à-vis paperwork. 'Did we get him a dentist?'

'He said he didn't deserve a dentist.' Martinez paused. 'Not after what he'd done.'

Sam felt a familiar prickle in his spine, and waited.

'He told the uniforms who arrested him that he was one of "the four", and then he started to cry. I mean they said he bawled his eyes out.'

'He confessed?' Hope sprang.

'Not exactly,' Martinez said. 'But while the guys were putting him in the car, he was talking to himself, and they both heard him mumble something about letters to Becket.'

Sam pulled over to the right.

So he could enjoy it.

One of those *moments*.

'There's more,' Martinez said. 'Another name.'

'Hit me,' Sam said.

'Virginia,' Martinez said.

The only name they had for him so far was Miguel.

Written with a shaky hand inside a small birthday card folded into the back pocket of his denim jeans. *A Miguel, mi niño especial. El amor siempre, Mamá.*

'To Miguel, my special boy. Love always, Mama.'

Caution being exercised all round, because

dealing with spontaneous statements could be worse than tricky, leading to a potentially corrosive situation – though soon as they'd realized what they might be dealing with, knowing that detectives would be getting involved, the patrolmen had refrained from reading Miguel his Miranda rights.

So far, so good.

No one in Dewey's had admitted to knowing him, the bartender adamant he'd never seen him before, but describing Miguel as an amateur drinker desperate to blot out the world.

No ID, nothing in his vinyl wallet except two tens and a five. No drivers license, no Social Security card. Nothing else on him except a bottle of Advil and Excedrin, both almost empty, a handful of loose change and his Nokia phone. Search warrant needed before anyone would look at that.

The drunk was sleeping it off in a single cell, being monitored in case he became ill, because *nobody* wanted this guy choking on his own vomit and not waking up.

Sam took a look at him, comparing what he saw against a photo of 'the four'.

'I guess he could be the smallest guy. Then again, he could be just about anyone.'

'"Virginia" could've been leaked,' Martinez said. 'But seems like he knows the messages were addressed to you.'

Sam nodded.

'Gut feeling?' Duval asked.

'What am I now, the local psychic?' Sam said sourly.

'You're the hunch-man of Washington Avenue, man,' Martinez reminded him.

'Nothing coming through,' Sam said. 'Except maybe sympathy. He looks pathetic.'

They left the holding area and went up to the squad room, all three men quiet now, working things through from as many angles as they could.

Miguel had not asked for a lawyer yet. But he'd been drunk, maybe drugged – probably just on the meds he'd been carrying – so they were going to have to assess his condition when he woke, decide if he needed to be cleared at the ER.

For now, he slept.

Cathy woke again to a headache and an instant sense of depression because Gabe had not called. Which meant that he was still mad at her.

And now, in the bright, beautiful light of another Côte d'Azur noontime, she found that her own annoyance with him had completely dissipated, only regret, remorse and anxiety remaining. She tried his phone again, then Rafael's. Left another voicemail on Gabe's cell.

'Please call me, Gabe. We need to talk. I need to see you so I can apologize. I get why you were so upset, and I'm so sorry, but there's news about the poisoning, which you may know about from Jeanne – and oh, Gabe, I should have walked out with you, I know that now. Please call me.'

She winced as she ended the call, not keen on groveling but knowing it was necessary, because she had been wrong.

She picked up the phone again, redialed. 'I forgot to say don't come to my place, because I'll be out looking for you. Just call me, please.'

She ran to Forville, but Rafael had already left, so she bought a big bunch of sunflowers – Gabe's favorite – hurried to the rue de la Miséricorde, pressed Rafael's buzzer and waited.

Nothing, and neither Rafi's Harley nor the Ducati were outside, but still, when another man came out of the street door, Cathy ran inside and up to the second floor.

She knocked, called Rafi's name then Gabe's, pressed her ear to the door, listening, though she doubted that he'd skulk inside, refusing to answer.

No one there, which left, she guessed, the bus to Golfe-Juan. Or a taxi, she thought – regularly forgetting that even at Cannes prices, she could afford taxis every single day.

This time of day in June, she decided, it might take longer to find a taxi.

Gripping the sunflowers in one hand, checking for messages again with the other, she headed for the Croisette.

At eleven a.m. Miguel was bleary, but awake and ready for interview.

He was about five-nine, one hundred and fifty pounds, Latino with minimal accent, probably Mexican. He was perspiring, trembling, unshaven and, without question, in pain, but the consensus was that since he seemed in no danger and could, in any case, not be administered more painkillers

217

for several hours, he was just going to have to suffer for now.

Hard to see this wrecked young man as a monster.

A patsy, Sam was guessing, maybe a fall guy, guilt oozing from every pore.

One of the four, if his drunken ramblings were to be believed.

And he knew about the letters from Virginia. Which meant that he was, at very least, connected with some or all of the murders.

Sam remembered the victims. Looked at this man, cradling his jaw.

Knew that he deserved no sympathy.

This was their break, for sure.

Three against one. Sam, Martinez and Duval. Captain Kennedy on his way to observe through the one-way mirror; Lieutenant Kovac and Riley both keen to see how this might play out.

Martinez read him his rights, though the prisoner scarcely seemed to be listening, too absorbed in himself, perhaps by his pain, maybe his conscience.

'Did you understand your rights?' Sam asked.

'This thing is killing me,' Miguel said, clasping his jaw.

'Seems to me like you'd be best off talking to us,' Martinez said.

'Might take your mind off your pain,' Sam added.

'After all' – Duval's tone was kindly – 'they say confession's good for the soul, so maybe that goes for toothache too.'

218

'You think?' Miguel's desperate eyes turned to him.

'Might as well give it a try,' Sam said. 'You already told the officers at the bar that you were "one of the four". So why not tell us the rest?'

Miguel groaned softly. 'OK.'

'So,' Sam repeated patiently, 'did you understand your rights?'

'Yes.'

'Then how about we start with your full name?' Sam said.

'Miguel Ernesto López.'

'Thank you, Mr López.'

'We're going to run your name,' Duval told him. 'But how about you save us some time and tell us what we're going to find?'

'You mean, like a record?' López shook his head, winced. 'Nothing. You won't find anything. I've never been in trouble.'

'You're in trouble now,' Martinez said.

López's eyes filled with tears.

'It's OK,' Sam said. 'Talk to us. You'll feel better.'

'I'll never feel better,' López said.

Miguel Ernesto López, aka – to Mrs Hood and the other three members of her kill team – CB, began talking anyway, feeling he had no real choice. He told them he was thirty-one and worked as a cleaner, was unmarried, without children, but that he had to earn money to send to his mother and younger brother in California, who would be in great trouble if he could not.

219

He spoke freely for about a minute, then stopped abruptly, shut his eyes, muttered to himself.

'We can't hear you, Mr López,' Sam said.

'I said too much already,' the man said.

'Seems you just told us your name,' Martinez said. 'And that you're a good son and a person who never had any trouble before.'

'Where do you work, Mr López?' Duval asked.

'I don't want to lose my job.'

'OK,' Sam said, easily. 'So tell us about "the four" instead.'

'I need the bathroom,' Miguel López said.

'Sure,' Sam said. 'But first, you need to tell us a little more.' He looked into the other man's dark eyes, held his gaze. 'About what you've done, Miguel.'

'I really need the toilet bad,' López said.

And began to weep.

At five-twenty p.m. in Cannes, Chauvin was back in the ceiling space above the ground floor, waiting, listening.

He'd escaped for a while to exercise and check around for anything he might have forgotten, working through his strategy for the umpteenth time, mentally arranging the final touches. Back now, safe and sound, untouched by claustrophobia, which might have afflicted him before he'd learned to breathe efficiently.

It seemed to him a safe bet that Catherine would return at some point to see her buddy, Luc, though if she and Ryan had made up their quarrel and she did not come back or perhaps returned with the waiter, then he'd have to put everything on hold.

But Chauvin was an optimist, always had been.

His time – *their* time – was coming.

He knew it.

It was time, having found no record of the prisoner's existence on every database the FBI had to offer, to get tougher. If he'd told the arresting officers the truth about being a part of these killings, then he'd been a participant in some of the worst crimes any of them had ever investigated. So they would not go through the Miranda again; they had it on record that he'd heard it, there was no question of deafness or language issues, and if the scumbag wanted pain relief more than a lawyer, that was fine with them.

What they wanted was the other three.

What they wanted was 'Virginia'.

'So, Miguel,' Sam said, 'are you going to talk to us or not?'

'Because it's going to go easier on you if you do talk,' Duval said.

López's eyes were still suffering. 'I'm just scared, man.'

'What are you scared of?' Martinez asked.

'Not for myself,' López said. 'There's nothing you can do to me that's going to be worse than . . .'

'Worse than what?' Duval asked.

'Worse than who?' Sam said.

López shook his head.

Sam gave him three seconds. 'OK, Miguel, if you don't want to help us, you can just go before the judge on the disorderly charge and you can

221

walk – that's if Homeland Security and Customs Enforcement – or maybe you know about ICE?'

'Immigration,' López said miserably.

'That's right. So if they do let you walk, I'm guessing your . . . What shall we call them? Your "colleagues", your "killing buddies" – or maybe they're the scum, not you, maybe they *made* you do those terrible things. Whichever, I'm betting they know you got yourself arrested, and I doubt they'll believe you when you say you didn't tell us anything.'

'But if you help us now,' Duval said, 'we'll help you all we can.'

'You mean like a deal?' López said.

'We don't do deals,' Duval said.

'Nine people dead,' Sam reminded him. 'Not counting an unborn child.'

They all stopped, watched him.

Miguel, aka CB, saw their eyes on him.

He didn't know what to *do*.

He'd never been real sharp – smarter than his baby brother, for sure, but Mateo had not been right from the start. Alicia, their older sister, had been the smart one, had married a rich American, a tight-fisted bastard who laid down rules. If Miguel didn't send money every month for his mother and Mateo, they'd go the same way as their father, who'd been deported when Miguel was still a kid. And *Mamá* had worked so hard and worried so much that she'd gotten sick, and if Miguel stopped paying or got in trouble, she and Mateo would be sent back to Mexico, with no health insurance and no pension . . .

Mrs Hood had persuaded him to spill his worries, had seemed to care, had made him believe she had the answer to all his troubles. Enough money to take care of his family for keeps, and to hell with his brother-in-law. Money and rewards on top, and she knew he had bad teeth, said she'd pay for dental treatments into the bargain, and so long as he 'kept it zipped' and was loyal to her, she'd always look after him.

All he had to do was kill innocent people.

At the start he'd told her no.

'Think about it,' she'd said. 'That's all I ask. Just don't talk about it.'

He'd sworn he'd never tell.

'Because if you do,' Mrs Hood had said, 'I won't be able to help you, and your mother and brother will be finished in America.'

She'd told him about her reasons, her motivations, had sat him down, explained her beliefs. She'd quoted the Bible, told him about the great and good people who felt the same way, said that everyone had a duty to make things right, which was what she was trying to do now, only she needed men like him to help.

Miguel had known it was racist bullshit, had seen that she was wicked, maybe crazy. The most dangerous person he'd ever encountered.

But he had supped from her spoon, done as she'd ordered, taken her money and dental treatment. And then everything had overwhelmed him, he'd mixed pills and alcohol and here he was.

Struggling just to *think*. On one hand, he badly

needed help, and they'd said that if he couldn't afford a lawyer they'd provide him with one. He had his blood money now, but they wouldn't let him spend it on his defense – and anyway, having his own lawyer didn't mean that his mother and brother would be any better off.

There was no defense for what he'd done.

And the pain was blocking everything out like a massive boiling thunderhead.

'OK,' he said.

Catherine was back!

Though things might not be going entirely his way, because having taken until after six to return, she'd gone straight up to see Meyer on the top floor, and before long – tomorrow at the latest – the restaurant would be teeming with activity, cleaners moving in, maybe more pest control, maybe even the cops . . .

Still, if necessary he'd fix it, get to her another way, probably at her apartment, and her building was easy and he knew her routines and the waiter's too, though with the restaurant closed until—

Voices.

Cathy and Meyer coming downstairs.

He heard her lovely voice say she was going out to get pizza.

Perfect.

Life changing on the spin of a pin, on the joys of fast food.

Time to get ready.

No, not yet.

Not a *sound.*

He commanded himself to do his mind exercises, to be calm.

He waited till she'd been gone for five whole minutes. Counted them through silently.

Breathed.

Needing to be *certain* where Meyer was. Remembering exactly where everything was.

He had all he needed – most of it wrapped up in himself, his body strong these days.

And the meat tenderizer mallet he'd stolen from the kitchen earlier.

Along with the small knife.

Just in case.

He'd finished counting.

Meyer was back upstairs, and now Chauvin needed to get him out again – but on *his* terms.

Now.

Soigneusement. Carefully.

He tucked the mallet into his waistband, eased himself into a low crouch – no room for more up here – found the trapdoor, raised it silently, got a grip, lowered himself, sprang down quietly onto the floor, moved to the stairs, up to the first floor, stopped just behind the dumb waiter, focusing on a chair in easy reach.

He turned, breathed, kicked the chair over – hard and *loud*.

Retreated again into position. Heard the door two floors up open.

'Cathy?'

Meyer.

Coming down.

* * *

'I can give you their names,' Miguel Ernesto López said. 'And I can tell you where they work – not all of them all of the time. One only comes in a few times a week, and not always, and I don't know where any of them live. She's the only one who knows that.'

'She?' Sam's tone was light.

Miguel shook his head. 'I won't tell you her name. I'm afraid of her. You have to guarantee you'll keep me safe from her, otherwise I won't tell you anything at all.'

'Can't guarantee you anything,' Duval said.

'Certainly not unless you tell us,' Martinez said.

López fell silent, until the pain flared again. So intense, they saw it in his eyes.

'You tell us' – Sam was gentle – 'you'll feel better.'

Miguel gave a sharp, bitter laugh, and then he spoke the names quickly, one after the other, like a schoolboy reciting history dates.

Antony Copani.

Frank Blazek.

Jimmy Bodine.

'They print them on our name tags,' López said. 'We leave our IDs in our lockers before we go home.'

'So you all work in the same place?' Martinez asked.

'We all had different names for when we did the jobs.'

'The "jobs" being what?' Sam asked evenly.

'The boss said our names were after people she admired. Copani's called Leon. Blazek is Jerry. Bodine is Andy. I was CB.' López shook his

226

head. 'I don't know what that was about. She didn't explain and I didn't ask.'

'You want to quit stalling?' Martinez said.

López cradled his face again. 'I'm sorry.'

'Where do you work, Mr López?' Sam asked.

'If I tell you that you'll go straight there, and then they'll know I sent you. And I know I have to tell you, I know it, only I'm scared, so please let me tell you the rest first, like what I know about the others.'

'Sure,' Duval said.

'So long as he isn't jerking us around,' Martinez said.

'I don't think he is,' Sam said. 'Are you, Mr López?'

'I'm too sick to do that,' López said.

'You're not sick,' Martinez said. 'You got a toothache.'

'I got the king of all toothaches,' López said, 'which is what I deserve.'

'Yeah, yeah,' Martinez said.

'Hey,' Sam said. 'Even I'm getting impatient here, and I'm the calm one.'

'So tell us about the others,' Duval said.

He told them that Copani – aka Leon – was some kind of fitness coach, the one who came to work a couple of days a week. That Blazek – Jerry – was a nurse. That Bodine – the one called Andy – was an orderly.

'That's all I know about them,' he said. 'Except Leon – Copani – thinks he's something special, like our leader.' Another pause. 'I think he enjoyed doing it.' He stopped again, buried his head in his hands.

'Come on, López,' Martinez said. 'Don't quit now.'

'I can't.'

'Sure you can,' Duval said.

'How about you take a look at this?' From a folder on the table, Sam produced a copy of one of the images of the four men walking back to their boat, set it down in front of López. 'Take it easy for a moment, and tell us who's who.'

His head was still in his hands.

'Hey,' Martinez said. 'Get your head up and take a look.'

López's eyes were wet again. 'I can't.'

'Do it,' Sam told him.

López dropped his hands, looked at the photograph and shuddered. And then he pointed at one of the men. 'That was me,' he said.

And then he identified the others, while Duval made notes, for the record.

'That wasn't so hard, was it?' Sam said.

López said nothing.

'I'm guessing,' Sam continued, 'from what you've said, that you all work in a hospital. Or maybe a nursing home.'

'I need the bathroom again,' López said.

'Jesus,' Martinez said. 'You just went.'

'I need to go,' the other man said. 'Just let me go and then I'll tell you.'

'Interview suspended,' Sam said, 'at one thirty-seven p.m.'

At ten past seven, Cathy was back with the pizza.

228

'Hey,' she yelled from the bottom of the stairs. 'Coming right up.'

She'd tried Gabe three times in the last hour, tried once more now.

Still voicemail.

'Gabe, I'm back at the restaurant, taking a pizza up to Luc. My battery's running low, and I don't have my charger with me, so if you can't get me, try Luc's number. Just please, please call me.'

She started up the staircase, paused at the first floor.

Something not feeling quite right.

'Luc?'

No answer.

She continued up, found his door closed.

'Luc?'

She knocked, then opened the door.

He wasn't there, had probably gone out for wine.

She set the box on the worktop beside the microwave, looked at her phone again.

Down to one bar.

'Call me, Gabe,' she said, softly, willing him.

'He won't,' a voice said from behind her.

Cathy froze.

Turned.

Saw him.

'Surpri-ise,' Thomas Chauvin said, singsong.

'How the hell did you get in here?' Cathy said.

'I've been here a while,' he said. 'Came in with the lunch crowd on Sunday.'

She felt sick, remembered getting suddenly creeped out a few days ago in case he was one of the visiting photographers . . .

Don't get scared, she told herself now. *Take charge.*

Best way to deal with this creep.

'Get out,' she said.

'We're both going out,' Chauvin said.

Cathy laughed, because weird as this was – as *he* was – she was not scared.

'I love the sound of your laughter,' he said. 'Though not so much when you're laughing at me. You shouldn't do that.'

'You need to leave,' Cathy said. 'While you still can.'

'Why's that?' Chauvin mocked. 'Because someone's coming here any minute?'

'Yes,' she said. 'They are.'

'No,' he said. 'They're not.'

She stared at him, realized that he'd changed since she'd last seen him. He was thinner, leaner, he looked *stronger*, and – no glasses anymore, contacts, presumably – there was a look in his blue eyes that was sending warning signals.

'What have you done?' she said. 'Where's Luc?'

'Out of harm's way,' Chauvin said.

'Where is he?'

Her mind planned her escape. She'd ask him again, get upset, then push past him and *run*, and she had the advantage, knew every inch of *Le Rêve*, and hell, she was even wearing khaki cargo pants – combat gear, as if she'd known . . .

'Don't,' Chauvin said. 'Don't do anything foolish. If you value Luc Meyer's life,' he added, 'you'll do what I tell you.'

Cathy suddenly felt ice cold but she shook her

230

head, made herself laugh again. 'You sound like a shitty movie.'

'I don't like it when you swear,' Chauvin said.

'I don't give a fuck what you like,' Cathy said.

'If you make me mad,' he said, 'Meyer could die.'

'Where *is* he?' Her sham calm was gone. 'What have you done to him?'

'That's for me to know,' he said.

'What do you want?' she asked.

'That's easy. You.'

'You can't have me.'

'I can,' he said. 'I will.'

'No, you won't.' Cathy kept her tone hard. 'And I suggest you stop this and leave right now, before my boyfriend gets here.'

'Ryan's not going anywhere right now,' Chauvin said.

It felt like having her circulation cut off with an axe. The strength drained out of her. 'What have you *done*?'

'Come with me now,' Chauvin said, 'and I'll explain it to you.'

'I'm not going anywhere with you.'

His eyes were definitely bluer – tinted contacts, then – and his brown hair, which had been wavy, was almost buzz cut now, and this man *was* different now. She needed to take him seriously.

'I don't want to hurt you, Catherine,' he said.

'So tell me what you've done, and we can put it right.'

'Later,' he said, 'I'll tell you everything. But right now, you're coming with me so that I don't have to hurt you, and so that both your friends may survive until tomorrow.' He looked at the pizza box. 'We have good food where we're going, but if you're in the mood for that, you can bring it along.'

'It's for Luc,' Cathy said.

'Luc won't be eating anything,' Chauvin said.

She looked into his eyes, knew that she was going with him.

That she had no choice.

In the interview break, they'd run the three names López had given them and sent out for enough Markie's roast beef sandwiches to keep them going.

None of the four – *if* those names were legit – had a prison history or warrants outstanding, which was pretty much all they could have hoped to find at this stage, in the absence of drivers licenses, Social Security numbers or dates of birth. And they might have surmised that the lack of rap sheets indicated skillful criminals, but López appeared such a loser that seemed improbable. In which case, perhaps 'Virginia' had chosen her team partly because if they screwed up, left prints or DNA, she'd have the security of knowing there'd be no DNA matches in CODIS or NDIS or print matches in the AFIS.

'Weirdest interview I've ever been in on,' Martinez said before they restarted. 'It's like we're using torture, except we're not doing anything. All we got to do is wait, and his fucking diseased mouth makes him spill.'

'We need him to spill more,' Sam said. 'Before he changes his mind about a lawyer.'

'Or demands medication,' Duval said.

Sam took a moment. Torture not sitting well with him.

And then he remembered the bodies in the cars.

'Let's go suck him dry,' he said.

It took less than ten minutes.

'Thing is,' Sam said, the machine back on, 'we're not sure we buy what you've been telling us.'

'What do you mean?' López said.

'He means why should we believe you?' Duval said.

'You think I'd lie about something like this?' He looked incredulous.

'You want us to believe you cut those people's throats,' Martinez said.

López gaped. 'I never – we never did that. We just tied them up and then the cars did the rest, and we had guns to make them do what we wanted – what *she* wanted – but we didn't shoot anybody and we never cut anybody. We tied them up, and Leon did that thing with the noose, and . . . oh, Jesus, you have to believe I didn't do that, oh, God . . .'

'Go on,' Duval said.

'Do you believe me now?' López begged.

'Yes,' Sam said, gentle as a priest at confession. 'We believe you, Miguel.'

'And if I tell you where to find them' – López's brown eyes were pleading – 'will you help me?'

Sam wondered if the victims had looked at

233

Miguel López like that, felt no guilt for lying to him now.

'We'll do what we can,' he said.

López crossed himself, whispered a prayer.

'Like that's going to help you,' Martinez said.

'Hey,' Duval said quietly.

'Rosemont House,' López said. 'On Alton Road.'

Duval was typing it into his iPhone.

'I'll give you the name we called the boss.' López's eyes were wet. 'Which is not her real name, OK?' He wiped his eyes with the back of his hand. 'It's Mrs Hood. Like Robin Hood.' He shuddered again. 'She called us her Crusaders.'

'Got it,' Duval said. 'Rosemont House on Alton.'

López laid his head on his arms on the table and wept.

'Warrants,' Sam said, ignoring him.

'On it,' Duval said.

'How near my house?' Martinez asked quietly.

'Close enough,' Duval said.

'Holy shit,' Martinez said.

'Interview suspended,' Sam said, and turned off the machine again.

Gripping Cathy's arm firmly, Chauvin had pushed her into the passenger seat of his white Peugeot 307, tossed the pizza box onto the back seat, then leaned across to buckle her seatbelt. The car was parked a hundred meters along the rue de la Rampe – she might have passed it any number of times, *oblivious* – and as Chauvin walked around to his side Cathy had thought of bolting, but the threats against Gabe and Luc had held her there, and even if she'd yelled for help, the road had been deserted.

On the move now, heading in evening traffic out of Cannes, La Bocca to their right, the almost empty beaches to their left, and Chauvin had enabled the childproof central locking, though he didn't appear to be hurrying, seemed to be enjoying the ride, and to strangers, Cathy realized, they must look like any couple, perhaps on their way to dinner . . .

'Why are you doing this?' she asked.

'To give us a chance.' They were on the Boulevard du Midi. 'All I ask is one or two days and nights.'

'You're crazy.'

'In love. Not crazy.'

Cathy remembered Sam calling this man a 'dope', a 'jerk'.

'I think you're bluffing. I think Luc went out, and you've invented the rest.'

'Believe what you like,' Chauvin said. 'It'll be his funeral.'

'You're out of your mind.'

'To get your attention for a while? I don't think so.' He checked the mirror. 'They'll be OK, you know, so long as you do as I ask and try to enjoy yourself.'

'*Enjoy?*'

'You haven't asked what I've done to your waiter.'

'His name is Gabe, and I don't believe you've done anything to him.'

'As I said, believe what you like,' Chauvin said.

Mrs Hood knew that CB had not come in to work this morning.

She had a feeling. Not a good one.

Something was going on.

Going wrong, maybe.

'Hold your nerve,' she told herself.

Not that she had any alternative, but she was made of strong stuff. Superior stuff. Part of her heritage.

And maybe this feeling was nothing, maybe López had met with an accident – preferably fatal – or maybe he had the flu or food poisoning, and if that was the case, all she had to do was what she'd already decided on: pause the operation, consider ridding herself of this band of Crusaders and start again when Becket and his task force had disbanded or gone into hibernation mode . . .

She poured herself a shot of vodka – early in the day for her, but to hell with that.

She raised the glass.

'To fatal accidents,' she said.

Though life, as she'd learned over the years, was rarely that convenient.

They'd left the coast, turned right just past the Pullman Hotel into avenue de la Mer. Chauvin had stopped talking, and Cathy was trying to focus on their route.

Golf course to the right, sign for a campsite, right again . . . Boulevard des Ecureuils . . . Left into a residential road: substantial houses, some hidden by high walls, but she'd missed the street sign . . .

He slowed, and Cathy caught a glimpse of a rough stone wall and a small white house as they turned into its driveway, stopping close to the front door, and her stomach clenched as she looked around frantically, took in blue-shuttered windows, red bougainvillea, no neighbors visible . . .

'Don't be scared,' Chauvin said softly.

'Take me back and I won't be.'

'There's nothing to be afraid of.' He smiled. 'I hoped for Monaco, obviously, but I knew it was impossible. Beyond anyone's wildest dreams – even yours, Catherine, with your newfound wealth.'

She sat very still. 'Have you been following me all this time?'

'Keeping up with you. The way we do, when we love.' He turned off the engine. 'Let's go inside.'

She thought of escape again as he got out – pause, then kick him *hard*, scream and run – but his threats were still buzzing like hornets in her head, so she'd have to wait till she was certain he was bluffing. And anyway, he was too swift, pulled her out of the car and close to him again. She caught his scent, a soft, citrusy sandalwood fragrance which smelled like a cologne that Sam sometimes wore, and the thought that Chauvin might know that, the possible *implications* of that, were so repugnant that she thought, for an instant, that she might pass out . . .

'You're OK,' he said, and opened the door. '*Voilà.*'

Darkness inside. Cathy tried to pull back, but Chauvin drew her inside, turned on the light.

She blinked, registered an open-plan sitting room and kitchen. Window shutters closed. Floors tiled, white with navy edging, bare fireplace, couch, low pine coffee table, small round dining table and chairs in one corner. A flat-screen TV on one wall, DVD player on a shelf beneath.

Immaculate and tidy, probably a rental awaiting occupancy.

'Is this yours?' she asked.

'For now.'

'Legally?'

'You think I broke in? That I'm what, a burglar, maybe a squatter?' He held up the keys. 'Mine – ours – for two weeks,' he said.

He locked the door, pocketed the keys, released her arm.

Cathy's stomach felt hollow. 'You said one or two nights.'

Just the thought of this one evening – *night* – enough to freak her out.

A known stalker. *Her* stalker.

He moved into the kitchen area, and Cathy took another look around. Navy-and-white straw baskets with rope handles, one by the fireplace, another beside the sofa filled with magazines, a third filled with white pebbles and matchboxes. Cushions on the couch, a stack of cloths in the kitchen and two caddies, all blue and white. No signs of cooking, yet she smelled an aroma of something, and maybe, if she hadn't felt sick – if

238

she hadn't been *abducted* – it might have given her an appetite.

Her mind scrambled, but she thought of something, grabbed hold.

He'd been arrested more than once, but had never been convicted. Which meant he'd never done anything seriously bad.

She made herself breathe. 'OK if I sit down?'

'Of course.'

She sat at one end of the small couch, watched him open the fridge, used the moment to open her bag.

'Do you need something?' Chauvin closed the fridge.

Cathy could see her phone, thought about keying in 112, for emergency, but the battery had been almost gone back at the restaurant, and the operator would ask questions, and Chauvin would hear, know what she'd done.

'I'll take that.' He leaned over, plucked it out, opened it, took out the SIM card, put that in his back pocket and dropped the phone back in the bag. 'I'll return the SIM.'

'I'd like to go home now,' she said.

'This is your home for tonight.'

'Like hell it is,' she said.

'So would you like to see upstairs now, or would you prefer a glass of champagne?'

She looked toward the small, narrow staircase, her stomach churning. 'Neither.'

'I'd like champagne,' he said.

'Don't let me stop you.' She thought he sighed. 'Honestly, Thomas, what is supposed to be the point of this?'

'Love,' he said. 'Destiny.'

'God,' she said. 'You're a walking cliché.'

'Don't be unkind, Catherine.'

'My name isn't Catherine.'

'You decide, Catherine,' he said. 'Upstairs first, or champagne?'

'Could we have a window open?'

'I'm afraid not.'

'I'd feel better with some air.'

'A drink instead.'

'Jesus,' Cathy said. 'One drink, then home.'

Chauvin smiled. 'Dinner first,' he said.

The task force had teeth, it seemed. Everyone cooperating, favors being pulled in where necessary, arrest and search warrants dropping into place, a major operation almost ready to roll.

Their intel had it that Rosemont House was a licensed in-home elderly care service owned by Caesar Care, a company headed by one Constance Cezary. The building was four stories high with front and rear exits and fire escapes.

Elderly care.

Suddenly Hildy felt so close, Sam could almost smell her.

No information yet on Cezary.

No way of knowing if she was, or had any connection with, Hildegard Benedict.

López had shut down.

Time would tell.

The waiting was driving them a little nuts.

They wanted to hit the place during day shift

hours – not that López had been specific about work hours, but neither had he mentioned night shifts, so the one most likely to slip the net was Copani, the fitness coach, aka Leon, who presumably gave old people stretching exercises part-time, and tortured and killed innocent victims for reward.

No one knew for sure if Constance Cezary was their 'boss'.

Mrs Hood might, for all they knew, be a resident or even another employee of Caesar Care. But they all doubted that.

'Your image of Hildy plotting from her wheelchair's still ringing bells with me,' Sam told Martinez in the squad room. 'Though I'd imagined something glitzier for her.'

'I don't know,' Duval said. 'Caesar Care sounds pretty megalomanic to me.'

'Is there such a word?' Sam asked.

'Who gives a fuck?' Martinez said.

'Hildy or not,' Sam said, 'let's just hope we end this.'

They'd been talking dates. The first murders on June third. The Gomez killings just four days later on the seventh. Then a whole week until the Dickens Avenue homicides.

Five days since then.

One of the four in custody. Three more to come. Not forgetting the boss. Miguel López's 'Mrs Hood'.

'Crusaders, my ass,' Martinez said now.

Duval's cell phone rang.

He answered, listened, responded with a curt affirmative, looked at the other two.

'Ready or not,' he said.

* * *

At ten minutes past nine on Tuesday evening, the Ducati Monster growled to a halt on rue de la Rampe, and Gabe, pulling off his Shoei helmet, stomped up to the back door of *Le Rêve*, rang the bell and waited.

No one came.

It had been a very long day, during which Gabe had ridden more kilometers than he could remember, stopping several times for a drink, looking without interest at any number of views. Sulking, he guessed.

Not his finest day, and even if he'd been justified in losing his cool with Jeanne, none of that had been Cathy's fault; and maybe, in an ideal universe, she might have walked out with him, but loyalty, he guessed, cut more than one way, and Nic had given her an amazing opportunity. *Le Rêve* had been targeted repeatedly by *someone*, and Sunday night had pushed Jones and Jeanne to the brink.

Of course Cathy hadn't wanted to storm out.

Gabe had begun feeling ashamed of himself hours ago at a brasserie near Grasse, after downing a good bowl of onion soup, a large bottle of Vittel and two espressos, then looking at his phone and seeing all the missed calls. He'd listened to Cathy's generous apology and pleas for him to call, then the final message just after seven, telling him her battery was running low and that he should try Luc if he couldn't get her.

'Just please, please call me.'

So he had, repeatedly, and he didn't have Luc's number, so he'd called the restaurant several

242

times, but no one picked up, just a message apologizing for their brief closure and assuring them of the speediest possible reopening.

He'd come to *Le Rêve* earlier on reaching Cannes, had given up when no one had answered the door and tried Cathy's apartment instead; then, calling Rafi – just back from visiting friends in Antibes – he learned that he, too, had received multiple messages from Cathy, all looking for him.

Now, back outside the restaurant, frustration was setting in.

Even if Cathy wasn't here, Meyer was surely upstairs – the guy seldom went anywhere, was almost a monk – so either they'd shared the pizza and a bottle of wine, and maybe they were both asleep, or Luc had guzzled down the whole thing himself, in which case he was almost definitely in bed.

Or maybe something was wrong.

The security shutters hadn't been lowered – one of Luc's last tasks every night. And if he had gone out and left the place empty, he'd certainly have closed them.

What if Sunday's poisoner had done something even worse?

What if something had happened to *Cathy*?

He glared at the entry system, useless without the altered code. He didn't have Nic's private number, and though he could call Jeanne, she patently had no faith in him, so to hell with that . . .

All his instincts were suddenly clamoring, telling him he had to get inside.

He'd broken rules before, a few laws. He'd smoked weed, done some coke, and he did grow cannabis alongside herbs and wild flowers on his *lopin de terre*, the dope meant for his uncle's arthritis (though Yves used it regularly recreationally, when he wasn't drinking himself into oblivion); and he broke the speed limit all the time, and he'd gotten into a jam with loan sharks back in his Boston college days . . .

He'd never broken in anywhere.

But if Cathy was in danger . . .

He tried to think what an opportunistic thief might do. No shutters down, so *maybe* no alarm system set either – so all he had to do was smash the glass in the rear door . . .

He opened his toolbox, found his tire iron set, chose the one that looked toughest, pulled off his T-shirt and wrapped it around his right hand and arm. Looked up and down the road. Saw no one. Thought about what he was about to do, about the possible ramifications. Dismissed them.

Took a swing with the tire iron.

Nothing.

Serious force needed.

He took a breath, got himself into batting stance, readied himself – and swung . . .

Loud enough to wake the dead – but the toughened glass shattered into thousands of tiny fragments, and nobody yelled or came outside and no alarm sounded, and maybe Nic's alarm was silent, through to the cops, or maybe some neighbor was calling them even now . . .

Gabe stopped thinking, punched his wrapped fist and arm through the glass, cleared a gap big enough for him to climb through, and it was a squeeze, fragments flying, and he felt small cuts on his chest and leg, but his adrenalin was pumping, and then he was inside.

'Cathy!' He ran through the kitchen, out through the bar area to the staircase, taking the steps three at a time. 'Luc?'

The door on the top floor was open. No one inside.

And then he heard it.

A voice – male – calling from somewhere below.

'Luc?' Gabe called again. 'Where are you?'

He walked back down to the upper floor of the restaurant, looked around, unwrapped the T-shirt from his arm, shook it out, pulled it back over his head.

'Luc?' he called again. 'It's Gabe.'

The voice came again, words not distinguishable, from somewhere farther below.

'Luc, keep on calling.' Gabe moved down to the ground floor. 'I'll find you.'

A little louder, but still not close enough. From one of the storage rooms maybe, perhaps one of the coolers. He sprinted back through the kitchen – heard the voice again. From farther down. The cellar.

'Hold on, Luc!' he yelled. 'Coming to get you.'

At four-thirty, everyone was in position.

Spotters and marksmen on the roofs of neighboring houses both sides of Rosemont House, because there was a heck of a possibility that

Cezary, Blazek, Bodine and Copani – especially Copani, the part-timer who, according to López, *enjoyed* killing – might not be in the building, and if they were spotted outside, there were cops ready and waiting to apprehend under the protection of police snipers.

Sam would have preferred to have closed Alton and the two closest side streets, but that would have been a red flag to any gang member not within Rosemont's walls, so they'd had to settle for the exercise of sending officers into neighboring houses to ensure the safety of occupants.

Sam would also infinitely have preferred to be among the first into Rosemont, but it was a given that if Constance Cezary was 'Virginia', then she and her gang knew exactly what Sam Becket and Martinez looked like. So the two of them were waiting in an FBI van parked on Alton in sight of Rosemont House, dependent on radio and cell phone contact with the operation.

Special Agent Joe Duval heading in first any moment now alongside Thomas G. Grove – the commander of the SWAT team that had taken down the 'Couples Killers' a few years back. No such storming planned today, not with the likely presence of frail seniors on all three main stories of the 'in-home elderly care service' – assuming that Caesar Care's operation was what it seemed.

As it was, any one of those residents might be in grave danger.

Tactics had been thrown back and forth, fast as a US Open finals rally, speeding through alternative scenarios. Ideally, they'd have put the place under surveillance until they knew for sure that all three men and 'Mrs Hood' were inside, but they couldn't risk the wait.

'We could wait for them to come out,' Duval had said. 'Pick them up outside.'

'Except if that doesn't go down well,' Sam had said, 'someone might get word to Cezary.'

'And then we could get ourselves a hostage situation,' Martinez had said.

'Nice PR,' Kovac had said. 'Houseful of old folk.'

Sam had to agree. 'All we need.'

No one else had argued.

They were going to buzz at the entrance, claim to be from the Department of Health, show fake IDs to get them inside, then ask for the manager – and *maybe* that was Cezary, in which case that might be an arrest, nice and clean – but no one was buying that. And this was not a fancy nursing home with a meet-and-greet receptionist; this was a big house where senior citizens tried to get by in a protected environment, so Duval and Grove were going to have to find someone in charge, someone who knew names. Then identify themselves for real.

Ensure no warning was given.

Hope that the 'someone in charge' was neither 'Virginia', nor her ally.

Find out where *they* were.

Then bring in the troops.

'It's a go,' Sam heard through earphones.

He gave Martinez a nod, and both men raised

their binoculars, Sam focusing on the entrance, Martinez scanning back and forth – others doing the same from vantage points overlooking the rear.

Duval and Grove, wired for sound, got themselves easily inside, admitted by a nice old lady who might, Sam suspected, have let in *anyone*, unaware that she'd been living with Florida's five most wanted criminals.

He kept his gaze steady, listened intently.

Seven seconds before they were intercepted.

'How can I help you, gentlemen?'

That was all Sam and Martinez heard before a vacuum cleaner drove seventy-something decibels over the conversation, but after fifteen seconds Grove's voice, low but precise, came across, probably aimed down toward his miked-up chest.

'Barbara Kellerman, manager,' he reported. 'Moving to a quieter spot.'

Quiet enough, they had to guess, for Duval to have put the manager in the picture, because the next time they heard her voice, it was hushed, tense, efficient.

Duval told her the names of the three men they wanted to speak to.

'Let me check the computer,' Kellerman said. They waited.

Bodine and Blazek were both on duty.

Copani was not.

'Unless Miss Cezary – that's the owner – had him come in to give her a treatment.' She was checking a computer. 'Nothing's logged, but they might have made a private arrangement. Miss Cezary likes her privacy.'

Sam bet she did.

'I could call to try and find out,' Kellerman offered.

'Please don't call anyone, ma'am,' Duval said.

'Do you know where Bodine and Blazek are right now?' Grove asked.

'Mr Blazek should be doing rounds on the second floor,' the manager replied. 'And Mr Bodine is probably in the basement kitchen loading up the hot servers for dinner at five forty-five.'

'How many other people in the kitchen?' Grove asked.

'Three,' she said. 'Is this going to be dangerous for them?'

'We'll do our best to keep everyone safe,' Duval said.

'The residents are usually in their rooms at this time,' Barbara Kellerman said. 'They tend not to come out until dinner, and some of them eat in their rooms, so if you're patient, you should only have to wait for Mr Blazek to exit whichever room he's in, and then he'll be at the medication cart preparing for the next resident.'

'You all get that?' Grove said softly.

'Affirmative,' his second-in-command told him.

'Final question, ma'am,' Duval told her, 'and then we're going to secure you and everyone else on this floor. Where is Miss Cezary?'

'She's at home, where she always is. In the penthouse.'

'Does she have surveillance?' Grove asked. 'Could she be watching us now?'

'I doubt it.'

'Why the smile?' Duval asked.

'Because Constance Cezary is just a very sweet, friendly old lady.'

The front door opened again less than two minutes later.

What looked, from the confines of the van, like a small dark-clad army, the equivalent of at least four SWAT teams, flowed into the building, while a team of MBPD officers shut down Alton one block each way.

If Copani was not inside, they might lose him, but Grove had made the decision for public safety.

Sam and Martinez readied themselves.

Their turn next.

Two more silent, tense minutes passed, and then:

'We have Blazek,' Duval radioed.

Less than thirty seconds later: 'We have Bodine.'

'Detective Becket, that's a go,' Grove said.

'Are you ready to go up now?' Chauvin asked Cathy.

'I'm fine right here,' she said.

It had been dark outside for a couple of hours now, making little physical difference in these shuttered rooms, yet nightfall had sharpened her fear.

She'd accepted his offer of dinner as delay tactics – Hostage 101 – and though she'd thought about the possibility of his using a date-rape drug, Cathy doubted it, because the man seemed to

250

think he was *romancing* her, for God's sake. The aroma she'd noted earlier was *boeuf bourguignon*, which Chauvin had served at the small table with mashed potatoes and green beans, and she'd told him she had little appetite, that having her closest friends threatened and being abducted were not conducive to eating rich food.

'I worked hard to make it for you,' Chauvin had said.

'I can't imagine when,' she had said. 'Since you claim to have been holed up in *Le Rêve* spying on people and . . .'

Her voice had trembled, and she'd stopped, mad at herself for showing fear.

'Try and eat a little something,' Chauvin had encouraged.

Cathy had shivered, despite herself.

'Are you cold? There's no wood, or I'd light the fire.'

'I'm not cold. Just ready to go home.'

'That's not the deal.'

'I didn't make a deal.'

'The deal is we spend some time together. You have to get to know me.'

'I don't have to do anything.'

'No, you don't,' Chauvin had said. 'Just stay with me awhile.'

'Then just get *on* with it.' Her patience had evaporated. 'Take away this ridiculous dinner and tell me what you really want so we can get this over with and I can go back.'

'What about your friend and the waiter?'

'His name is Gabe Ryan.' Cathy had pushed back her chair, stood up.

251

'Sit down, please.'

'No.' She'd walked toward the front door.

'It's locked,' Chauvin had reminded her. 'Please come back to the table.'

'*No.*'

'If you act like a child, I'll have to treat you like a child.'

'I wouldn't try.'

Chauvin had regarded her for a moment. 'You've heard of Qi Gong, Catherine?'

'Please stop calling me that. Of course I've heard of it.'

'I would commend it to you.'

'What does that mean?'

Though she'd guessed it meant that the *jerk* had been in some kind of training, which had toughened him up, and to her knowledge, Qi Gong was not a martial art, but still she thought that 'commending' it to her had probably been another threat: 'unless you know what I know, don't think about standing up to me'.

'Fuck you, Chauvin,' she'd said, and sat down on the couch.

He had sighed. And then he'd cleared away the dinner, humming some old song that she recognized but couldn't place, and now he was taking his time over his chores, cutting shrinkwrap with precision, placing plastic containers in straight lines on a worktop.

OCD into the bargain, Cathy thought.

'Would you like to go upstairs now?' he said, startling her.

'I'm fine right here,' she said from the couch.

'Coffee then?'

'OK.' Anything to buy time. 'So what is it you want me to understand?'

Grace came into her mind, and Cathy yearned for her psychologist mom's wisdom almost as much as she longed for Sam to magically come busting through that locked door.

Chauvin was making coffee, humming again, then singing softly as he reached for cups. She did know the song, 'Grace Kelly', a hit from some years back, had liked it, and it hadn't been about Kelly, but in Chauvin's head, Cathy knew it had to be linked with his obsession with the late princess and . . .

Any moment now – she reined in her thoughts – he was going to *make* her go up those stairs. She had to *focus*.

He'd put the keys in his pocket.

Front right-hand pocket.

No way she could get them from him unless he got out of those jeans.

Jesus.

Chauvin stopped singing. 'It's strange. I know so many things about you, but not how you like your coffee.'

Black was how she wanted it – needed it now.

Then again, anything that bought more time.

'Could you make a cappuccino?' she asked.

Faces on the way through the hallway, more pale bespectacled faces behind the glass window of a door, penned in, staring. Elderly people and staff, too, all unnerved, some excited, because this had to feel like a movie, unreal, strangers swarming, taking over, wearing dark bullet-resistant vests, holding *guns*.

Duval and Grove were leading the way, Sam and Martinez right behind them, everyone checking back and forth at every turn, because Blazek and Bodine were out of the picture, but Copani was not, nor Cezary, nor '*Virginia*'; and no one knew how many others might be involved in the operation, so no one was safe, and their Glocks were out of their holsters, police all over, keeping the innocent safe, looking out for each other.

There was an elevator but they used the stairs – special grip handrails, anti-slip stair-edging, and if it weren't looking as if this place had been set up by a monster, the house might feel OK, a place of safety.

The stairs ran out on the third floor.

An elevator marked Private over to the right, leading to the penthouse, the boss's private domain where, according to Barbara Kellerman, Cezary lived alone, having no need of permanent care, drawing all the help she needed from Rosemont House employees.

Kellerman had told Duval that the elevator ran from the basement, and reports from the rear confirmed that no one had entered or exited that way since they'd arrived, and officers were now in place near the two top floor fire exits; everyone exercising extreme caution, since someone might have tipped off Cezary, or maybe the 'friendly old lady' did have a personal surveillance system that her manager didn't know about.

If Kellerman was telling the truth.

Sam had spoken to her briefly downstairs, had been impressed by her calmness, but had seen no intense shock, felt unsure about her.

Unsure about *everyone* in this place.

He'd paused momentarily in the entrance hall, noting a black-and-white photograph on a wall to his right.

'That's her,' Kellerman had said.

Sam had taken a closer look.

A silver-haired woman, elegant in a dark dress, single strand of pearls around her neck. Intelligent eyes that might be blue or gray, mouth curving in a slight smile. Humor of a kind in there, Sam thought.

'How old is she?' he'd asked.

'Seventy-two,' Kellerman had said. 'And sharp as a tack.'

Not Hildegard Benedict.

Another old lady in a nursing home.

Big lesson for him and Martinez to learn.

Coincidences *did* happen.

Kellerman had told them she had a key to the private elevator which she said triggered a light on every telephone in Cezary's five rooms: living room, bedroom, treatment room, kitchen and bathroom.

'There's another phone inside the elevator. I buzz before I go up.'

'What if she doesn't want you to?' Grove asked.

'She tells me. And she can disable the elevator if she chooses to. Though there is an emergency override; a coded keypad next to the phone.'

'How many people have that code?' Martinez had asked.

'Just me. If I'm going to be absent, the code is passed to my deputy, and is altered again when I return.'

'Is there a camera in the elevator?' Sam had asked.

'No.'

Now, on the third floor, Sam turned to the others.

'I think we need Kellerman up here.' His voice was barely above a whisper. 'She calls Cezary and we four ride up. If she turns Kellerman down, we use the emergency code. Either way we need to synch with the fire exit teams.'

'Are we trusting what Kellerman told us?' Martinez asked.

'We'll soon find out,' Sam said.

'She'll stay under guard,' Duval said, 'so no warnings possible.'

'Can't be sure she hasn't warned Cezary already,' Grove said.

'We could be walking into an ambush,' Sam said.

Anything possible, given who they were dealing with.

Upstairs, in Constance Cezary's private residence, Anthony Copani was eating dinner.

Fine food. Filet mignon with sauce Béarnaise and tiny crispy fries, going down well with a bottle of Pinot Noir.

Mrs Hood had called him a few hours ago to invite him.

'Will you be wanting a treatment?' Copani had asked.

256

'Probably a massage.'

'Will the others be there?'

'Not tonight, Leon. Will four be too early for you?'

'Not for you, Mrs Hood.'

There was something else on the lacy white cloth, a dish of something beneath a silver-domed cloche cover with a brass knob.

'It's my gift for you, Leon,' she told him now. 'After your dinner.'

'Another reward?' His dark eyes glinted.

'You deserve it,' Cezary told him.

She watched him accelerate, then slow down for the last few mouthfuls, wanting to relish the final morsels.

'That was terrific, Mrs H,' he said.

'Glad you enjoyed it.'

She had not sat with him, had moved around the room, regarding items, photographs, books and ornaments, touching a polished leaf on an orchid plant, walking to an alcove, looking at a small screen.

She did so again now.

'Something good?' Copani asked, wondering what kind of TV this sharp-eyed old lady, this buyer of killers, enjoyed.

'That depends,' she answered, 'on your outlook.'

She turned, saw the greedy third generation Italian-American eyeing the covered dish again, and smiled. Copani was a barely adequate fitness instructor who got off on bullying and gazing at his reflection, who could be sweet to the residents but regularly ridiculed them and had been known to get impatient, even hurt them if he felt pissed off. Copani would do anything for money, believing – and in this he was not wrong – that it equaled power.

Except you needed more than money to achieve power. You needed a brain.

You needed to know how to manipulate people.

It had been so easy. A stash of kiddy porn planted in an envelope in his basement locker; one of Cezary's cameras ready to catch his expression when he found it, then a little editing to remove the disgust, keep the moments when he looked excited – and those close-ups had been cruel but authentic.

And after that he'd been hers.

Frank Blazek – a nurse with a cruel streak, was a recovering addict. Cezary had studied him for a while before creating a situation exposing him to an unlocked drugs cabinet. Blazek had swallowed some tabs on the spot and pocketed more, all on video.

Jimmy Bodine, an orderly without ambition or scruples, had been raised in Chicago, hated his family and the cold, had come south for sun, sex and whatever else was on offer. He'd stolen valuables from two patients, had been caught and reported to Cezary, and he'd heard terrifying tales about Florida jails, but the boss had been kind, had told him she'd keep quiet, take good care of him, so long as he did her bidding when the time came.

Blazek: her Jerry. Bodine: her Andy. López: her CB.

All finished.

So be it.

Only Copani – her Leon – left now.

And then, her Plan B.

Education. Of others.

She was old, with no certainty of how much time was left, and she'd squandered too much of that, stuck up here with all her comforts, though at least these past several years, planning how to end her years honorably, finally being true to her beliefs – saying her piece – had been stimulating.

This past month had been little short of sublime.

And all good things had to end.

A phone rang in the alcove. She turned, picked up, took a look at the screen.

'Got it,' she said.

Time.

She returned to the table.

'Allow me,' she said to Leon, and removed the cloche with a flourish, the way waiters did in expensive restaurants.

Copani stared at the dish beneath.

An envelope.

'Better than money,' she told him.

She saw doubt on his stupid face, knew that Copani could imagine nothing finer than money, with the possible exception of a Golden Opulence Sundae from Serendipity 3.

'It's your freedom, Leon.'

He frowned, picked it up.

'It's everything I had on you,' Constance Cezary said.

He opened it tentatively.

'I'm setting you free,' she said. 'You've followed my orders well, been the best of my Crusaders. You deserve to follow your own destiny now.'

'You serious, Mrs H?' he asked, not sure at that moment how to feel, because this had been the time of his life, and if he was honest with himself, he wanted more.

'Always,' she said.

'You're OK,' Gabe had kept telling Luc.

OK, considering the guy had been struck on the shoulder with a mallet, then, while he was still stunned, threatened with a knife, bullied down into the wine cellar and tied with cord to a pipe.

'Where's Cathy?'

The most important thing Gabe had wanted to know once he'd established that Meyer wasn't badly hurt. He'd been sufficiently composed to have given Gabe the number of the security company so he could make the call about the smashed window, give the code, assure them there had been a minor accident but all was secure, and the operator had accepted it, though both men still expected a police car any moment.

Neither of them wanted that, not once Luc had told Gabe what had happened.

'It was a meat tenderizer,' Luc had said, still trembling. 'The mallet. From our kitchen.'

'You told me that already,' Gabe had said.

Meyer had told him something else, too, something that had made the small hairs on the back of Gabe's neck stand up.

'He told me to keep quiet for three hours, that if I made a noise and the cops were called, Cathy would be the one to suffer.' He'd hesitated. 'Except he didn't call her Cathy, he called her Catherine.'

Gabe had sat him down at a corner table, poured him a cognac and Luc had gone over it again. How Cathy had gone for pizza, and he'd heard a bang from below, had gone to see if she'd come back, maybe had a fall.

'He was waiting for me. On the first floor. He jumped me.'

'And you don't know who he was?'

'Not then.' Luc had rubbed his shoulder.

'But now?' Gabe had wanted to shake the guy. 'Luc, come on.'

'I need to find the photo.'

'What photo?'

'Of the man Cathy's father told me about, back in Miami.'

'What man?' First Gabe had heard about it.

'The Frenchman,' Luc had said. 'Hasn't Cathy talked about him?'

Gabe had watched Luc reach for more cognac, leaned over, laid a hand over his glass. 'Luc, be more specific. What photo?'

'Upstairs.' Luc had stood up. 'My room.'

'I can't believe she never mentioned him to me,' Gabe said now. 'She's told me so much about her past.'

261

'Maybe it didn't loom very large, by comparison.'
Gabe stared at the picture. 'You sure it's him?'

'I think so, though this guy wasn't wearing
glasses, and his hair was short.' Luc shook his
head. 'But it figures, doesn't it? The way he called
her "Catherine" – and Sam said Chauvin had
been arrested for stalking in the past.'

'So this bastard tracked Cathy down in Cannes'
– Gabe started pacing Luc's living room – 'and
got in here somehow—'

'He said he'd been here watching. I forgot he
said that. Oh, God, I'm such an idiot.'

'Doesn't matter,' Gabe said. 'What matters is
he must have been waiting. Cathy wouldn't have
let him in, and the door would have locked behind
her when she went for pizza, so he had to have
been inside already.'

'The cops haven't come,' Luc realized abruptly.
'The alarm people must have bought your story.'

'That's something.'

'Is it?' Luc was doubtful. 'I think we could use
some help.'

'Not yet.' Gabe headed for the door.

'Where are you going?' Luc asked. 'We need
to do something, call Sam.'

'We need to look around first.' Gabe was on
the stairs. 'If he's been watching . . .'

'He must have had a hiding place,' Luc said,
following.

Everyone poised, *again*.

Enough men and firepower to take down a
small terrorist cell.

Maybe all for just one seventy-two-year-old woman.

A woman possibly behind the brutal wiping out of ten innocent lives.

Ten that they *knew* of. Who knew how many more over time?

The three assault teams were all in radio contact.

Commander Grove replaced by Special Agent Casey Newton, compact build but exuding power; Grove now outside one of the fire exits, still in overall command.

Which was fine by Sam.

'I still think there must be a huge mistake,' Barbara Kellerman said.

'Ma'am,' Sam said, raising an index finger to his lips.

She nodded.

All set now, contingency plans in place, should Cezary refuse Kellerman access.

'Let's do it,' Duval whispered.

Sam inserted Kellerman's key, turned it, and the elevator door opened.

Tight squeeze for four men.

Martinez handed Kellerman the phone.

She pushed two keys, waited.

They *all* waited.

'Miss Cezary,' she said, 'I need to see you.'

A moment of deathly silence.

'Thank you,' Kellerman said.

She handed the phone over to Martinez and stepped back.

The elevator door slid shut.

They began to move.

* * *

263

'How about a cigar, Leon?' Constance Cezary opened the lid of a rosewood humidor which stood on the marble surface of a cabinet. 'Cuba's finest.'

Copani still sat at her table. 'I wouldn't say no, Mrs H.'

She took out a cigar.

'I don't think I want you calling me that any more.' She handed it to him. 'Just roll it under your nostrils.'

'I'll do just that,' he said appreciatively. 'Thank you, Mrs Cezary.'

'You're welcome,' she said. 'Help yourself to the cutter and lighter, Anthony.'

She took something else out of the humidor.

A Heckler and Koch P2000 compact pistol.

Waited for the elevator door to slide open.

'For the avoidance of doubt,' she said.

And shot him through his left temple.

The sound still reverberated in the air as the other two teams crashed their way through the two fire exits and thundered into the sitting room.

'Put down your weapon,' Thomas Grove ordered.

'By all means,' Cezary said, and laid it on the table.

They were on her in less than a second.

No one thrown by the strangeness of patting down an old woman, while two FBI agents approached the shot man slumped sideways in his carver chair, frisked him, then, despite the blood- and brain-spattered evidence of his fatal injury, checked his pulse and pronounced him dead.

264

'Detective Becket,' she said, 'I'm glad you're here. Will you be the one to cuff me?'

'It'll be my pleasure.' Sam stepped forward, caught a whiff of jasmine. 'Put your hands behind your back.'

'Cuff me, by all means,' Constance Cezary said. 'But please do not touch me.'

The room went silent.

'I don't want your skin touching mine,' Cezary said.

And there it was, right out in the open.

The hideous, flesh-crawling stuff that made 'Virginia' tick.

'Hands behind your back,' Sam said, more sharply, and gripped her hands.

Cezary gave an intense, theatrical shudder, and Sam suppressed the urge to yank her wrists violently into the cuffs, felt Martinez's furious, protective gaze on him, was aware of other eyes watching.

'I asked you not to touch me,' Cezary said.

'You have the right to—'

'Wait. Please.' She twisted around, faced Duval. 'In that drawer, please. My gloves.'

Beside Sam, Martinez made a small explosive sound.

'Ma'am,' Duval said, pleasantly. 'No gloves.'

Sam restarted the Miranda. 'You have the right to remain silent. Anything you say—'

'You,' she said, to Duval again. 'You may touch me.'

Anger seared through Sam and he checked her cuffs again, laid his hand on her wrist.

They all heard a weird, low sound in her throat.

A growl. Like a vicious dog on the brink.

'Someone else read her rights,' Sam said, disgusted, 'and get her out of here.'

'No problem,' Newton said.

'In case you're wondering,' Cezary said, 'I shot that man in your presence so you would see that I am capable of murder. His name was Anthony Copani, and he was one of the men the media have called "The Four". He enjoyed what he did for me, I think, but he was a terrible glutton who would probably have eaten himself to death, had he lived.'

Sam turned his back on her, heard Casey Newton beginning the Miranda again.

'I do look forward to speaking to you, Detective Becket,' he heard Cezary say. 'I shan't mind that at all. After all, you need to realize how much of the responsibility you and your wife bear for all these deaths.'

'Someone shut her the fuck up,' Martinez said.

'Only you all need to learn,' she went on. 'Because as Virginia said, I knew I couldn't stop you all. I just needed to say my piece.'

June 19

At midnight-thirty, Gabe glanced up at the ceiling over the bar and saw the trapdoor, scarcely visible. Three minutes later he was up there in Chauvin's space, Luc halfway up a short ladder, head and shoulders in the gap, holding a flashlight so Gabe could take photos.

They looked at a small pillow, glucose tablets,

Evian bottles – two filled with urine – and wondered how long the man had spent up here spying.

'There's something in the pillow case,' Gabe said.

'Maybe you shouldn't touch it,' Luc said. 'Evidence.'

'Video me. Use your phone.' Gabe withdrew a large white envelope, took a photo himself, then opened it carefully, shook out its contents.

Two photographs of Cathy, plainly altered to resemble Grace Kelly.

'Definitely Chauvin, then,' Gabe said grimly.

'We need to call Sam,' Luc said.

'Shine the light.' Gabe took photos of the pictures and a piece of paper folded around something. He unfolded it, saw it was a letter encasing two more photographs, and took his own shots, careful of clarity.

'Seems the bastard wants us to find him,' he said. 'Look.'

Luc leaned in, stared at a picture of a small white house with blue shutters and a red tile roof. No house number or street sign.

'Could be anywhere,' he said.

Gabe picked it up by a corner, turned it over. Blank.

The second was more help: part of a signpost at the entrance to a camping and caravan site. *Park "Les Cigales"*.

Gabe put the photo down, then, taking the torch from Luc, started to read the letter.

'Oh, man,' he said after a moment. '*Now* we call Sam.'

Hectic scenes at Rosement House just after seven, Tuesday evening – Eastern Daylight Time.

A homicide scene now, the building and surrounding area cordoned off, police vehicles everywhere, media penned up as far away as possible, locals rubbernecking behind yellow tape.

Inside, residents were still penned up for their own safety, some of them protesting, others scared. Rumors flying that the single gunshot heard by some had been the suicide of their benefactor – for that was how they thought of the wealthy lady who'd opened her home to them and said to call her 'Connie'.

The body of the man believed to be Anthony Copani was still slumped on a dining chair in the penthouse living room pending the ME's arrival.

Cezary, Bodine and Blazek were at South Beach, along with López, all in separate holding cells awaiting interrogation, Task Force investigators exercising the greatest care; *no* slip-ups, all efforts now going into driving the arrests toward multiple charges, successful prosecutions and justice for the victims.

Barbara Kellerman, too, had been taken in for questioning.

'Someone has to be left in charge here,' she'd protested.

'You mentioned a deputy earlier, ma'am,' Sam had said.

'On vacation,' Kellerman had said.

'The Florida Department of Elder Affairs will be ensuring the welfare of Rosemont House residents,' Joe Duval had informed her.

'You think they'll close us down?'

'Too soon to say,' Duval had said.

Sam's guess was that it would close almost immediately, and he felt bad about the upheaval for the residents. Major change never easy for the elderly or frail.

More of Cezary's victims.

Photographs taken, sketches made, Crime Scene at work, he and Martinez returned to the station, to an atmosphere of relief as well as jubilation. Mary Cutter passing the news to the families, Beth Riley organizing the press conference they'd all hoped for, telling South Florida and beyond that four arrests had been made, one suspect was dead, and one individual, still to be named, had been arrested for his murder.

'Don't forget to tell them that Hildegard Benedict's off the hook.' Kovac poured cold water, as per usual. 'Some screw-up there,' he went on. 'Don't be surprised if the Benedict family sues our sorry asses, Becket.'

'At least we got them all,' Captain Kennedy said. 'Good job, Sam.'

'Good job, Task Force,' Sam said.

'Lucky break,' Kovac said. 'If that Mexican scumbag hadn't gotten pissed out of his skull and taken a swing in that bar, we'd still be whistling in the dark.'

'Degree of luck in most big breaks, Ron,' Kennedy gently chided.

Sam's cell phone rang. He frowned, saw who was calling, answered.

'Just a minute, Luc,' he said, saw Martinez's questioning eyes on him, left the hubbub of the squad room to take the call.

'What's up?' he asked, walking down the stairs.

Less than a minute later, emerging from the building onto the plaza, his legs suddenly so weak that he needed to sit down on a low stone wall, he was already checking flights on his G1 while listening to the agitated voice of his daughter's friend.

'Put Gabe on,' Sam said.

June 19

One-forty a.m. Wednesday in Cannes – Central European Summer Time – and Gabe was fighting to be coherent.

'Chauvin *must* have figured we'd find it.'

In Miami Beach – still Tuesday, seven-forty p.m., Eastern Daylight Time – Sam stopped checking flights, listening intently.

'The letter's handwritten,' Gabe went on. 'Writing's steady, so I guess he was calm when he wrote it, which I'm hoping is good.'

'Just read it to me,' Sam said.

'"Dear Detective Becket,
    I suppose that someone at the restaurant is reading or scanning this to you. It can only be a matter of time before this letter is found, and if it's taken a little longer,

that's OK, since more time alone with Catherine can only be wonderful for me.

So please, dear Sam – for this is how I think of you, as my friend, as Catherine's treasured papa – don't be alarmed, and I send the same message to dear Grace – or Grace-mère, as I call her now. I will not hurt Catherine. I love her too much. She is everything to me.

But you must come.

The only way any harm could befall Catherine would be if you were to notify the police. If I see a single cop, or the waiter, if I see anyone but YOU, dear Sam, I will have no choice. She will be hurt. And that would break my heart. It would kill me.

More than anything in life, I want Catherine. But I want your blessing too.

I've left two photos to aid your search for us. Maybe Jones or the waiter will work out where we are, but tell them NOT TO COME. Only you.

I'm guessing you'll be on the next flight.

(She is a little mad at me, which is to be expected, but she will remain safe so long as you come ALONE.)

Your admiring future son-in-law,
Thomas.'"

Gabe stopped reading. 'Mr Becket, I'm pretty sure I know where that campsite is, and I'm assuming the white house is somewhere nearby.

I know what I want to do, but I'll take my orders from you.'

'You do nothing, Gabe.'

'But I'm here, and you're nearly five thousand miles away.'

'And he's happy to wait for me to get there – the longer the better. Which probably makes you want to kill him, but you are *not* going to do one single thing to increase the danger to Cathy, do you understand me?'

'I do.'

'I'm about to walk out on my case, and as soon as I know my ETA, I'll call you. Meantime, your number one job is to make sure *no* one calls the cops and no one goes looking for that house.' Sam paused. 'Gabe, listen, I won't be armed. I can't take a weapon on a plane, and I'm coming as a private individual, not a cop.'

'I already thought of that. My uncle has two shotguns at his place in the country.'

'I'm assuming it's illegal for you to think of taking those, Gabe.'

'I don't care,' Gabe said.

'Do not do anything crazy,' Sam said, 'and I repeat, do *not* try finding Cathy till I'm with you. Don't even go near the neighborhood. I know you ride a Ducati, so I'm sure Chauvin knows that too, might recognize its sound. We can't risk a kneejerk reaction.'

'Agreed,' Gabe said.

'If we play this right,' Sam said, 'we'll get her back safe and sound.'

'Just get here, please,' Gabe said.

* * *

272

'You look tired,' Chauvin said to Cathy. 'It's almost two a.m.'

'I'm tired of this,' she said. 'Time has nothing to do with it.'

She'd run out of ways to procrastinate, had drunk two cappuccinos, even feigned interest in his career, his home life in Strasbourg.

'You'll come there with me some day,' he'd said, 'and you'll love it.'

'I have till next spring in Cannes. Then I'll be going home.'

'Our home could be anywhere,' Chauvin had said.

She'd wanted to slap him for actually seeming to believe that, but there was still a long night ahead, and what she needed was to get his keys, and then she'd do whatever she had to, hit him over his idiot head with the casserole dish if need be and get *away.*

He'd gone upstairs a while ago, and Cathy had swiftly, quietly, unhooked the interior shutters and tried the windows – all locked – and then she'd heard a lavatory flush and had returned to the couch.

'I really need some air,' she said now.

'You should have eaten. I could find you something now.'

'I'm not hungry. Being kept prisoner kills the appetite.'

'Then I guess it's time for bed.'

'In your dreams,' Cathy said.

'I've told you, you don't need to be afraid. I won't force myself on you.'

'Because you're such a gentleman.'

'I hope I am.'

Cathy's laugh was brief, harsh.

'Don't laugh at me.' His eyes were suddenly sad. 'Please, go upstairs. I've bought you something to change into.'

'Don't you see how weird this is?' Cathy said.

'Can't you see that I'm only asking you to give me a chance?'

'But this isn't the way,' she said, weary again.

'Just go upstairs,' Chauvin said. 'I'll show you what I bought, and then I'll leave you to get changed, and you can sleep for a few hours, and then it'll be dawn, and everything will seem better.'

She thought of the keys.

If she didn't go up and put on whatever flimsy negligee she supposed he'd bought, then he wouldn't take off his damned jeans either, and he had to be getting tired too, and maybe, if she seemed to be caving in, he might relax his guard . . .

'How can I sleep if I don't know that Gabe and Luc are safe?' she said.

'They're safe,' he said. 'I'm a man of my word, Catherine.'

She sighed, and stood up.

'You win,' she said.

Candles everywhere, lit when he'd gone up earlier.

'God, Thomas, this is beyond cliché.'

She stared around, saw several doctored photographs of herself with Chauvin beside her, and

274

felt sick again. Saw a small double bed made up with silk sheets, a white cardboard box on top, an ice bucket on a stand near the window – and closed shutters here too.

'You need to let me out of here,' she said, struggling against panic.

'You need to understand what I'm offering you. We'll go to Strasbourg. My parents will adore you. We'll have a fine home, and my photographs of you will sell – you'll become famous, Catherine.'

She looked into his face, saw that he believed it.

Knew she had to play along.

He picked up the box, opened it, removed something tissue-wrapped. 'For you.'

Not a negligee, at least. Black silky pajamas with a camisole and long-sleeved top.

She took a look. Elle Macpherson. If Gabe had bought them for her . . .

'I wanted to find something you might have chosen yourself.' He nodded at a door beside the stairs. 'You can change in there.'

Cathy picked up the pajamas, forced herself to step into the tiny shower room.

No lock, just a flimsy, easily breakable bolt, but she slid it shut, turned and stared at her face in the mirror, saw anger and fear. And even now, most of the fear was for Gabe and Luc, not really for herself, because this man was still Sam's 'dope', wasn't he? Not a real threat, still just Chauvin-the-jerk . . .

Get undressed.

She took off her jeans, used the lavatory,

washed with Coco Mademoiselle soap, opened the sealed toothbrush and toothpaste – neither her own brand, thankfully, because that would just have been too creepy for words.

Like this wasn't?

The pajamas fitted perfectly, so maybe he'd been in her place, looking at . . .

Don't.

She took a breath, emerged, saw him by the shuttered windows.

'Perfect,' he said.

'So now you go downstairs,' Cathy said.

'Now we go to bed,' he said.

Her flesh crawled. 'No way.'

'Just to sleep. We both need rest.' He sat on the side of the bed, took off his sneakers.

'I'd appreciate it if you'd undress in the bathroom.'

'I'm not undressing. You get under the covers; I'll stretch out on top.'

Not getting naked, thank Christ.

No access to the keys either.

She pulled back the covers, got under them, considered asking him to blow out the candles, except then they'd be in the dark . . .

'First light,' she said, 'I'm out of here.'

'I don't think so,' he said.

'Fuck's sake,' she said, and shut her eyes.

She felt him lie down.

'If you so much as touch me,' she said, 'I'll scratch your eyes out.'

'I won't,' he said.

Boulder-heavy weariness invaded her. If she wasn't careful, she'd fall asleep.

Got to stay awake.
No chance.

'I'm going to head up to my uncle's now,' Gabe said.

'I think you should wait till morning.' Luc, feet up on a chair, hated himself for craving sleep when Cathy was in such trouble. 'Sam won't be here till God knows when.'

'I'm not waiting for Nic or Jeanne to stop me,' Gabe said.

'You'll come straight back here, right?'

'Sure.' Gabe fished for the black Ducati key he always kept apart from the irreplaceable red key needed to program the bike's electronic control unit.

'Don't do anything crazy,' Luc said.

'Nothing crazier than coming back here with two shotguns.'

'You still think I should wait till five to call Jeanne?'

'No earlier. And make sure they don't call the cops.'

'Nic's never called them before,' Luc pointed out.

Gabe headed for the kitchen. 'Cathy was never abducted before.'

'I'll lock up after you.' Luc followed. 'Call when you're back so I can let you in. Call any time so I know you're OK.'

'Get some sleep.'

'You haven't slept,' Luc said.

'Sleep's not what I need,' Gabe said.

277

The only flight leaving Miami Tuesday night was the British Airways to London; *impossible*, except that Martinez – covering for Sam until he was en route – had a contact at MIA who'd promised to do his best to get Sam on board, and skulking off during an investigation did not sit well with Sam, but he was out of options.

As it was, he'd told Grace – home to pick up his passport and bare essentials – he'd be traveling, including the Heathrow wait, for upward of fourteen agonizing hours.

'I want to come,' Grace had said, following him around.

'Can't be done. Even if I knew what I was heading into—'

'I can't believe this is *happening*.'

Sam had kissed her frantic face, blown a second kiss at their sleeping son from the doorway and sprinted down and out to his waiting cab.

At MIA, running again, scooping coins out of his pockets at security, leaving them – *no time* – he'd called Martinez.

'How'd they take it?'

'Lotta grim faces,' Martinez said quietly. 'I told them family emergency, and I'm guessing you'll have a shitload of trouble when you get back, and I'm also guessing that right now you don't give a damn.'

'Who's going to interview Cezary?' Sam asked.

'As it stands, me and Duval.'

'That's good,' Sam said. 'Gotta run, Al.'

278

'Sure you don't want me to call my pal at Interpol?'

'No officials, no cops. Get Cathy to safety, then get the hell back is what I'm hoping.'

'I hear you, man. Fly safe.'

Sam's flight had been in the air for about fifteen minutes when, in an interview room at 1100 Washington Avenue, Constance Cezary was informed by Duval that Detective Becket was unavailable.

'What does that mean?' she asked.

'Not available is what it means,' Martinez said.

The look she cast his way was ice-cold.

Martinez smiled back at her.

She turned her attention back to Duval. 'If I were you,' she said, 'I'd get Becket back here. That is, if you want me answering questions any time soon.'

'Not possible,' Duval said.

'We know how much you like writing to him,' Martinez said. 'But it's us or nothing.'

He was glad, briefly, that Sam wasn't here. Anything that pissed off this bitch had to be good news. Pissed not the word for how she looked right now. The murderous old broad looked ready to pop, fury sizzling in her eyes.

If she stroked out here and now, Martinez thought, he might just get on the next flight to France to help Sam, even if it meant losing his job.

Cezary wasn't ready to die. 'You have half an hour to get Becket here.'

'Detective Becket won't be here in half an hour or any time soon,' Duval said.

For a moment, the rage was replaced by interest. 'I hope he hasn't gotten himself in trouble for screwing up,' she said. 'Looking for the wrong old lady, for instance.'

'Detective Becket is on vacation,' Martinez said.

The anger sparked again, turned to ice.

'I'll have my lawyer now. Until then, I'm exercising my right to remain silent.'

June 19

Weird sounds woke Cathy.

Only two candles still alight, flickering palely near the window.

Enough light to confirm that Chauvin was not beside her.

She sat up, listening.

The sounds were human, from downstairs.

She took a moment, then climbed quietly out of bed, checked that the shower room was empty, then crept to the window, picked up a candle, held it up to her watch.

Three thirty-four.

She put down the candle, touched the edge of a shutter. A hinge squeaked and she backed off, waiting to see if he'd heard, but the sounds went on – and even if she did open the shutter, the window would be locked. She had to go down, see what was going on.

Silent on the stairs, she stopped two-thirds down, seeing him.

He'd lit more candles around the room, was in front of the dead fireplace, wearing only a thong, working through some kind of exercise, chanting. Qi Gong, she supposed, his absorption appearing total. She looked around, saw his jeans, folded on a kitchen worktop.

Chauvin was still immersed, his movements smooth, flowing.

She made it soundlessly to the foot of the stairs, padded over to the worktop, peered at the jeans.

Only one chance. The slightest jangle, her chance was gone.

She slid a hand into a pocket. No keys. Not even her SIM card. All pockets empty.

She turned to the drawers from which he'd taken cutlery earlier, snuck a glance at the crazy man still going through his paces. Opened a drawer. No knives, not even a *fork*. She moved to another drawer, holding her breath, started to open it.

'Which of these were you hoping to find?' he said behind her.

She turned around, her heart hammering.

Keys in his left hand. A knife in his right.

A medium-sized chopping knife, sharp enough to be lethal.

'I shouldn't be surprised,' Chauvin said. 'But I'm very disappointed.'

'I didn't mean to disturb you,' Cathy said. 'I was looking for—'

'Escape,' he said.

She didn't answer, couldn't read his eyes.

'Time,' he said. 'That's all I was asking for.'

He leaned past her, still holding the knife, put

down the keys, retrieved his jeans, stepped into them, pulled them up, zipped them one-handed, put the keys back in his pocket and gripped her right arm.

'*Viens.*' He steered her to the table, drew out a chair. 'Sit.'

She obeyed, and he moved back into the kitchen.

She stood up.

'Sit *down*.'

She sat, turned to watch as he took something from beneath the sink.

Narrow cord, plenty of it.

'Three strand polypropylene, very strong,' he said.

'You have a very strange idea of romance,' Cathy said.

'I hoped I wouldn't need it.' Chauvin cut off a length with the knife. 'Put your hands behind your back, around the chair.'

'You don't have to do this.' Her heart was pounding harder. 'I don't have the keys, so I can't leave.'

'But I can't trust you anymore.' He tied her wrists together, then wound a long length of cord around her waist.

'Screw you,' Cathy said, and kicked him.

'Temper.' He knelt on her thighs. 'I'm strong, Catherine. Much more so than when you met me in Miami. It's surprisingly easy to strengthen your body.' He finished winding the cord, tied it tightly behind her. 'The mind, too.' He cut more line, moved around the chair. 'Don't try kicking again. I don't want to hurt you.' He knelt, tied her ankles together, then attached the cord to the chair legs. 'It's interesting, in a way.'

'What is?'

'Sam's working on a case right now where the victims have been tied up before dying. They were hogtied, then gassed in their cars.'

'How do you know that?' For the first time, real, hard fear gripped her.

'I keep a close eye on your papa. *Père-noir*, as I think of him.' Chauvin sat on the floor in front of her, legs crossed, resting the knife on his right thigh. 'Easy to do these days.'

'So you're obsessed by us all,' Cathy said. 'Not just me.'

'I don't like that word,' Chauvin said. 'I prefer love.'

'Love doesn't work like this,' Cathy said.

'Your doing, not mine,' he said.

Gabe's arrival at the farm just after four a.m. was acknowledged with no more than a wagging tail by his uncle's elderly German Shepherd.

If Yves Rémy had made it to bed, he might have locked up and turned out the lights, but as it was, there'd been no need for Gabe to use his keys or grope his way around, because his uncle was snoring in an ancient armchair in the sitting room, three empty wine bottles giving Gabe more than enough confidence to go to the gun room – never locked – and help himself without fear of argument.

The gun room was empty.

Gabe swore softly, searched the kitchen and

scullery, then the bedroom, in case his uncle had gotten it into his addled brain to stash them in a closet or under his bed.

No guns, and for all he knew they'd been stolen, or Yves might have given them away or left them in a field or an outhouse.

No way he was going to find them now, since he doubted if his uncle would make any sense this side of noon.

'Thanks for nothing,' Gabe said softly, leaving.

He bent to pat the dog's head, closed the big front door quietly behind him.

And was on his way.

Somewhere over the Atlantic, in the sleepy twilight of the BA jumbo, Sam gave up on sleep and forced his mind away from Cathy back to the case.

Constance Cezary's preparedness for their entry had bugged him. The theatrically timed shooting of Anthony Copani – how had she put it?

'For the avoidance of doubt.'

Sick bitch.

They'd found her CCTV setup, three monitors, one in an alcove, one in a closet and one that doubled as a TV. No shortage of funds, clearly, but still, quite a setup.

Which someone else had surely helped organize – and maybe a security firm had installed the system, but it was the mind behind it – whether Cezary's or someone else's – that intrigued Sam now.

One of the four, perhaps, but he doubted it.

Certainly not López, and interrogation would tell them something about Blazek or Bodine: a male nurse or orderly, capable of moonlighting as cold-blooded killers, might feasibly have a technical mindset, but he doubted that too, though perhaps Copani . . .

Constance Cezary, with those sharp, ice-blue eyes, might be capable of just about anything, but someone else had to be involved in the organization.

Barbara Kellerman, perhaps, her unflappable manager.

Someone.

If he'd stayed in Miami, he'd be chewing this over with Martinez and Duval, Sam thought, staring past silent flickering screens and blanket-covered bodies; though by now they'd probably both have been told that he was off the case. Lead investigator no more.

Lucky if he had a job to come back to.

To hell with that.

He had a daughter in danger.

Gabe had not intended to do it this way.

But when it came down to it, it just made sense.

To at least *find* that house.

Near the camping site called *Les Cigales*, which Gabe had now confirmed was located on avenue de la Mer just outside Mandelieu-La Napoule – a stone's throw from Cannes.

He'd stopped a mile back, had found a text from Cathy's father, telling him his ETA – more than twelve hours away, for crying out loud – and then he'd taken a look at his photo of the house. Nothing significant to help identify it, especially before dawn, so Gabe had put away the phone and made his way to *Les Cigales*.

He found the sign. A few caravans visible from the road. No signs of life at five a.m. – not that a tourist would be able to help anyway – and his TomTom was confirming how hard it would be trying to pinpoint a single house.

Except he couldn't give up now, not when he might be so *close*, and Sam had told him not to do this, but if he kept the bike's growl low . . .

Bottom line, he was here and Sam was not, so he started looking, rode with lights off, up and down every residential road in a square kilometer from the campsite, and if darkness was keeping the houses under wraps, it had to be doing the same for him.

They all looked the *same*, and if the cops were involved, they might be able to track Cathy's phone – if Chauvin had let her keep it, though anyway, her phone had been almost out of juice and Gabe didn't know if they could track phones with dead batteries.

He didn't even register what he'd seen until he was about twenty meters past. He took the next left turn, pulled over.

Thought about it.

A girl he'd dated a couple of years ago. Nice time, nothing intense. But she'd come from Strasbourg. Same as this creep.

Her Renault Clio had been her great passion, and during a boring conversation about French license plates, she'd explained her own car's

286

number, saying that '67' was the number of the département Bas-Rhin in the préfecture of Strasbourg, and Gabe had yawned, and the relationship hadn't survived long past that.

He thanked God for her now.

And for the street light that had illuminated the license plate of a white Peugeot in the small driveway he'd just passed.

Strasbourg registered.

Not conclusive, for sure. But the crooked angle of the car had made it look as if it had been parked by a drunk or learner.

Or maybe by a man about to move an unwilling woman from his car to the front door as quickly as possible.

Gabe killed the engine, took out his phone, checked out the house in Chauvin's photograph again.

His heartbeat stepped up.

If Cathy was in there, in Christ knew what kind of trouble . . .

Her dad had told him *not* to do this.

Gabe got off the bike. He'd take a closer look, then decide his next move, but just in *case* . . .

He'd left the biggest of his tire irons at *Le Rêve*, too busy breaking in to think about returning it to his toolbox, counting on having his uncle's shotguns. But there was a second iron, and a screwdriver, and he didn't plan on going in, though if he saw a real chance of getting Cathy out . . .

And even when Sam did arrive, it wouldn't get dark again till way after nine, and that was *unthinkable*.

He scrabbled for commonsense, knew he needed to let Luc know where he was.

He tucked the two lousy weapons in his belt, walked to the corner, checked the street sign. Rue Saint Vincent de Paul. Took a photo of the sign and attached a swift message: 'Think I found it.'

Then he walked slowly back toward the house, looking for a name or number, found none, counted houses from the corner, typed that information for Luc to pass on.

And finally, moving in closer, he added the clincher: the Peugeot's license details.

Sent the message and turned the phone off.

He regarded the house from the other side of the road: windows shuttered, no signs of life – and maybe this wasn't it, maybe innocent strangers were asleep inside.

He crossed the road, stepped into the driveway, bent to look through the Peugeot's windows, and it was too dark, but he could just see . . . A pizza carton.

Cathy had gone out for pizza. Half the world went out for pizza most nights, yet he *knew* it meant something. He straightened up. The door was just feet away.

Time to make a decision.

He could go back to the bike, wait, keep watch from the corner, call Luc or Nic . . .

He heard a muffled cry from inside.

Cathy.

Gabe eased the screwdriver from his belt, scanned the shuttered windows.

'Come on in, Ryan.'

288

Male voice, French accent.

Chauvin.

Gabe stared at the front door, saw it was ajar. The scumbag had opened the fucking *door*.

Realization slammed home. The light in his phone – the bastard had seen him coming.

'Come and join us,' Chauvin said.

Gabe heard Cathy cry out again, stood still, took a breath.

Kicked the door open with a bellow of anger.

The light inside flickered, candles everywhere.

Cathy was tied to a chair, Chauvin's left hand covering her mouth, his right hand holding a knife to her throat, her frightened eyes staring at Gabe.

Chauvin was bare-chested, wearing jeans and sneakers. Taller and leaner than he'd appeared in the photo and, as Luc had said, shorter hair, no glasses.

Gabe wanted to *kill* him, but the blade was right up against Cathy's skin.

'Saying "drop the screwdriver" sounds ridiculous,' Chauvin said. 'But humor me and drop it anyway.'

Gabe hesitated.

'You want me to cut her?' Chauvin said. 'I don't want to, but I will.'

The screwdriver clattered on the tiles.

'And that other little thing too,' Chauvin said. 'In your belt.'

Gabe withdrew the tire iron and dropped it. 'If you've hurt her . . .'

'You were right, Catherine.' Chauvin kept his eyes on Gabe. 'It is like a shitty movie.'

He removed his hand from her mouth and Cathy gulped in air.

'He said he'd done something to you and Luc, that if I didn't come . . .' Tears flooded her eyes. 'I didn't know what to believe.'

'He locked Luc in the wine cellar,' Gabe said. 'He's OK.'

'Kick your *weapons* over to me,' Chauvin said.

Gabe kicked them and the tire iron spun before coming to a rest.

'*Merci*,' Chauvin said. 'Now sit there.'

He indicated a second chair about five feet from Cathy's.

Gabe glanced at the chair, then spotted what looked like meters of cord resting on the couch. 'I'll pass.'

Chauvin transferred the kitchen knife to his left hand, returned it to Cathy's neck, then, with his right hand, unbuckled his belt, deftly made a loop and passed it over Cathy's head.

'What the fuck are you *doing*?' Gabe said.

Cathy's face was ashen.

'A trick I once learned, but never thought I'd need.' He pulled something from his pocket. 'Very still now, Catherine.'

Another knife.

'This is a Falcon folding knife.' Chauvin opened it, then swiftly, smoothly, tucked its handle inside the belt around Cathy's neck. 'I need both hands for a moment – but I wouldn't risk anything, Ryan, not now.'

'Thomas, what are you *doing*?' Cathy was rigid with terror.

'Be still.' He tightened the belt a little more. 'Can you breathe?'

'No,' she gasped.

'Clearly you can.' He arranged the knife so that its tip touched her throat. 'This is so I can use my hands to take care of the waiter, Catherine. If you move, or if he fights me and we knock against you, then the blade . . .' He shrugged.

'Strange kind of love,' she managed.

'Don't talk or move. As for love, I guess you killed it.'

'Jesus,' Gabe said.

'Sit down, Ryan,' Chauvin ordered him.

Gabe kept his eyes on the knife at Cathy's throat.

'If you do anything, I will kick her and she will be cut, or maybe worse. It's a tactical knife, very sharp.'

Gabe sat on the chair.

Sam had told him to wait, but he'd known better . . .

His eyes left the blade for an instant, saw Chauvin moving, coming at him, cord in one hand, kitchen knife in the other, knew he'd only get one chance.

He sagged back against the chair.

Chauvin paused, making a noose.

Now.

Gabe launched forward, headbutted Chauvin, heard his grunt, and they both went down, Cathy crying out, and Gabe brought his right arm back and swung, caught the other man on the side of his head, rolled sideways—

Felt fire as the blade stabbed his right shoulder.

'*Salaud!*' Chauvin spat at him, pulled the knife out, dragged at his arm. Gabe yelled with pain, and Chauvin kicked him hard, then rolled him onto his stomach, knelt on his back, yanked his arms behind him, got the noose around his wrists, pulled hard and sank back on his haunches.

'OK,' he said, gasping.

And then he looked over his shoulder at Cathy.

'So much for your waiter,' he said.

Nic and Jeanne arrived at *Le Rêve* with the sunrise.

Luc filled them in, starting at the end, with Gabe's text.

'It's unbelievable,' Jeanne said when he'd finished, after he'd shown them Chauvin's hiding place and the letter.

'Nothing from Gabe since then?' Nic asked.

'Not a word.'

'So he may have gone in.'

'But he knew Cathy's father wanted him to stay away,' Jeanne said.

'Let's hope he hasn't made things worse,' Nic said.

'At least she won't be alone any more,' Luc said.

'OK.' Nic motioned to them to follow and headed back into his office, where he opened a cabinet behind his desk, exposing a floor safe, crouched to key in a combination and took something out.

'God,' Luc said softly.

Nic laid the gun on the desk. 'It's a Glock 22.'

'Nic, this is not a good idea,' Jeanne said.

'It's a damned good idea,' he said. 'Unless Becket's arranged to meet someone on arrival, he won't be armed. This is for him.'

'It doesn't look real,' Luc said, mesmerized.

'Believe me,' Nic said. 'It's very real.'

'So what now?' Jeanne asked.

'I make a call,' Nic said.

Chauvin had stuck three-inch sticky tape over Gabe's mouth, but he had not done that to Cathy, and he'd removed the looped belt and tactical knife from around her neck, so *maybe* he still cared about her.

His behavior had become increasingly erratic since taking Gabe prisoner, pulling on and taking off a black T-shirt, beginning Qi Gong exercises, then stopping abruptly, pacing, muttering in French, abstracted.

'How's your shoulder?' Cathy had whispered.

Gabe had nodded, his eyes reassuring.

'*Arrête.*' Chauvin's voice, like a whipcrack. 'Talk to him and I'll separate you, and just remember I have *this*.' He took out the folding knife, held it close to Cathy's face, then Gabe's.

'I won't talk to him,' Cathy had said.

Chauvin had turned away again, back in some whacked-out zone, and Cathy had wondered if he'd taken something, and if so, when might it wear off, and *then* what?

Now, threads of daylight filtering through the shutters, he was still intermittently pacing, exercising, rambling, and Cathy longed to ask Gabe who else knew he'd come here.

'Beauty, the great deceiver,' Chauvin said abruptly, and sank onto the couch.

Tired, Cathy hoped, maybe enough to fall asleep . . .

'When I first saw your mother, I almost believed *she* was alive again, and then there was you. And Sam.' He looked at Cathy. 'I think I long for his approval more than anything. Even more than your love.'

She heard the words but had no idea what to say, was not *equipped* for this.

He got up, then sat down on the floor again, crosslegged.

'Grace-*mère* scares me a little, which is mad, because Sam should be far more frightening. But Grace can see inside my head, and I don't like that.'

Gabe coughed suddenly, and Cathy glanced at him anxiously.

'Please,' she said. 'Take the tape off his mouth.'

Gabe coughed again, his eyes watering.

'Thomas, he might choke. You don't want him to choke.'

'Not especially,' Chauvin said.

'You bastard,' Cathy said.

Chauvin shrugged. 'Your fault,' he said.

At eleven-thirty, British Summer Time, Sam called Martinez from Heathrow.

'Hey.' Six-thirty in Miami Beach, and Martinez sounded fuzzy. 'You in London already?'

'For three damned hours, and Cathy's boyfriend isn't answering his phone. I'll call Meyer soon, but I wanted to check in with you first, talk about the case.'

'You don't need to think about that now.'

'It's the only thing keeping me sane,' Sam said. 'Cezary's security system, for instance, and the fact that I'm betting there's someone else involved in all this.'

'We'll be finding out who installed the system.'

'Cezary's probably way smart enough to have organized the Rosemont surveillance, but we still don't know how she knew the Gomez family's travel plans – and OK, Lorna and Jay's trip to Sarasota was publicized, but the Burton barbecue wasn't a special occasion, so it seems to me we got *someone* maybe eavesdropping on the victims, and I'm thinking we should go back to Mo Li Burton's and Dr Gomez's offices, check for listening devices.'

'Good idea,' Martinez said.

'Probably too late.' Sam looked around at the glitzy shops and bars, figured he needed to stoke up on carbohydrates. 'Whoever installed them would have gotten them out already.'

'Might not,' Martinez said. 'Kellerman's coming in again later.'

'Good. I don't buy her not knowing about the security cameras.' Sam paused. 'Has someone checked to see if Cezary could have seen the Bodine and Blazek arrests? She certainly couldn't have seen López being picked up in the bar.'

'She'll have known he didn't show up for

work,' Martinez said. 'And yes, she could have seen the other arrests.'

'We need to know why she shot Copani. Just because she knew it was all over, so what the hell? Or maybe he had more on her than the others. Otherwise, why kill the one man who might have helped her when she knew we were coming up?'

'We don't have much on Copani yet,' Martinez said. 'But Duval's on it.'

'Good.' Sam yawned. 'I'm going to make a couple more calls, get some breakfast, then try and get my head down while I can.'

'Keep me posted, man.'

'Count on it,' Sam said.

Gabe Ryan's phone was still on voicemail, so he called Luc Meyer.

'I've been waiting for your call,' Luc said, and filled him in.

'I told him to stay away,' Sam said. 'Jesus.'

'I know.' Luc paused. 'Nic says he'll meet your flight along with a trusted friend, a PI named Jac Noël – like Christmas.'

'Last I spoke to Gabe, he was going to his uncle's place to pick something up.'

'I don't know if he did that,' Luc said, 'but Nic says not to worry on that score.'

Sam thanked Meyer, checked his watch and called Grace.

She picked up after two rings.

'Hey, sleepyhead,' he said. 'Don't wake up. Just wanted to tell you I'm safe in London, waiting for my connection.'

'No news?' Wide awake, tension already back.

'Only that I'll have plenty of help when I get to Nice, so try not to worry too much.'

'You should have let me come, Sam.'

He heard her anger, knew it came from fear and frustration. 'How's our son?'

'Sleeping. Didn't even wake up when I started baking in the night.'

Sam conjured up a picture of Grace in their kitchen, flour in her hair. He'd never actually seen her stress-baking because, more often than not, the stress had been exacerbated by his absence.

'I'm sorry, Gracie,' he said.

'Whatever may be wrong with that man, Cathy's not trained to deal with any of it.'

'Our daughter's smart, and she's been through worse.'

'Even before she came to us,' Grace said. 'Too much.'

Sam heard tears in her voice.

'Hey,' he said. 'You be strong, Gracie.'

'You just get Cathy away from him. And you stay safe too, please. Don't underestimate Chauvin. He's not as naïve as you thought when you kicked him out of Miami.'

Blaming him, Sam registered, which was not surprising, since he'd been doing the same thing himself.

'I'll text from Nice,' he said. 'I'll be running soon as my feet touch the ground.'

It never ceased to amaze Connie Cezary how easy it was to persuade people to do terrible

297

things. Threats and inducements, and you had them.

There were, of course, some 'decent' human beings you couldn't buy with money or menace. The art lay in recognizing those you could, then assessing and consolidating their vulnerability.

She'd known that her reign of terror would be limited, had actively risked curtailing it by addressing the messages to Becket, knowing it would galvanize him.

It had thrown her, hearing that he'd gone on vacation.

She doubted now if it was true, though she would learn the truth presently.

For now, she would simply remain silent, let her lawyer speak for her.

She'd been looking forward to speaking with Detective Becket, to needling him about his marriage, their family, their little boy, but for now that seemed to be on hold.

Always good to have something *special* to look forward to.

In the meantime, she had a prison population to study and probe and play with, time to devise ways to use her fellow inmates to her advantage.

And she had the comfort, too, of knowing that her reign on the outside was not quite over. That there was something more to anticipate.

Not in nearly as much comfort as she was accustomed to.

But still, with relish.

* * *

True to his word, Nic Jones was waiting in arrivals at Nice Airport. Forty-five minutes late, the flight having landed at six-twenty, and even without baggage to retrieve, Sam had had to pass through immigration again, questions being asked about the reason for his late booking and last-minute boarding in Miami.

'My daughter's sick,' he'd explained. 'I need to be with her.'

'We're OK,' Nic told him now, recognizing controlled desperation when he saw it. 'I have a buddy waiting for us outside. His name's—'

'Jac Noël. Meyer told me.'

The air outside was warm, pleasant, with none of the humidity Sam had left behind, though he doubted he'd have blinked if it had been snowing. Jones led the way toward a dark gray Land Rover Freelander, illegally parked, its driver, a stocky man with short white hair, wearing a black T-shirt and jeans, waiting for them.

'Come on, guys.' Noël shook Sam's hand firmly, opened the rear door. 'I don't need another ticket.'

'This is good of you both,' Sam said. 'I take it we know exactly where we're going?'

'We do,' Nic said from the passenger seat. 'Thanks to Gabe.'

'Still no word from him?'

'Nothing,' Noël said.

'He was planning on picking up shotguns from a farm,' Sam said. 'But even if he did, I'd . . .'

'Not to worry.' Nic unholstered his Glock, showed it to Sam.

'Good.' Sam met his eyes, remembered their

brilliance from their first meeting in Miami. 'Let's hope we don't need it.'

'Agreed,' Nic said.

As Noël took the Freelander onto the autoroute, Sam texted home: 'No more, Gracie, till I have Cathy back safe and sound,' he typed, then added: 'Knock on wood. Love you.'

He put the phone away, asked Noël why he wasn't driving faster.

'It's not far,' the PI said, 'and we'll need to wait until dusk to make a move.'

'Sunset's not till nine-fifteen,' Nic added. 'There's time to prepare.'

'Main thing, we know where she is,' Noël said.

'You know where the house in Chauvin's photo is,' Sam said grimly. 'And where a white Peugeot with a Strasbourg license plate was hours ago. Chauvin might be playing mind-fuck games with us, or they might have moved.'

'Judging by that letter, he seems to want you there pretty badly,' Nic said. 'Seems you're a major part of his obsession.'

'Sonofabitch can have me,' Sam said.

'I was thinking a little more *taking* from him than giving,' Noël said.

Chauvin was resting, but not sleeping.

He'd stood up a while ago, gone to the sink to wash Gabe's blood off the blade of the chopping knife, drying it and tucking it into the belt now back around his jeans, and then he'd come back and sat down on the floor crosslegged, as before,

300

taking out the Falcon knife, unfolded and ready for use, resting it on his thigh.

'I need to pee,' Cathy said suddenly.

'Too bad,' Chauvin said.

'And I'm worried about Gabe. He's lost so much blood.'

'He stopped bleeding hours ago,' Chauvin said. 'And I'm sorry you're uncomfortable, but what can I do? If you hadn't tried to escape . . . If *he* hadn't come . . .' He stood up, went to the front window, peered through a narrow slit in a shutter. 'Your father should be here by now. I left him a letter.'

'You did?' Cathy glanced at Gabe, saw his nod.

'When he comes . . .' Chauvin stopped.

'What?' New fear shook Cathy.

'When Sam comes, we'll talk, and it'll be OK.'

'If you untie us now,' Cathy said, 'let us go, it'll be OK sooner.'

Chauvin reassumed his position back on the floor.

Cathy glanced at Gabe again, thought Chauvin was right about the bleeding, and she'd realized a while ago that Gabe was trying to work the cord around his wrists but she doubted he was getting anywhere because of the scarily efficient job Chauvin had made of that in her case . . .

'Your papa will come,' Chauvin said.

'I'm sure he will,' Cathy said.

'I told him to come alone. Let's hope he does.'

Cathy said nothing.

'Ryan's a nobody, Catherine,' Chauvin said, abruptly.

She looked at him. 'And what are you, Thomas?'

His expression was unreadable.

'Hard to say,' he said. 'Insane, I guess.'

'OK,' Noël said, rounding a corner. 'Rue Saint Vincent de Paul.'

He drove the Freelander sedately down the narrow one-way residential road, eyes flicking left and right.

'White car to the right,' Sam said.

'Not a Peugeot.' Noël drove on.

'*There*,' Nic said. 'Keep going, Jac.'

Sam was turned around in his seat. 'You saw the license?'

'Enough,' Nic confirmed. 'Strasbourg registered, parked badly.'

'Eyes left – is that Ryan's Ducati?' Noël yanked at the wheel, turned into Traverse Dante Alighieri.

'Yes,' Nic said.

The PI took the Land Rover a little farther along the road, pulled over.

'No question now that Chauvin has them both,' Nic said.

'Which suggests he's probably armed,' Sam said grimly. 'And just one Glock between us.'

'Actually,' Noël said, 'we can do a little better than that.' From an inside waistband holster, he produced a second Glock 22. 'For you' – he passed it over the seat to Sam – 'since I figure your hands are too big for a baby Glock' – he magicked up a subcompact 27 – 'which is fine for me. So that's fifteen rounds each for you and Nic, nine for me.'

'Needless to say,' Nic pointed out to Sam, 'you're not licensed to carry here.'

'I'm guessing,' Sam said, 'that neither of you are licensed for any part of this operation.' He saw Jones shrug. 'Grateful doesn't begin to express how I feel about you both being here, but are you sure you're up for this?'

'Wouldn't be here if we weren't,' Noël said.

'I've grown very fond of your daughter,' Nic said.

'And this man is my favorite client and a very good friend,' Noël said. 'So while we're waiting for the sun to get the hell down, let's talk tactics.'

'Just so long as we remember one thing,' Sam said. 'That's my kid in there.'

Enfin,' Chauvin said. 'Finally.'

So softly that Cathy and Gabe could barely hear him.

Dark again outside, and the waiting had become intolerable, the bizarre quality of the nightmare rising and falling, peaks and troughs of physical discomfort and fear of the unpredictability of the man with the knives.

He'd been standing at the window for a while, staring through the slit in the shutters, gazing out as dusk became night.

'Sam is here.' He sighed. 'With company.'

He took the Falcon knife from his belt, turned to look at Cathy.

'*C'est fini,*' he said.

And then he turned again, and ran lightly up the stairs.

*   *   *

303

They came seconds later, with a crash so sudden, so *violent*, that Cathy cried out with shock.

Sam through first, the tallest, toughest of them, kicking in the door – Nic and Noël right behind him, framing him to left and right, weapons made ready.

'Upstairs!' Cathy's voice was shrill. Sam already on his way up, Noël behind him. 'He's got two knives! Be careful!'

'They'll get him.' Nic crouched beside her, scanning her. 'Are you OK? Are you hurt?' He laid down his Glock between them, took a Swiss army knife from his back pocket. 'Let me get you out of—'

'Gabe first,' Cathy broke in. 'Chauvin *stabbed* him.'

From upstairs they heard doors slam, footsteps back and forth, steeled themselves for gunshots, Nic moving quickly, peeling the tape off Gabe's mouth.

Gabe sucked in breath. 'Thanks. I'm OK.'

'Where'd he cut you?' Nic sawed through the cord around his wrists.

'Shoulder.' Gabe was hoarse. 'No big deal.'

Nic freed his ankles, turned back to Cathy.

'Gone!' Sam came down the stairs ahead of Noël, crouched beside Cathy, took the knife from Nic and began freeing her. 'You're OK now, sweetheart. He's not here.'

'Window's open,' Noël said. 'He must have jumped.'

'He's on foot.' Nic picked up his gun. 'We blocked his car.'

'So let's go.' Gabe was up, stretching, getting his circulation going.

'You have to find him.' Close to tears, Cathy

grabbed at Sam's arm. 'He was so weird – I think he might do something crazy.'

'He didn't hurt you?' Sam checked Cathy out, rubbed her wrists.

'Not me,' she said. 'Gabe fought him and got cut.'

They all heard the sound.

A motorbike being gunned.

'Shit,' Gabe said. 'He took my Ducati key.'

Sam went out into the driveway, saw the bike, headlamp on, stationary in the road twenty yards to the left, Chauvin revving gently now.

'What's he *doing*?' Gabe was behind Sam.

'Guess he wants me to follow him,' Sam said softly.

'Not alone,' Cathy said from the doorway.

The bike began to move, passed the driveway – wrong direction along the one-way street – then turned, front tire hitting the pavement, reversing, coming back their way.

'I could shoot a tire,' Noël said.

'And wake the neighbors?' Sam said. 'Too many questions.'

'Please,' Cathy said. 'Just stop him.'

Noël came out, holstering his gun. 'Nic, you stay with Cathy, sort this mess out.'

Gabe looked back at Cathy. 'You OK with this?'

'*Go*,' she said. 'Just be careful!'

The Ducati moved suddenly, roaring off down the road, swerving.

Noël ran for the Freelander.

'Take care of my daughter, Jones,' Sam said, and followed.

* * *

305

Not headed for Monaco.

Sam had voiced that best guess soon as Noël had started the engine. Some crazed last showdown at Devil's Curse, which, according to some reading back at Heathrow, was the hairpin bend where Grace Kelly had met her end. Obsessed with the late princess's life, so logic suggested why not her death?

Logic not on Chauvin's agenda. He'd made a right onto avenue de Cannes, then another right, but then he'd turned left onto rue Jean Monnet and all bets were off.

'So not a Kelly pilgrimage,' Noël said.

'Plenty of other hairpins you wouldn't want to ride a bike off,' Gabe said.

'Maybe he's not suicidal,' Sam said, unsure how he felt about that.

Relief his greatest emotion for the moment, now that Cathy was safe.

He was in the Freelander's passenger seat this time, Gabe in the back, oblivious of any pain from his cut shoulder or the plentiful bruises from his scrap with Chauvin.

The road was two lanes, four vehicles between them and the Ducati, and it was hard to be sure of anything in the dark, but they felt that Chauvin knew they were there, was staying in range, using his mirrors, and that was a concern, Gabe said, because the guy was clearly an inexperienced biker and too much time spent focusing on what was behind him was time not looking ahead. And he'd be a liar if he said he cared what happened to Chauvin, but he was sure it would impact heavily on Cathy – not

306

to mention that he was quite fond of his Monster . . .

'Sonofabitch,' he said suddenly, seeing the autoroute to their left, leading to Fréjus and Saint-Raphael, the road known as La Provencale.

'What?' Sam looked up sharply, had just texted Grace: *Cathy OK. More soon.*

'Nothing, I guess,' Gabe said. 'That's the route I sometimes take to my uncle's farm – just made me wonder how long this bastard has been watching us – me too, for fuck's sake.'

'Has Cathy been there with you?' Sam asked.

'Not yet.' Gabe felt a thump of guilt, shook it off. 'So, do we have a plan?'

'Just keep him in sight for now,' Sam said.

'Nothing that's going to spook him into a crash.'

'He seems to be mastering your bike,' Noël said.

'Must have ridden before,' Gabe said. 'I was betting he'd come off in the first mile.' His shrug made his shoulder hurt. 'But then, I was dumb enough to think I could take him in a fight.'

'He had a knife,' Sam said.

They'd parted company with the highway, dark woodland sloping away now, and looking at it made him feel dizzy, so he redirected his gaze, found the Ducati; just three vehicles between them now, no other visible traffic ahead on the winding road, and he realized that fatigue, jet lag and anxiety over Cathy were catching up with him, and he wished he knew what the hell Chauvin was planning now . . .

'I just don't get why he bolted,' Gabe said. 'He'd been waiting for you – it really mattered to him that you were coming.'

'I guess he wasn't expecting three armed men,' Noël said.

Sam kept his eyes glued to the Ducati's tail and wished, not for the first time, that he'd brought binoculars. 'Do either of you know where this road leads?'

Noël pointed to the dash satnav. 'The domaine of Le Grand Duc – a kind of estate, I think. Expensive homes. Not sure what comes after.'

'Maybe his family have a place there,' Gabe said.

A sudden thought crashed Sam's mind like a shotgun blast. 'Call Jones. *Now.*'

Noël glanced his way. 'What's up?'

'How do we know that's Chauvin?' Sam's heart was hammering.

'He hasn't been out of my sight since—'

'Sam's right.' Gabe hunched forward, gripped by alarm. 'It was dark when he rode by the house. We didn't see him clearly enough to be sure it was him even then.'

Nic's number was already ringing as they passed a big house set back from the road, one of the cars ahead turning in through tall gates.

'Jac?' Nic's voice. 'You got him?'

'Not yet,' Noël said. 'Everything OK with you?'

'All quiet.'

'Is Cathy safe?' Sam's voice resonated in the car. 'Let me hear her voice.'

'Dad, what's up?' Cathy, anxious, strung out. *Safe.*

'Nothing's wrong, sweetheart.' Sam's pulse was still in overdrive. 'Just checking.'

'Pass the phone back to Nic, please,' Noël told Cathy.

'What was that about?' Nic asked.

'We still have Chauvin in our sight, but we can't see his face, and Sam wanted to be certain he hadn't pulled some stunt.'

'Unlikely,' Nic said. 'Gabe said Chauvin took his key, and I don't buy this nutjob having an accomplice.'

'I'm sure we're following the right man,' Noël said.

'We'll be vigilant, anyway,' Nic said. 'And Sam, the door and windows are all secure.'

'Just take care of her,' Sam said.

He took some breaths, steadied himself, knowing this was no time for a meltdown. 'Sorry, guys. Needed to be sure.'

'But are we?' Gabe asked.

The vehicles ahead were slowing down.

'Barrier up ahead,' Noël said.

'The Duke's estate, I guess,' Sam said.

The traffic moved slowly to the right, around a small oval central island planted with palms and flowers, the lighting brighter here, and the barrier lifted to allow a truck and a VW Golf to exit – and suddenly the Ducati roared into life, swung around the oval island and passed them, going back the way they'd come.

Chauvin for sure.

'Sonofabitch,' Sam said.

Noël nosed the Freelander out of the line, hit his hazard lights and cut in front of a Toyota, wheels screeching as he got back on the south-bound lane.

'Fuck,' he said, watching the Ducati weave out to the left, overtaking first the VW, then the truck, really gunning it now. 'Do we stay back or go with him?'

'Stay back as long as we can see him,' Sam said. 'We don't want to push him into something.'

Suicide by cop coming to mind.

Off-duty cop *way* out of jurisdiction.

A friend had given Chauvin some lessons on his Suzuki years ago in Strasbourg, but he'd made a critical error cornering, had not leaned in at the right moment, had come off unscathed – which was more than could be said for the Suzuki. Yet still, tonight, as soon as he'd got Ryan's bike moving, the fundamentals had returned. He'd known about the black key, had researched the Monster after seeing Catherine one afternoon riding with her arms around the waiter (such a surge of jealousy that he'd pulled off his Ray-Ban Aviators, ripped them apart); and fragments had instantly come back about judging corners and the 'vanishing point'. And stealing the Ducati had felt good, and using it to make Sam follow him – all the way from Florida and he was *still* calling the shots – had felt better than fine even in the depths of the one crushing, annihilating blow of realization.

That Catherine was never going to love him.

He hadn't planned to run, hated that she would think him a coward at the end, though he had felt afraid seeing those three men coming for him – but once he'd found the Ducati, the fear had gone. And he'd thought, instantly, of getting to the *perfect* place, but reality had kicked in,

310

because they wouldn't let him get near Monaco, would find a way to stop him – and he would not let that happen, not now that he'd made up his mind . . .

They were still with him, two vehicles back, and he was still in charge, the winding road ahead, blackness to left and right, and the motorbike's power was filling him now, and maybe, after all, he was still capable of *anything*. He could leave them behind, outride them and regroup, start another campaign, and maybe it wasn't all over for him and Catherine after all – and here came another bend, and he was improving with every curve, feeling more at one with the bike, and he would master this bend, would *show* Sam . . .

The skid shocked him, and he fought to control it, but the front tire clipped the curb – and after that he knew what was coming.

The Ducati mounted the pavement, and in the glare of its headlamp, Chauvin saw a low wall of sand, saw it spray to either side like clouds of shimmering moths' wings, and he heard a horn blaring, brakes squealing—

'*Catherine!*'

He screamed her name because here it came – here it *came* – and it felt OK, was the way it had to be, and maybe now, maybe after all he might get to see her, the *real* Grace.

He started to sing 'Grace Kelly' again, one last time.

One phrase in, the Ducati smashed into a tree, and Thomas Chauvin flew away, propelled into the blackness of forest and night, and it didn't hurt at all, he was really *flying*.

And then there was landing, and absolute darkness descending.

And silence.

'Jesus!' Sam said.

'Fuck,' Gabe said, staring, horrified.

Jac Noël said nothing, just took the Freelander
on along the road, edged carefully past the Golf
and the truck, both stationary, people getting
out.

'What are you *doing*?' Gabe said.

'Jac, we have to stop,' Sam said.

'Be calm.' Noël drove around the next curve,
then pulled over, turned on his hazard lights
again. 'Wait.' He laid a hand on Sam's left arm.
'You have to stay in the car.' He looked back at
Gabe. 'You too. You still have blood on your
T-shirt. I'll go.'

'I can't just sit,' Sam said.

'You must.'

Noël got out, walked back to the spot where a
third vehicle had pulled over and three men and
two women were now gathered, all peering,
exchanging grim words, one of the women on
her phone, reporting the accident, saying that two
men had climbed down to help. Looking over
the edge, Noël saw that one held a flashlight, and
in its beam he saw a man lying prone on the hill,
another man on his knees beside him.

'*Ou est le moto?*' the second woman on the
road asked the man beside her.

'*Là,*' he said tersely, and pointed.

Noël looked, saw, in the moonlight, the smashed

remains of the Ducati, saw that Chauvin and the machine were a distance apart and knew, before the men began to make their way back up the slope, one on his phone, the other man shaking his head.

'*Mort,*' he heard a man say, and the woman on the phone passed on the information.

'*Trop vite.*' A man to Noël's right sighed.

'*Tous fous, ces motards,*' the second woman said.

Noël muttered something, shook his head, turned and walked slowly back around the bend to the Freelander, got in and locked the doors.

'He's dead.' He turned off the hazard lights, started the engine.

'Are you sure?' Sam felt surreal, out of control.

'Ninety per cent.' Noël checked his mirrors, signaled and moved off.

'What are you *doing*?' Gabe demanded again.

'I didn't get close.' Noël was calm. 'I saw him from the road, but two men went down, came back and told the others he was dead.' He looked in the rearview. 'There's nothing we can do. There are seven people on the scene, it's been reported, there are no cameras to say we were here, and we were not involved.'

'Of course we were fucking involved,' Gabe said. 'He was riding my bike.'

'Which he had stolen, and which you will be reporting as soon as we have our story straight.'

Sam was listening, but remembering Chauvin's vacation rental papered with photographs of Cathy and Grace, and though he felt real sadness at the death of a young man, the greater part of

313

his thoughts were already with his daughter, fearing her reaction.

'What story?' Gabe's voice was disbelieving.

'Number one,' Noël said, 'we need to get away from here. Cathy's not hurt, thank God, and you, my friend' – he glanced at Sam – 'don't need to get snarled up in all kinds of bad legal shit in another country, am I right?'

'You're not wrong,' Sam said, his conscience telling him the opposite.

'We were *chasing* him,' Gabe said.

'We were not chasing him,' Noël insisted. 'We were never right behind him. We played no part in the accident. We did not force him to ride faster than was safe, and we definitely did not cause him to lose control.' He paused. 'Sam, I hardly know your daughter, but after all she's been through, do you think she needs an unpleasant, long-drawn-out investigation? Surely she needs to recover and put it behind her?'

Sam stared at the dark road ahead, thoughts jamming his shocked, exhausted brain, aware that this was wrong on many levels but knowing at the same time that Noël was right. Three Americans and a PI versus one mentally ill Frenchman. No guarantee of a good outcome, certainly not an easy or straightforward one.

'I'd have to ask Cathy,' he said, 'but I know which I'd choose.'

'The guy is *dead*.' Gabe was badly shaken. 'I hated him for what he did to Cathy, but he was sick. He didn't deserve to die.'

'Of course not.' Sam turned in his seat. 'But

314

he's dead because he stole your bike and rode it recklessly.'

'Not forgetting abduction, imprisonment and stabbing,' Noël said briskly. 'None of which – if you ask me – the cops need to know about.'

The sound of sirens chilled them all, coming closer.

'They may already know,' Sam said.

'Not if Nic's had anything to do with it.' Noël paused. 'We're going to need a cover story.'

'What we need,' Sam said, 'is to get back to the house.'

'Not necessarily,' Noël said. 'Nic can get Cathy out of there, get the door fixed.'

'I'm going back to her,' Gabe said. 'I'll walk if I have to.'

'There's no guarantee we'll be able to cover this whole thing up,' Sam said. 'Neighbors might have heard me kick the door in.'

'Just a little bang,' Noël said. 'No shots fired.'

'Doesn't mean they didn't call it in,' Sam said.

The sirens pierced the air and two emergency vehicles flashed by at high speed.

'I think we might get lucky.' Noël leaned across and opened the glove box, pulled out a flat sealed plastic bag. 'Clean T-shirt for you, Gabe. Put the stained one in the bag and give it to me. I'll deal with it.'

'Maybe I'd rather deal with it myself,' Gabe said.

Sam glanced at him, saw his tension and understood his anger, even if it was being directed at the wrong man.

The right man beyond anger now.

315

Justice self-administered.

Maybe that was what Chauvin had intended at the end.

'I'm going to tell Nic we're on our way back.' Noël paused. 'I'm guessing you both want to be with Cathy when she hears about Chauvin.'

'For sure,' Sam said.

'And then we can all agree on the same story,' Noël said.

'Whatever,' Gabe said.

'Makes sense,' Sam said.

And shut his eyes.

June 20

Cathy had wept when she'd learned of Chauvin's death.

'How can I cry for him, after all he did?' she'd said, bewildered.

'I think I'd be more troubled if you didn't feel for him,' Sam had said.

'The guy was a total headcase,' Gabe said, 'but he loved you.'

They were all still at the house in the early hours of Thursday, Noël continuing the work Nic had already begun, starting with the door repair, a 'safe' repairman fixing the wood and putting in a new lock, which the owners would presumably believe their tenant, the late Thomas Chauvin, had installed.

'What can I do?' Sam asked Nic.

'Take care of your daughter. Leave the rest to us.'

316

The 'rest' including photographing, then obliterating from the scene all evidence of crimes committed. Keeping certain items, in case the truth emerged. The Falcon knife found in the back garden, dropped by Chauvin when he jumped, photographed and bagged, along with the cord and tape used to bind Cathy and gag Gabe; and Sam believed Jones when he said that Noël had ways and means of safeguarding as well as disposing of key things, depending on the outcome.

He was getting that surreal sensation again, unused to being out of control at a crime scene, yet finding it almost comforting right now to sit back and let others take charge.

Their territory, after all.

He'd wondered, briefly, how he felt about Cathy working for a man as complex and secretive as Nic Jones. Had decided that, given what that man had just gone through for his daughter, he felt just fine about it.

'Have we even apologized to you for that debacle at the restaurant?' Nic asked Gabe suddenly, in the midst of things.

'Not yet,' Gabe said. 'Not that it matters a damn.'

'Did Jeanne get a chance to tell you Michel Mont was responsible?'

Gabe shook his head.

Cathy remembered the young Parisian waiter, recalled him complaining, as several others had, about being treated like suspects during the long night after the poisonings.

'He did all those things?' She felt baffled. 'Why?'

317

'Mostly for money,' Nic said. 'Paid by a guy who's not my greatest fan.' He looked back at Gabe. 'I'm deeply sorry. I hope you'll let us make it up to you.'

'No need,' Gabe said. 'It was a bad scene.'

'Mont's being prosecuted,' Nic told them. 'I had no choice this time, with clients being harmed.' He shook his head. 'More than enough police involvement for me.'

'Cops not your favorite people?' Sam said.

Nic smiled. 'Let's say we've had our moments.'

Which did not, having witnessed him and Noël in action, greatly surprise Sam.

Cathy's wrists were bruised, she was exhausted, and the trauma might come back to bite her at a later date, but she'd come through relatively unscathed. Noël had photographed Gabe's shoulder wound before cleaning and dressing it, but insisted that a doctor look at it.

'Another friend,' he said. 'Will you be at Cathy's?'

'What I'd like,' Cathy said, 'is to book us all into the Radisson Blu. There's no room for my dad at my place, and the hotel's so close to *Le Rêve*, and' – she smiled at Sam –'you're going to have to get some sleep before you fall down.'

'Maybe you and Sam would rather be alone?' Gabe asked.

'After you risked your life to save my daughter?' Sam said. 'I don't think so.'

'I made things worse, not better,' Gabe said.

'You were here with me,' Cathy said. 'Better doesn't begin to describe that.'

* * *

318

Another dawn had arrived by the time they got back to the restaurant, Sam standing back again, observing the warm embraces between his daughter, Luc and Jeanne Darroze.

Everyone fit to drop, but all singing from the same hymn sheet.

The cover-up version.

No one but those present ever to learn what had happened.

The ceiling crawlspace photographed again, including Chauvin's belongings, then carefully removed by Noël.

Gabe's story – soon to be reported to the police – would be that he'd left his Ducati in the rue de la Rampe some time Tuesday afternoon and had gone for a stroll. He'd gotten talking to a bunch of tourists, shared several bottles of wine with them and taken the bus back to his apartment in Golfe-Juan, where he'd spent all of Wednesday.

It was only when he'd come to *Le Rêve* this morning because he'd had a call about a vandalism issue, that he'd discovered that the bike – and his Ducati black key – were missing, the assumption being that someone had seen him leaving the bike, had followed and picked his pocket.

'What if someone saw Gabe ride the bike away?' Cathy asked.

'Then he'll say he came back again after that,' Nic said. 'Got the time frame wrong.'

'What if they saw me break the window?' Gabe said.

'I think they'd have come forward by now,' Jeanne said.

319

'Probably,' Gabe said.

'Just focus on the story,' Nic told Gabe.

'Which is that I'm a careless drunk.'

'You drank and chose not to ride your bike,' Noël said. 'Responsible.'

'And soon, the cops will inform you that the thief met with a fatal accident, and that your Monster is a write-off,' Nic said.

The dead man almost forgotten, it seemed to Gabe, in the concoction of a lie.

'I'm not sure I'm a natural liar,' he said.

'Me neither,' Cathy said.

'Seems to me,' Sam said slowly, 'this lie's as much for Chauvin's family's sake as it is ours. If their son hadn't crashed Gabe's bike, he'd be facing a long jail sentence.'

'And we'd all have to testify.' Gabe sounded brittle. 'Which makes his death kind of convenient, doesn't it?'

'His death is tragic,' Sam said. 'His whole obsessive young life seems tragic to me.'

'Oh, God.' Cathy covered her face with her hands. 'I hadn't even thought about his parents. How selfish am I?'

'You're exhausted and traumatized,' Sam said. 'I think you can let yourself off that guilt trip.'

'I wonder if they even know yet,' Gabe said.

The morning seemed to darken.

'I've been worrying that Chauvin might have had a photo of Cathy on him,' Sam said to Grace two hours later, calling from his hotel room. 'Or worse, a copy of his letter to me.'

'What if he did?'

'The letter would be a major problem, but I doubt if the cops would care about a photo. The accident was clear-cut, with witnesses, no other vehicle involved. Another joyrider getting himself killed.'

He sighed, rolled over on his bed, gazed out at the blue sky.

'You OK?' Grace asked.

'Wishing you were here. Under different circumstances.'

'I'd settle for having you home.' Grace paused. 'Cathy says she won't fly back with you.'

'I know. She says she's OK, and she won't leave Gabe.'

'I suggested he come too,' Grace said.

'They're not about to walk out on Nic after this,' Sam said. 'And I don't blame them. I wish I could just say to you, come over with Joshua, but I walked out in the middle of a major case.'

'I know it,' she said. 'When are you coming?'

'I might stay till Sunday. Think that's too long?'

'To be with Cathy, after all she's been through? Hardly.'

'Are you remembering to set the alarm?' Sam asked.

'Sure,' she said. 'Though aren't we off red alert?'

'We are,' Sam said. 'All in custody or dead.'

Yet still, something was playing at the back of his mind.

Maybe once he'd had a few hours of sleep, it would come to him.

'I'm going to stretch out, catch a few z's,' he said. 'Call you later.'

'It's expensive,' Grace said. 'You might be out of a job soon.'

Sam smiled. 'Our daughter's trying to pay for everything.'

'Don't let her,' Grace said. 'She needs to save for her old age.'

'I'll be sure to pass that on,' Sam said.

June 21

Dinner with the kids Thursday evening had been wonderful, despite events. Gabe had made his police report and been informed about the accident; it remained to be seen if anything further would emerge. The city was hectic with Cannes Lions, a massive creative communications festival, restaurants jammed, but Nic had organized a table for Sam, Cathy and Gabe at the Saint-Antoine, a relaxed seafood restaurant in Le Suquet with a view of the harbor. They'd shared a huge seafood platter and several glasses of *rosé de Provence*, and Chauvin being strictly off the menu lent the evening an air of almost magical unreality.

And then, taking a stroll Friday morning along the promenade, Sam's phone rang.

Nic calling from *Le Rêve*. 'There's someone here who needs to see you, Sam.'

Cold foreboding slapped at him. 'Cops?' he asked quietly.

'Chauvin's father,' Nic said.

Paul Chauvin, having left his wife sedated with her sister, had paid a visit, before leaving

322

Strasbourg, to their son's apartment, a place that had been off-limits to them for some time.

'Thomas felt that we disapproved of him,' he told Sam now in perfect English, 'but the truth is we feared for him.'

He was in his mid-fifties but looked older – the way parents seemed to instantly age when news of their children's sudden death struck them. Sam had seen it too often.

Nic had brought them coffee and had gone, with Jeanne, to his office.

'How did you know about *Le Rêve*, sir?' Sam asked Chauvin.

'My son's apartment led me here. A locked room filled with photographs of a beautiful young woman. Your daughter, Catherine.'

'Cathy,' Sam corrected.

'When I looked at Thomas's computer, it became clear that he'd been following your daughter's life in a disturbing way. It took less than an hour to learn where she worked and lived.' Paul Chauvin paused. 'He seems to have become almost equally fascinated by you, Detective Becket.'

Sam said nothing.

'I came here hoping to meet Cathy, but Monsieur Jones told me that you were in Cannes, and that it might be better for Cathy if I spoke to you.'

'How can I help you, sir?' Sam asked.

Paul Chauvin looked into his eyes. 'I'm terribly afraid of what my son might have done before he died.'

Sam frowned, sat forward. 'You do know that his death was accidental?'

'Yes. The police seem certain of that. Witnesses, apparently.' He paused. 'He died in a motorcycle crash, riding a bike that did not belong to him.'

Again, Sam was silent.

'May I ask you a question?' Chauvin said. 'You don't have to answer.'

'Of course.'

'Putting things together as far as I can, I'm guessing' – his tone was measured – 'that since Thomas died so close to Cannes, there may have been a connection between his feelings for your daughter and whatever led up to his accident.'

Sam took a moment. He could lie outright, but certain facts were bound ultimately to find their way to the Chauvin family: the presence of their son's Peugeot outside the house on rue Saint Vincent de Paul, for instance; things possibly overlooked by Jones and Noël; and Thomas's computer had already brought his father here. If his mother discovered the truth, she might look for someone to blame.

Time to listen to his gut.

'There are things you might be better off not knowing.' He paused. 'Things we've decided not to report to the authorities. In part, because I'd prefer my daughter to put certain experiences behind her. Also because I believe your son was unwell and because he isn't here to defend any charges against him.'

'So he did commit a crime?' Paul Chauvin's face seemed paler.

'A number of serious crimes,' Sam said. 'Not only against my daughter.'

324

The bereaved father leaned back, closed his eyes. 'Tell me, please.'

'Are you sure?'

'I have to know. My imagination will never let me rest otherwise.'

A half-hour or so later, after Nic had brought the older man a cognac and after Paul Chauvin had thanked him for all he'd done, he turned back to Sam.

'What can I do to make restitution?' His eyes were distraught. 'Is there anything I can offer – any kind of compensation? Please don't be offended, but I have to ask. Anything you might feel appropriate.'

'My daughter and her friend are safe,' Sam said. 'You've lost your son.'

'But so much fear – terror, even . . .'

'Thomas was unwell,' Sam said again.

'You had to fly from Miami at short notice. These things are shockingly expensive.'

'We all do things for our children,' Sam said. 'And we don't want compensation.'

'I have offended you.'

'Not at all.' Sam paused. 'Will you tell your wife?'

'No.'

'Are you sure? It might be easier for you both. You mentioned your imagination. Your wife may be experiencing the same thing.'

'On the whole, my wife prefers being cushioned from reality,' Chauvin said.

'Your decision,' Sam said, grimly aware that should this man ever change his mind, or should his wife decide that Cathy might be even minimally to blame for her son's death, they would still be vulnerable to disruption.

Too many people already who knew what had happened.

'I'm more grateful to you than I can ever express,' Chauvin said, 'for not exposing Thomas.'

'It's a two-way street. Better for my daughter, too.'

'The least she deserves,' Paul Chauvin said.

'I agree,' Sam said.

June 23

He arrived back at MIA early Sunday evening after a relaxing Saturday, Gabe taking off after a while so that he and Cathy could have some time alone.

They'd gone shopping on the rue d'Antibes, bought gifts for the whole family, then taken off their shoes and walked along the beach, the atmosphere everywhere hungover after the wild Friday night climax to the festival.

'I'm flying you all over here in the fall,' Cathy had told Sam.

'Your mom says you need to keep your money for when you're old.'

'Who knows I'll even get to be old?' Cathy had said.

'Don't.' Sam's heart had contracted.

'Hey.' She'd hugged him. 'Only kidding.'

Only half kidding, he'd realized, spending the short flight to London dunking himself in

326

emotion, semi-happy and grateful, semi-sad and angst-ridden.

Reality, workwise, setting in on the longer leg of the journey home.

He'd told Martinez he was returning, but there'd been a noticeable dearth of information flowing back his way, and perhaps that was because Cezary and her three surviving hitmen had been pleading the Fifth, or maybe Martinez had been ordered not to pass on any case details to him.

Off the case, perhaps permanently.

Maybe even out of a job, period.

All Sam did know was that given the same set of circumstances, he'd have done the exact same thing again.

His probable departmental troubles hadn't stopped him switching back to detective mode on the flight – and then, halfway through dinner, the thing that had been nagging at him off and on since Thursday suddenly emerged.

He'd gone back to pondering the possible existence of a second brain behind the homicides.

Back, too, on the old 'no coincidence' theory.

It was what Cezary had said, just after her arrest.

'Because as Virginia said . . .'

And soon after that, Gabe had called and blown away his concentration.

Two elderly women, one in her late sixties – if alive; the other seventy-two.

Both of Eastern European stock.

Similar – on the face of it – racist ideologies.

If Sam voiced his suspicion now, no one would

pay attention. Except Martinez and perhaps Duval, and maybe one of them should put the thought over as their own . . .

Constance Cezary and Hildegard Benedict or Benedek.

Not one and the same individual, he accepted that much.

But maybe, just *maybe*, two minds working as one.

At the very least, Sam figured, something worth ruling out.

He reached his decision in the cab on his way home.

If he waited till tomorrow, he'd be dealing with disciplinary issues, and if he made a call now, he might achieve little more than an extra complaint on his file.

And Harper Benedict's apartment was, after all, in Bal Harbour. Just a hop and a skip from home.

He'd called Grace on landing, said he couldn't wait to see her and Joshua. No brownie points to be scored on *that* front if he delayed getting back now. Then again, he'd be no more popular if he went home, kissed his wife and son and then went straight out again.

He bit the bullet and called Grace. 'Something's come up,' he said.

'How the hell did you know?'

Harper Benedict stood at her front door, staring at Sam.

He'd sent his cab ahead to the island, had paid the driver, taken his number and shown him his own ID before entrusting him with the gift bags to deliver to Grace.

'Know what?' Sam asked.

She stepped back. 'Come in.' She appeared distracted, closing the door. She wore a white linen dress with a tan belt and matching shoes, the dress a little creased.

'I apologize for just showing up,' he said. 'But tomorrow's going to be hectic, and I wanted to know if you'd had any luck locating your mother.'

She looked startled. 'I didn't think you were still . . . You made arrests.'

'What is it you think I know?' Sam asked.

She turned, walked ahead into the living room. 'You'd better sit down.' A quilted tan bag with large gold charms dangling from the handle lay on the sofa, and she sat down and delved inside for a pack of Marlboro and a lighter. 'You don't mind, do you?'

'It's your home,' Sam said. 'No laws against that yet.' He sat in an armchair, watched her light up. 'I don't think I've seen you smoke before.'

'It's been quite a day. I'd offer you coffee, but I need to get this said.'

Facing her, doubt hit Sam suddenly, because maybe this had not been his best move, maybe he ought to call Martinez even now, have him drive up . . .

Too late.

'My mother is dead,' Harper Benedict said.

* * *

329

Grace was not in the best of moods, having just finished sharing with Martinez (who'd phoned to welcome Sam home) her feelings about her husband – her *off-duty* husband – not coming straight home so he could follow up one of his damned hunches.

'It's not fair on Joshua. Sam calls to say he's on his way, so we're both sitting waiting with all his favorite goodies from Epicure and silly grins on our faces and then it's "something's come up".'

'Did he happen to say what that something was?'

'Only that he wouldn't be long,' Grace said.

'Then if you're still on speaking terms when he does get back, would you ask him to call me? I promise not to keep him for long or take him away.'

'No problem, Al. Thanks for listening.'

'If he doesn't show, call me. I could come eat his goodies.'

She put down the phone, took a deep breath, wanting to stay upbeat for Joshua.

After eight already, and she'd given him a snack earlier, because even if things had gone to plan, they'd have been keeping him up way after his bedtime.

Go to plan? With Sam Becket?

Happy voice.

'Joshua!' She called him now from the foot of the stairs.

No answer, no running feet, which meant he was probably playing dinosaurs, and she was tempted to leave him for as long as possible, because as soon as he set eyes on her he'd be wanting to know where his daddy was.

Though, maybe, if she suggested they set up the Dinosaur Train set in the den, so they could play with Daddy when he got home . . .

'Oh, Joshua!' she called again and started up the stairs.

Not *too* loud in case he'd fallen asleep, and she'd kept him busy today, had taken him to the beach and then, after lunch and fingerpainting, they'd gone to Publix and then Epicure, and then she'd brought him home and they'd played Marble Run.

She heard it, halfway up.

Not a cry, exactly, but something *wrong*.

'I'm coming,' she called.

The door to his room was closed.

It was never fully closed.

She felt her heart begin to hammer, no real reason for it, just instinct.

'Joshua?' Quieter this time.

She knocked – they were teaching him about knocking and privacy – then opened the door.

Felt her heart stop.

Seeing her worst nightmare – a totally *incomprehensible* nightmare.

This man – this man she *knew* – was holding Joshua tight against him with one strong arm, his other hand clamped over her son's mouth.

'Hello, Grace,' he said.

'She killed herself,' Harper Benedict said.

'I'm sorry for your loss,' Sam said. On automatic. Needing a moment.

331

'She was found by her housekeeper on Thursday. I received a letter by special courier on Friday morning.' She took a drag of her cigarette. 'I've just come back from the funeral home – first time I've seen her in years. She'd been living in Naples, apparently. Two hours drive, and I had no idea.'

'I am sorry.' This time he meant it.

'Not so much a loss, as you know. More a confirmation.'

He said nothing.

'It has been quite a shock, though,' Harper said.

'Suicide,' Sam said. 'Very hard on those left behind.'

'That wasn't the shocking part,' Harper said flatly. 'Best thing she ever did.'

Sam watched her face. 'How did she do it?'

'Pills.' Harper looked him in the eye. 'Not carbon monoxide.'

He felt a sharp kick of excitement, unsure why.

'She left something for you.' She took another drag, tilted the cigarette in a big crystal ashtray, reached for her bag, drew out a white rectangular envelope, leaned across and placed it in his hand.

Sam looked at the printing center front. *S.B.*

The font was italicized and bold, but still, he thought, Baskerville.

Same as the windshield messages.

Same as the fake letter sent to City of Santa Barbara PD from 'Joshua Becket'.

'I wonder,' he said, 'if you might have

something like a Ziploc bag.' He paused. 'And I don't imagine you have plastic or latex gloves, Ms Benedict?'

'I thought we'd moved on to first names, Sam.' Harper stood up. 'I have both, in the kitchen.' She paused. 'I was rather hoping you were going to read it.'

'I am,' Sam said. 'Believe me.'

He watched her leave the room and it occurred to him, abruptly, that she might, after all, be part of it, that she might return with a knife or even a gun. He thought of texting Martinez, making him aware.

She was back before he'd reached for his phone.

No weapon. Only what he'd asked her for.

'Would you like a pair of tweezers?' she asked. 'For handling. Though I've held it several times, as did the undertaker.'

Sam smiled. 'It's OK. I'll be careful.'

'May I stay while you read it?' Harper asked.

'Be my guest.' He smiled wryly.

She sat on the sofa, then rose again. 'Letter opener.'

'Thank you.'

She moved smoothly to an antique writing desk, opened a drawer, and Sam tensed.

'Here.' She turned, handed him a silver opener, sat down again.

Sam slit the envelope along one side, preserving possible prints and DNA that might be present over and beneath the flap.

A vague sense struck him that he was delaying.

Not exactly procrastinating.

Just dreading.

He had a gun in a shoulder holster.

'Please,' Grace said. 'Give me my son.'

'No can do, Mrs B,' he said.

Joshua's wide dark eyes were brimming with tears, and his small face was contorted by his efforts to cry, the man's big hand still covering his mouth.

'At least take your hand off his face.' She wanted to scream, fought to stay calm. 'What's the difference to you now if he cries?'

'Difference is if he starts bawling, I might smack him.'

'He's just a little boy,' Grace said. 'Please, just put him down.'

'If I do that he'll either run to you or try running away, and then I'll have to shoot him, and neither of us wants that, do we?'

For an instant, Grace felt faint and she leaned against the wall for support.

Sam, where are you?

'I don't understand,' she said. 'Why are you doing this?'

'Sam will understand,' he said.

'He'll be back any minute.'

'Best get started then.'

Started.

'Please, just give me my son.'

On cue, Joshua wriggled fiercely, shook off the big hand and started howling, tears rolling down his cheeks.

'I warned you,' he said, and slapped the child hard across the face.

'You *bastard*!' Grace lost it, flew across the room, primeval rage taking over, and Joshua's screams intensified as she tried to wrest him away and kicked out hard with her right foot.

'Bitch!' the man said, and backhanded her.

Grace felt her head spinning from the blow even before she collided with the dresser to her left.

'*Mommy!*'

Joshua's scream masked the cracking sound of the back of her skull hitting the wood crafted by his uncle.

Out cold.

Ron Kovac set to work.

'I was wondering how to deal with this,' Harper Benedict said. 'On the drive back from Naples. I thought maybe I might need a lawyer – and I guess I would have arranged that, only then you showed up.'

'Did you write this?' Sam asked.

White letter-size paper folded over inside the envelope.

'Of course not,' Harper said.

'Then I don't think you need a lawyer,' he said. 'Though by all means call one, if you'd feel more comfortable.'

'I might feel more – or possibly less – comfortable if you would just read that.'

Sam nodded, extracted the paper with care, unfolded it, held it by one corner.

For the <u>Very</u> Personal Attention of Detective
Samuel Becket

I fear my piece has almost run its course.
Not quite, though.
The Main Event is yet to happen.
If my final planning has gone to order,
you may yet be able to attend. Perhaps
even to prevent it, who knows? You are
an adequate policeman, after all.
Though not so fine as to have spotted the
co-perpetrator right under your nose.

Constance and I could not have done it
without our trusty lieutenant. His Aunt
Connie's favorite patsy, blessed with a
working life of invaluable contacts, a
talent for snooping and a disconsolate,
greedy soul. He hates you and your wife
so much that we were never certain which
carrots were more irresistible to him. The
Cezary estate, which may, amusingly,
never come to him.
Or the knowledge that you and yours were
last on our shortlist.
You should have known better.
We can't stop you all.
But I am about to stop YOU.

Love Virginia

The words blurred.
'Sam?' Harper Benedict's eyes were concerned.
'What did she say?'

336

Colors spun in his head.

Get a grip.

He felt for his iPhone, photographed the letter, sent it to Martinez, then called him. The letter fell from his hand onto the floor, and Harper stared at it.

Sam ignored voicemail, called again, already on his way to the front door.

'Al, listen to me. Hildy Benedict was in it with Cezary, but they had help.'

'Sam—' Martinez sounded confused. 'What the—?'

'Kovac.' He was through the door, on the stairs. 'Al, I'm leaving Harper Benedict's apartment now, but I think Kovac might be at my house.' He passed the doorman, yanked the front door open himself. 'Hildy killed herself but she sent me a letter. Same style, same font as the windshield messages, telling me we're next. I just mailed it to you. He could be there *now*.'

'On my way.' All the shock in the world in Martinez's voice.

There was a taxi parked outside, the driver pacing the sidewalk. The man Sam had entrusted the bags with earlier.

'I didn't know what apartment you went to, and they wouldn't let me in.'

'No time.' Sam was moving away.

'No answer at your house, but I still have the bags in my cab.'

Running now, down Collins, Bal Harbour Shops on his right, dodging the cars queuing to enter, banging a fist on the hood of a Chevy in his way.

337

'This is costing me, man!' The cab driver was following, his voice trailing away.

On Harding, making the turn at 96th – he'd run this stretch a few times with Cathy: Kane Concourse, crossing the water, then onto the first of the Bay Harbor Islands . . .

More colors going off in his brain, images.

Cathy tied up in Chauvin's house.

The first two couples hideously dead in Gary Burton's BMW, the cord around Mo Li's neck, her *face* . . .

He was sprinting, elbows pumping, and Cathy would say he was doing it all wrong, that he might injure himself . . .

Not true. Cathy would just scream: 'Go *faster*!'

Over water again, and he needed backup, needed to call it in . . .

Martinez taking care of that.

Maybe it wasn't true, maybe it was another deranged old bitch fucking with him, with his heart, which was in some kind of overdrive now, keeping him alive, running *faster*, his eyes not seeing the Intracoastal or the cars, hanging left onto East Broadview.

Another image, of Chauvin flying off that bend . . .

Death everywhere.

Slow down.

Sam halted, stumbled, fell on his knees, and his breathing sounded like a tornado whistling by as he stared at his home.

Normal on the outside. Nothing out of place, twin palms, bottlebrush tree all present and correct, and this was crazy. Hildy Benedict had

338

made it up, had seen her Wanted notices, gotten mad, figured she was good to go, but maybe one last game before she left. Or maybe this was all Harper's doing, maybe *she* was the queen bitch on wheels . . .

He got up. Seeing, finally, what was out of place, what was missing.

Grace's VW Golf Hatchback – a gift from Cathy last birthday – was parked out on the street, which made sense, because Sam had dumped his Saab in the driveway last Tuesday before he'd caught the cab to MIA.

The Saab was not there now.

He began to walk, all his senses heightened, knowing that Kovac might be watching, whether from inside their house or maybe outside, perhaps opposite in the garden, and if the threat was real, he'd be armed with his Glock, minimum – who knew what else?

If it was true.

Aunt Connie.

Constance Cezary with her very own nephew in the same department as the couple who'd made the news a few times, black police detective, white child psychologist wife, the prototype target *and* detested by Kovac . . .

'*He hates you and your wife so much . . .*'

Sam knew Kovac had always disliked him – mutual feelings, well-known to all – but it was news to him that it – *hate* – had spread to Grace.

Still walking.

Breathing.

And then he heard it.

He knew the sound intimately, had been driving

339

his car more years than he could remember, loved its growl.

He heard the Saab now, idling.

Inside the closed garage.

'Oh, dear Lord.'

For an instant, Sam went limp, so weakened he almost fell again.

Get them out!

Running again, trying to find his keys, but he didn't *have* them, and the garage door remote was on the ring.

He was in the driveway, could smell the fumes.

'*Grace!*' he bellowed, bent, yanking at the handle, but it wouldn't shift.

He kicked it hard, but it didn't budge, and kicking wouldn't do it because the door was made to flip out and up from the base.

He wrenched at the handle again, yelled their names, pulled out his iPhone, hands shaking, needing to call it in, but then he heard sirens, knew that Martinez had gotten backup, was almost here, and now he couldn't find his *house* key either.

To hell with that.

Two kicks, and he'd busted through the front door.

Everything quiet.

'*Grace!*' He screamed her name. '*Joshua!*'

No entrance into the garage from this house, but Grace's car keys with the remote clicker were in the right place, in the dish on the shelf in the hall.

'Kovac!' he bellowed. 'I'm coming for you!'

Two MDFR trucks were drawing up outside,

but Sam was back outside the garage, clicking the door, nothing *happening.*

He sprinted to the first truck. 'My wife and boy are in there. You need an axe!'

'We're on it.' One of the men was hauling equipment.

'You need a Halligan, you need leverage – give it to me, I know the door.'

Another man materialized beside Sam, a Miami-Dade Fire Rescue Lieutentant.

'Detective Becket?'

Sam was back at the garage, pounding on the door. 'Grace, Joshua, we're *coming!*'

'You need to step away, sir,' one of the men told him.

'You need to get them *out!*' Sam wheeled around, saw two more guys coming, one with a Halligan, the other with a flat-headed axe. 'For God's *sake!*'

He heard Martinez's Chevy screech around the curve, grind to a halt. Heard the first blow of the axe, and his hands clamped both sides of his head, squeezing tight, and he was praying, and Martinez was beside him, talking, but Sam couldn't hear him, wasn't listening, there was too much rage, too much *anguish* . . .

The leverage end of the Halligan made swift work of the door.

The garage was filled with carbon monoxide.

'OK, man, they're going in.'

Martinez gripped his right arm but Sam shook him off, pushed his way past two firefighters, but there were two more ahead of him and he couldn't get through.

'Let me *in* there!' he bellowed. 'That's my *family*!'

The Saab's engine cut out.

The firefighters emerged.

'No one in there,' someone said.

'Let me *in*!' Sam yelled.

'Sir.' The lieutenant was by his side. 'There's no one in the car. No one in the garage. You have my word.'

'Let me see!'

'It's not safe,' the lieutenant told him.

'Fuck safe,' Sam snarled and pushed inside.

Saw for himself that they were right, came out, coughing. 'Where are they?' He stared at Martinez. 'Jesus!'

He turned, ran back into the house, Martinez behind him, through to the kitchen, then back-tracking, into the den, the living room, through the lanai, out to the deck, staring down at the water, turning away . . .

'Give me your gun,' he said to Martinez.

'Backup's on the way. If he's up there . . .'

Sam shoved him aside, ran inside, took the stairs three at a time.

Their bedroom door was shut.

Martinez was right behind him. Their eyes met and Sam nodded.

One each side of the door.

Silent count.

On *three*.

Sam kicked in the door, Martinez covering him.

Grace and Joshua were on the bed, both bound and gagged with tape.

Two pairs of beautiful eyes, filled with terror.

342

Both *alive*.

'Bathroom,' Martinez said softly.

He moved toward the door, saw Grace shaking her head.

Sam had the tape off her mouth first.

'He's gone,' she said.

Martinez checked the bathroom. 'Copy that.'

Sam sat on the side of the bed, breathing hard, and very gently peeled the tape off his son's mouth.

'Hey, brave boy,' he said.

'Daddy, you saved us,' Joshua said.

'Shit, shit, *shit*.'

He'd *had* them, just the way he'd planned it, had *him* in the palm of his hand, ready to squeeze that black, oh-so-holy heart of his into rubble, into *dust*, and then what did he do? He had to go and get himself a fucking *conscience*.

It was the kid, Becket's little cocoa-butter brat. He'd gotten to him with those damned coffee-colored eyes, and Aunt Connie was going to blow her little iron-lady stack when she heard that he'd failed.

He'd had his orders direct from Virginia, for the love of Christ, and hell, it was the mission he'd wanted more than any other, wasn't it? He'd been heartily glad that his involvement with the others had been purely strategic, and he'd been good at that, *damned* good. Tracking and bugging victims, using his privileges, his knowledge, his *expertise*, to help oil the wheels of the Mission, to help his aunt and the other 'Virginia' with one stolen powerboat, not to mention a whole bunch of firearms – and his years in Strategic Investigations had helped with all of that, and a man could learn all kinds of things if he was determined enough.

He'd only come back to Violent Crimes because Alvarez had gotten sick, and he'd preferred his life away from Becket and his sidekick, would have been happier staying away, but his Aunt Connie had decided it was better for the 'cause', as she called it. His mom had often referred to her sister as Crazy Connie, but his aunt had always been sweet to him, had always said he was her favorite, that one day, if he was good to her, all her wealth would come to him – it was in her will. And it was, she'd shown him a few weeks ago, when he'd been wavering a little; she'd brought out the big envelope with its seal and opened it, given it to him, then made a fresh seal herself, with red wax and a big gold ring that had been her grandfather's.

They'd shared special times, when she'd served him Polish delicacies and talked about her great Mission and about her friend – 'her *confrère*', she called her – Hildegard Benedict, whose mother-in-law, Alida Benedek, had written a great racist work, whose husband had not understood her, but who had spent her life seeking out like-minded fellow travelers.

A relationship born out of a chance meeting back in the eighties in Richmond, Virginia, both women at a gathering attended by admirers of white nationalist activist, William Pierce, a connection struck and continued over afternoon

344

tea at The Jefferson Hotel; the differences in their backgrounds brushed aside as they'd uncovered their remarkably similar ideologies. A staunch friendship forged in the Palm Court, the seeds of their Mission sown; Hildegard the intellectual lead, but Aunt Connie, the tougher of the two, the strategist.

He'd often thought, in earlier years, that his mother was right, that Aunt Connie did have a screw or two loose, was living in some weird aristo-type time warp, that the 'Mission' was a crock – and it was pretty loopy calling her hitmen her fucking 'Crusaders' because she claimed to be descended from Teutonic knights. But as time had gone on, he'd come to realize that her aims were solid, that they shared common principles, and sure, her approach was radical and criminal – but that depended, Aunt Connie said, on whose laws you lived by.

Biggest thing they had in common was their contempt for mixed marriages.

In her case, she'd had her top one hundred sinners to choose from.

In his case, it had just been the one couple.

'I'm not sure about the boy,' he'd said to her a while back.

'The boy is the whole point,' she'd answered.

'Shit, shit, *shit*,' he said now.

The Benedict woman was dead – her couriered letter informing him of that and commanding him, in view of his Aunt Constance's 'indisposition', to undertake the final part of the Mission. Aunt Connie was behind bars, her Crusaders likewise or dead – so it was only a matter of time

345

before one of them gave him up. He'd met Copani more than once, and he might have told the others, and he guessed he'd always known he might get found out, but he'd just gotten so pulled along by that crazy old broad's enthusiasm.

For execution.

'Shit, shit, *shit*,' he said again.

He'd come here, to this place, after he'd finished at the Beckets' – and it hadn't been easy fixing that garage door. Anyone could have walked by, challenged him, even called 911, and he'd had his ID ready for that eventuality, and his Glock and Smith & Wesson too; but no one had bothered him, and he'd been as good at that part of the job as all the other things he'd been ordered to do.

But then, when it had come to the task he'd wanted most, he'd failed. He'd failed Aunt Connie. Failed himself.

Only three things left to do now.

Wait for Becket to find him here, which he would.

Put a bullet through that jumped-up, righteous heart.

Then put one through his own skull.

No way was he going to be a killer cop in jail.

Martinez had taken care of business: alerting Duval first, then calling in the crime against Grace and Joshua and putting out a BOLO on Lieutenant Ron Kovac, wanted for imprisonment of a minor child and suspicion of nine counts of conspiracy to murder.

'Suspect armed and dangerous.'

They'd talked fast, while Sam was still engaged in priority number one: making sure that neither Joshua nor Grace were in need of urgent medical attention, and Grace was claiming to be OK, but Sam wanted them both checked out, and Mary Cutter was en route, guaranteeing to make damned sure Grace let someone look at her head.

Kovac might be anywhere by now.

Sam's best hunch that he was probably on his way, or already at, Rosemont House.

The elderly care home had been shut down, residents moved to alternative accommodation, searches and Crime Scene work complete, entrances and exits sealed.

'If Cezary really is Kovac's aunt, then I'm betting that's where he'll go to ground,' Sam said. 'Do we even know where the bastard lives?'

'Riley's on it,' Martinez said. 'Duval's on his way.'

'I'm not waiting,' Sam said.

'You're off the case, man.'

'Not officially,' Sam said. 'Not yet.'

'Can't take your car,' Martinez said. 'I'll drive, soon as backup arrives.'

Sam had already collected his Glock from its lock box upstairs, knew that Grace, sitting in Joshua's room, holding him in her arms, was aware that he'd taken the weapon; he'd seen her face, knew how unfair this was on her, because there was no way she was going to scare Joshua further by fighting his father about walking into more danger.

'Daddy and Uncle Al have to go out for a

347

while,' Sam had told Joshua, nice and calm for the child's sake, 'but there are going to be cops all over this house.'

'Don't go, Daddy,' Joshua said.

'I have to, sweetheart.'

'Do you?' Grace's eyes were cool, chilling him.

'After what he just did to you two,' Sam said, still quiet. 'No choice.'

'There's always a choice,' Grace said.

The troops had not yet assembled outside Rosemont House.

Sam and Martinez sat in the Chevy two blocks away, Sam using his Zeiss monocular telescope, moving window to window, floor by floor, seeing no sign of life, not expecting to.

'He might not be in there,' Martinez said.

'He's there,' Sam said. 'Hiding. Waiting.'

He'd hated that look on Grace's face, *hated* leaving them that way.

No choice.

Not for him, not now, not after what Kovac had done.

'All these years,' he said softly. 'Knowing he hated my guts, knowing he was probably a racist, but never dreaming . . .'

'We hated his guts too,' Martinez said. 'He's always known that.'

'You making excuses for him?'

Martinez glanced at him, hearing aggression, seeing it in his face. 'Take it easy, man.'

'Let's go,' Sam said.

'I told Duval we'd wait,' Martinez said.

348

'*You* told him,' Sam said. 'I'm not waiting.'
He opened the passenger door.
'Man, this is nuts.'
Sam shut the door, began walking.

He knew Martinez was right, yet there was no way he was going to stop. The craziness of the past days and nights, the helplessness. Feeling out of control while Jones and the French PI worked on his behalf, doing for his daughter what *he* ought to have been doing.

Then this.

Reading the letter.

The terror of not knowing.

The sound of the Saab in their garage, the inability to reach Grace and Joshua, having to leave it to other men *again*, then, finally, the greatest relief in the world because they were alive; and yet he felt – he *knew* – that nothing would ever be right again unless he found Kovac, made him pay.

He heard Martinez behind him, heard his breathlessness, his friend less fit than he should be, and he'd push him about that soon, when this was over, because a man needed his best friend. But for now, he wasn't even going to turn around to reassure him that he was only going in, not turning vigilante, that one rogue cop in the department was enough.

Sam wasn't going to tell Martinez any of that, because he couldn't.

Because he didn't know what he was going to do when he found Kovac.

He knew better than to kill the racist scumbag,

knew better as a cop and as a human being. But right now, moving fast, his Glock holstered, out of sight, he wanted to do *exactly* that. To kill him. Not only because of Grace and Joshua, but because of the other nine innocent victims and the tenth, the unborn child.

'To hell with him,' he said out loud.

'He's going there, man.' Martinez had caught up. 'But we need to do this right.'

'Sure,' Sam said.

'You don't want to give him what he wants,' Martinez said, breathing hard.

Sam didn't answer, nearly there now, and he was going to the back, was going to climb up via the fire escape, break in wherever he could. Or maybe the roof was the best place – he could sit it out there, either wait for him to emerge or go in from up there . . .

'Suicide by Sam Becket,' Martinez said. 'I'm betting that's what he wants. If he's here. Bastard might be long gone, someplace we don't know about.'

Sam was hardly listening. All he knew was he needed to get up there before the task force assembled by Duval arrived and this was taken out of his hands *again* – and he knew, deep inside, that his thoughts were *not* wholly rational, had been finally triggered by his little son's frightened eyes.

'Don't go, Daddy,' Joshua had appealed to him.

Then Grace, with her new cool eyes, and her flat statement: 'There's always a choice.'

'Not true,' Sam said now.

'What's not true?' Martinez said, still with him,

350

troubled, wondering what the hell was best to do with his partner, his closest friend. Nothing right now, he decided, except stay with him, stop him doing anything *really* crazy, anything that might get Sam fired – or worse.

Because then Kovac would have won, for sure.

His phone rang.

Duval.

He slowed to answer, saw Sam disappear around the corner, heard a sharp sound, Sam maybe kicking down some barricade.

'Units on the way,' Duval told him.

'We're here,' Martinez said.

'If that means you and Sam, you need to get him away from there.'

'Easier said,' Martinez said.

'He needs to stand down,' Duval said. 'We're on his side.'

'Tell me about it,' Martinez said.

He ended the call and went after Sam.

No sign of him.

No sign of Kovac on the roof.

Still, something telling Sam that this *was* the place to wait.

No time now for him to enter the interior, to search for him alone – as much sense in that as chasing a rat in a sewer. And his mind was working better up here, and it was still light, though another dusk was on its way, another night, closer to home, yet home still feeling a million miles away.

Martinez hadn't followed him up – too tough

a climb – and Sam guessed he'd be coming in with Duval, working his way up through the house.

On his own now, and it felt right.

'I'm here, Kovac,' he said, not too loud, like someone on stage, testing his mike.

His Glock in his right hand now, good to go.

He wondered how long he'd have to wait.

Wondered if maybe Martinez was right, and the rat might even now be heading Interstate or on a boat – and he remembered the Fountain used in the first killings, wondered if Kovac had requisitioned that . . .

A bullet whistled past his head and ricocheted off a steel door fifteen feet away.

Sam dove onto the sun-warmed bitumen, rolled, waited for a second shot, scanning all around.

No one else up here that he could see.

The door crashed open.

Martinez and Duval, both down in tactical crouch, seeking their target.

'You OK, man?' Martinez called to Sam.

'I'm good,' Sam called back.

'Got a team checking out the place,' Duval told him. 'I'd say go home, make the most of your time off, but maybe you'd best stay put.'

Another bullet.

Sam's head whipped around.

He saw him, got him in his sight.

'Adjacent roof,' he told the others. 'In plain sight.'

Ron Kovac stood about a foot back from the edge of the next building's roof, the sweat on his bald head glinting in the glow from the setting sun. Sam looked for some kind of arsenal, but all Kovac appeared to have on him was in his hands, held out straight-armed in front of him, his MBPD-issue Glock.

'Guess you might have been right, Al,' Sam said.

Kovac had taken two good close shots at him, and Sam figured that if he'd been aiming to hit him, he would have.

Didn't mean he didn't want Sam to die, but maybe he was waiting for the others to get him in their sights so he could get his star prize, a two-in-one result. Suicide by Sam Becket, Sam preferably dead or finished into the bargain.

Not going to happen.

Sam took a breath.

'Put down your weapon, Kovac,' Duval yelled across the divide.

Kovac's muscles shone with perspiration, and his arms didn't waver, but he shifted his stance, altered his angle by about twenty-five degrees . . .

Going for Duval or Martinez.

Not going to happen.

Sam took aim.

Squeezed the trigger.

Shot the gun right out of Kovac's hands.

'Going to jail!' he shouted.

Twenty or so feet behind Kovac, a door opened, men in tactical black moving out and across the roof, cutting off his escape.

Sam heard their voices, issuing orders.

Knew what Kovac was going to do.

'Don't do it, Ron!' someone yelled.

But he did it anyway.

353

He took a step back, then sprinted for the edge and jumped over the low barrier, looking, Sam thought, watching, like Elmer Fudd without his cap on, eyes shut, legs cycling as he fell, hitting the ground with no more than a thud.

Sam stood up, his mind feeling calmer than it had in a while, walked over to the edge, took a look over.

Not giving a damn which way it had gone for Kovac.

If he was dead, that was fine with him.

If he was badly injured and in pain, so much the better.

Sam wondered, briefly, if he was suffering some kind of compassion fatigue, knew he was not.

The last bad man standing in their case was down.

It was over.

He was conscious when Sam and the others reached ground level, paramedics tending to him.

Kovac had seen him, was saying something.

'Sir,' one of the paramedics called. 'I think he's talking to you.'

Sam strolled on over, looked down at him.

'I couldn't do it.' Kovac's voice was surprisingly strong. 'When it came to it, I couldn't do that to your wife or kid. That has to count for something, doesn't it?'

'Sam,' Martinez said from behind.

'It counts for something,' Sam said, 'that you wanted me to believe you had done it.'

'Hey, man,' Martinez said softly, touched his left arm.

354

'It counts for something that you terrorized my five-year-old son and my wife,' Sam went on. 'Not to mention your part in the killing of nine people and an unborn baby.' He looked around. 'Has anyone read this dirty scumbag cop his rights yet?'

'I should have shot your black head off while I had the chance,' Kovac said. 'I could have, if I'd wanted to.'

'Sure you could,' Sam said.

And walked away.

Going home.

About time.

A lot of trouble waiting for him at the station, but it could wait.

In the last few hours and days, Sam had seen three of his loved ones in mortal danger.

Nothing more important to him than protecting them.

Nothing more important now than getting back to Grace and Joshua.

No job on earth.

Nothing.